Blood in the Water: Tales of Shark Attack Horror

Myria Hopkins

Published by Sean Benoit, 2023.

BLOOD IN THE WATER: TALES OF SHARK ATTACK HORROR

First edition. March 18, 2023.

Copyright © 2023 Myria Hopkins.

ISBN: 979-8215655535

Written by Myria Hopkins.

Table of Contents

Foreword

Dear Reader,

I am so excited to share with you my book, "Blood in the Water: Tales of Shark Attack Horror". This collection of stories has been a passion project of mine for a long time and I am thrilled to finally see it in print. As an author, there is nothing more satisfying than seeing your words come to life on the page and I hope these tales will capture your imagination and leave you on the edge of your seat.

I want to take a moment to dedicate this book to the person who has supported me in everything I do: my mother, Robin Hopkins. She has always been my biggest cheerleader, encouraging me to pursue my dreams and follow my passions. Without her love and support, I would not be where I am today. So, thank you, Mom, for everything. This book is as much for you as it is for me.

And to you, dear reader, thank you for joining me on this journey. I hope you enjoy these stories as much as I enjoyed writing them. Be prepared for a thrilling ride as we dive into the depths of the ocean and come face-to-face with the ocean's deadliest predator. So, grab a copy, settle in, and watch out for the blood in the water.

Sincerely,

Myria Hopkins

Feeding Frenzy

Mia, Alex, Jules, Chris, and Sam had been planning this vacation for months. They were all burnt out from their jobs and needed a break, so they decided to take a trip to a tropical island. As they stepped off the plane, the warm breeze and the sound of the waves welcomed them.

"Wow, this place is amazing," exclaimed Sam, taking in the scenery.

"It's even better than the pictures," added Jules, grinning.

Mia had been researching the island for weeks, trying to find the best spots for adventure. She was eager to start exploring.

"Guys, I found this cove nearby that's perfect for snorkeling. Who's up for it?" she asked, looking excited.

"I'm not sure, Mia. Sharks live in these waters, and I'm not comfortable with the idea of swimming around them," said Alex, looking hesitant.

"I understand, Alex, but we can't just sit around on the beach all day. We came here for an adventure," said Mia, trying to convince him.

"I don't think it's a good idea," Jules chimed in, "I'm with Alex on this one."

"Come on, you guys, this is a once in a lifetime opportunity. We might not have the chance to do this again. Who knows when we'll be back here?" said Mia, pleading with her friends.

Chris was already onboard with Mia's plan, "I'm with Mia on this one. Let's do it."

"Me too," Sam added, excitedly.

Alex and Jules exchanged a look, and with a sigh, they both agreed to go snorkeling.

The group rented snorkeling gear and headed towards the cove that Mia had found on the map. As they walked along the beach, the water gradually got deeper, and they put on their snorkeling gear. Mia led the way, with Alex trailing behind her.

"Are you okay, Alex?" asked Mia, noticing his apprehensive behavior.

"I don't know, Mia. I've heard stories about shark attacks, and I don't want to risk it," said Alex, looking worried.

Mia tried to reassure him, "I understand your concern, Alex, but we'll be careful. We won't stray too far from the shore."

Jules and Chris were in the middle of the group, chatting and laughing. Sam was at the back of the group, keeping an eye on everyone.

Once they reached the cove, they waded into the water, admiring the colorful fish swimming around them. Mia dove down to get a closer look at the fish, and Alex stuck close to her, still feeling uneasy.

As they were swimming around, Jules suddenly let out a scream, and they all turned to see a shark swimming towards them. The group panicked and started swimming as fast as they could back to the shore.

Once they made it back to the beach safely, they were all shaken up by the close encounter.

"I told you guys we shouldn't have gone in the water. That was way too dangerous," said Alex, still looking worried.

"Come on, Alex, it's not that bad. We'll just be more careful next time," said Mia, trying to reassure him.

The group agreed to be more cautious in the water and returned to their hotel, grateful to be alive.

The next day, the group woke up early and prepared for their snorkeling expedition. They had learned their lesson from the previous day's encounter with the shark and were determined to be more careful this time.

As they made their way towards the beach, Mia checked her map to make sure they were heading in the right direction. "Okay, guys, this way," she said, pointing towards the cove.

They waded into the water, putting on their snorkeling gear, and started swimming towards the cove. As they dove deeper, they were surrounded by a school of colorful fish. Mia led the way, with the rest of the group following behind her.

But as they swam deeper into the cove, they realized that they had accidentally stumbled upon a feeding ground for sharks. The water started to get darker, and the group began to see more and more sharks swimming around them.

"Guys, we need to turn back. This is too dangerous," said Alex, looking around nervously.

Mia tried to stay calm and collected, "Just stay close to me, and we'll make our way back to the shore slowly."

But as they started to swim back, the sharks began to circle around them, getting closer and closer.

"Oh no, they're getting aggressive," said Jules, her voice shaking.

The group started to swim faster, but the sharks were getting more aggressive, nipping at their fins.

"We need to get out of here!" yelled Chris, fear in his voice.

Sam, who had been quiet the whole time, suddenly screamed, "Help! I'm caught in something!"

The group turned to see Sam struggling with something wrapped around her leg. They swam towards her, but as they got closer, they realized that it was a fishing net, and Sam was trapped in it.

"We need to get her out of there!" yelled Mia.

The group quickly worked together to cut the net and free Sam. As soon as they cut the net, they saw more sharks swimming towards them, attracted by the scent of blood.

"We need to get out of here now!" yelled Alex, his voice filled with panic.

The group started to swim as fast as they could back to the shore, with the sharks following closely behind them.

As they reached the shore, they collapsed on the sand, panting and shaking.

"That was too close," said Jules, tears streaming down her face.

"We're lucky to be alive," added Chris, his voice shaking.

Mia looked around at her friends, realizing that her adventurous spirit had put them all in danger. "I'm so sorry, guys. I didn't realize how dangerous it was."

"It's not your fault, Mia. We should have been more careful," said Sam, looking at her with gratitude.

The group realized that they had underestimated the danger of snorkeling in unknown waters, and they promised to be more cautious in the future.

After their close encounter with the sharks, the group was more cautious about their water activities. They spent the next few days exploring the island, hiking through the lush forests, and lounging on the beach.

But their adventurous spirit couldn't be contained for long. One day, while they were snorkeling near the shore, they noticed a small school of fish swimming frantically, as if trying to escape from something.

"What do you think is going on over there?" asked Jules, pointing towards the school of fish.

"I don't know, but let's go check it out," said Mia, putting on her snorkeling gear.

The group followed Mia towards the school of fish, but as they got closer, they realized that they were not alone. A group of sharks was feeding on the fish, and they were getting closer and closer to the group.

"Guys, we need to get out of here now!" yelled Alex, panic in his voice.

But it was too late. One of the sharks had spotted them and was heading straight towards Mia. She tried to swim away, but the shark was too fast.

"Mia!" yelled Sam, as she watched in horror.

The shark lunged at Mia, biting down on her leg. She screamed in pain as blood filled the water around her.

The group quickly sprang into action, swimming towards Mia and trying to push the shark away.

"Get away from her, you beast!" yelled Chris, hitting the shark with his snorkeling gear.

The shark turned towards Chris, giving Mia a chance to swim away. But the shark was not deterred. It circled back towards Chris, ready to attack.

The group worked together to fend off the hungry predators, hitting them with their snorkeling gear and throwing rocks at them.

"We need to get out of here!" yelled Jules, as she saw more sharks swimming towards them.

The group swam as fast as they could towards the shore, with the sharks following closely behind them.

As they reached the shore, they collapsed on the sand, panting and shaking.

"That was too close," said Alex, looking at Mia's bleeding leg.

"We need to get you to a doctor," added Sam, her voice trembling.

Mia winced in pain as she looked at her leg. "It's okay, guys. It's not that bad."

But the group knew better. They had witnessed firsthand the danger of the sharks and knew that they had to be more careful in the future.

Mia winced as Sam wrapped a bandage tightly around her leg to stop the bleeding. The group had made it back to their campsite safely, but the encounter with the sharks had left them shaken.

As they sat around the campfire that night, Mia suddenly remembered something. "Guys, I just remembered something strange. When I was getting dressed this morning, I found this metal tag attached to my swimsuit."

She reached into her bag and pulled out a small metal tag, holding it up for everyone to see.

"What is it?" asked Jules, examining the tag closely.

"I have no idea," replied Mia. "But I don't think it's a coincidence that I was attacked by a shark today."

The group fell silent, deep in thought. "Do you think someone is tracking us?" asked Chris.

"It's possible," said Sam. "But why would someone want to do that?"

Mia shrugged. "I have no idea. But we need to figure out what this tag is and who put it on my swimsuit."

The group spent the next few days investigating the tag, questioning locals and searching the internet for answers.

Finally, they came across a news article that caught their attention. It was about a company called Oceanic Solutions, a research organization that specialized in tracking marine life.

"They're tagging sharks and other sea creatures to study their behavior," said Alex, reading from the article. "Maybe they accidentally tagged you instead."

Mia's eyes widened in disbelief. "Accidentally? They put a metal tag on my swimsuit without my permission and endangered my life."

The group was outraged. They decided to confront Oceanic Solutions and demand answers.

The next day, they made their way to the organization's research center, located on the other side of the island. They were greeted by a stern-looking security guard, who asked them to state their business.

"We want to speak with someone in charge about a metal tag that was placed on our friend's swimsuit without her knowledge," said Jules firmly.

The guard hesitated for a moment before nodding and allowing them inside.

They were led to a small office where they met with the director of the organization, Dr. Martin.

"Hello, I'm Dr. Martin. How can I assist you?" he asked, looking up from his computer.

Mia stepped forward, holding up the metal tag. "We want to know why your organization put this on my swimsuit without my consent. It caused me to be attacked by a shark."

Dr. Martin's expression turned serious. "I'm sorry to hear about your experience. Our organization has strict protocols in place to ensure that our tagging activities do not harm humans. I assure you that this was an isolated incident."

"But why did you tag me in the first place?" asked Mia.

Dr. Martin sighed. "I believe it was a mistake. One of our researchers mistook your swimsuit for a buoy and tagged it by accident."

The group was skeptical, but they had no proof to the contrary. They decided to let the matter rest and continue with their vacation.

As they walked out of the research center, Chris turned to Mia. "Are you okay?"

Mia nodded, holding up the metal tag. "I'm just glad we found out what this is. But I can't help feeling like we're being watched."

The group nodded in agreement, silently vowing to be more vigilant in the future.

The group spent the next few days on edge, unable to shake the feeling that they were being watched. They spent most of their time on the beach, trying to relax and enjoy the rest of their vacation, but their minds were constantly occupied with thoughts of the metal tag and the mysterious organization that had put it on Mia's swimsuit.

One day, while Alex was scrolling through social media, he stumbled upon a post that caught his attention. It was from a local fisherman who had witnessed a strange event in the ocean.

"I saw these huge sharks swimming in the water, and they were all heading towards this one spot. It was like they were being called to something. I've never seen anything like it before."

Alex showed the post to the rest of the group, and they all agreed that it was strange. They decided to investigate further, asking locals if they had seen or heard anything unusual in the area.

Eventually, they came across a man who was willing to talk. He claimed to have worked for a government agency that had been conducting secret experiments on marine life in the area.

"They were experimenting with genetically engineered sharks," he said. "They were designed to target individuals who had been marked with a metal tag. It was supposed to be a way to eliminate threats to national security."

The group was shocked. They had never heard of anything like this before. "Why would the government do something like this?" asked Jules.

The man shrugged. "I don't know. Maybe they thought it was necessary for national security. But I couldn't be a part of it anymore. I quit and went into hiding. I'm telling you this because I think you have a right to know."

The group thanked the man and left, feeling both scared and outraged. They couldn't believe that their government would conduct such a dangerous and unethical experiment.

As they walked back to their campsite, Mia's mind was racing. "We have to do something," she said. "We can't just let this go."

The group agreed, but they knew they had to be careful. They couldn't just march into a government facility and demand answers.

They spent the next few days researching the experiment, gathering as much information as they could. They learned that the government agency responsible for the experiment was called the National Marine Research Institute, and that they had a facility on a nearby island.

The group decided to sneak onto the island and see if they could find any evidence of the experiment. It was risky, but they felt it was the only way to uncover the truth.

They rented a small boat and made their way to the island, hiding behind rocks and bushes as they made their way to the facility. They managed to sneak inside, avoiding the guards and cameras, and made their way to a room that looked like a laboratory.

Inside, they found a table covered in documents and a computer. Jules sat down at the computer and began searching through the files, looking for anything related to the experiment.

After a few minutes, she found what they were looking for. It was a report detailing the experiment, including the fact that the sharks had been genetically engineered to target individuals marked with the metal tag.

The group was shocked and angry. They had uncovered proof of a dangerous and unethical experiment, and they knew they had to do something about it.

As Jules read through the report, her heart raced with anger and disbelief. "This is insane," she muttered under her breath.

Mia paced back and forth, her fists clenched. "We have to stop this," she said. "We have to expose what they're doing here."

"But how?" asked Alex. "We can't just go to the authorities. They're probably involved in this too."

Jules nodded in agreement. "We have to be careful. We don't know who we can trust."

As they spoke, they heard footsteps approaching the lab. They quickly hid behind some equipment, holding their breath as the door opened and two men in lab coats entered.

"Did you hear about the group of tourists who were snooping around the island?" said one of the men.

"Yeah, I heard. They probably stumbled onto something they weren't supposed to see. We need to find them and make sure they don't tell anyone."

The group listened in horror as the men discussed their fate. They knew they had to act fast.

"We have to get out of here," whispered Mia.

They quietly made their way towards the door, but as they were about to leave, one of the men spotted them.

"Hey!" he shouted. "What are you doing here?"

The group took off running, their hearts pounding as they heard the men chasing after them. They weaved through the hallways, trying to find a way out of the facility.

As they turned a corner, they were met with a dead end. They were trapped.

The men caught up to them, grabbing them by the arms. "You shouldn't have come here," said one of the men. "Now you're going to pay the price."

The group struggled to break free, but the men were too strong. Suddenly, there was a loud crash as the door behind them burst open.

In walked the man they had spoken to earlier, the one who had worked for the agency but had gone into hiding.

"Let them go," he said. "They don't know what they're getting into."

The men hesitated, looking between the group and the man who had just arrived.

"Who are you?" asked one of the men.

"I'm someone who used to work here," said the man. "But I couldn't be a part of this anymore. I'm here to make things right."

The men reluctantly released the group, and they all ran towards the exit, with the man leading the way.

As they made their way through the facility, they heard alarms blaring and footsteps pounding behind them. They knew they had to move quickly if they wanted to escape.

Finally, they burst through the doors and into the sunlight, running towards their boat as fast as they could.

They could hear the sound of helicopters approaching, and they knew they had to leave before they were caught.

They climbed into the boat, starting the engine and pulling away from the island as fast as they could. As they looked back, they saw the helicopters hovering over the facility, and they knew that they had narrowly escaped a dangerous game.

As the group sailed away from the island, Jules let out a deep breath. "I can't believe we made it out of there," she said.

Mia nodded in agreement. "But what now? We can't just let those people get away with what they're doing."

As they pondered their next move, they heard a voice calling out to them from a nearby boat.

"Hey!" yelled the man on the boat. "You folks need some help?"

They looked over and saw a rugged-looking man with a thick beard and a weathered face. He wore a faded t-shirt and cargo shorts, and a harpoon gun hung at his side.

"Who are you?" asked Alex, eyeing the harpoon gun warily.

The man grinned. "Name's Jack. I'm a shark hunter."

Jules raised an eyebrow. "A shark hunter? What are you doing out here?"

Jack shrugged. "Just looking for some big game. But it looks like you folks could use some help. You look like you've seen a ghost."

Mia stepped forward. "We've just come from that island over there," she said, pointing back towards the facility. "We found out some pretty disturbing things about what they're doing there."

Jack nodded. "I know all about it. Those folks have been up to no good for years. I've been trying to put a stop to it, but they're always one step ahead."

Jules leaned in. "What do you know about them? Who are they?"

Jack scratched his beard. "They're a bunch of rich folks with a lot of power. They've been running all sorts of experiments on those poor sharks. But it's not just sharks they're after. They're trying to create a new breed of super predator, one that can survive in any environment."

The group exchanged a horrified look. "That's insane," said Alex. "We have to do something about it."

Jack nodded. "I've been trying to bring them down for years, but they're always one step ahead. But with your help, we might be able to finally put an end to it."

Mia stepped forward. "What do you have in mind?"

Jack gestured to his boat. "I've got a plan. But we're going to need to be careful. These folks don't mess around."

The group climbed aboard Jack's boat, eager to hear more about his plan. As they sailed away from the island, Jack began to fill them in on the details.

"We're going to need to get some evidence," he said. "Something that can prove what they're doing there. I've got a contact on the inside who can help us, but we're going to need to move quickly."

Jules nodded. "What do we need to do?"

Jack grinned. "We're going to need to do some diving. And we're going to need to be ready for anything."

As they sailed towards their destination, the group couldn't help but feel a sense of excitement and fear. They knew they were embarking on a dangerous mission, but they also knew that they had to do whatever it took to stop those responsible for the horrors they had witnessed on the island.

As they approached the coordinates Jack had given them, the group prepared themselves for the dive. They donned their wetsuits and checked their gear, making sure everything was in working order. Jules felt a twinge of apprehension as she looked out over the dark waters. She had always been a bit uneasy about diving, but she knew it was necessary if they were going to gather the evidence they needed.

As they began to descend into the depths, Jules could feel her heart racing in her chest. She focused on her breathing, trying to remain calm as she scanned the area for any signs of danger. Suddenly, she heard a loud noise, and she turned to see Alex struggling with something. She swam over to him and saw that he was tangled up in some kind of net.

"What's going on?" she asked, trying to help him free himself.

"I don't know," he replied, his voice muffled by his regulator. "I just got caught up in this thing."

As Jules helped him untangle himself, she couldn't shake the feeling that something was off. They had been diving for a while now, and they still hadn't found anything. She glanced around, looking for any signs of their contact.

Suddenly, she heard a noise behind her, and she turned to see Mia swimming towards them. But something was different about her. Her eyes were cold and distant, and she had a strange, predatory look on her face.

Jules felt a surge of fear as she realized what was happening. Mia had been the one working with the organizers all along.

"What's going on?" asked Alex, still struggling with the net.

Jules shook her head. "Mia's working with them. She's the one who set us up."

As if on cue, Mia pulled out a knife and swam towards them. Jules and Alex scrambled to defend themselves, but they were no match for Mia's speed and agility. She slashed at them with the knife, forcing them to retreat.

Jules felt a surge of anger and betrayal as she watched Mia swim away, disappearing into the darkness. They had trusted her, and she had betrayed them in the worst possible way.

As they made their way back to the surface, Jules felt a sense of despair wash over her. They had been so close to stopping those responsible for the horrors they had witnessed, but now they were in even greater danger.

"We have to get out of here," said Alex, his voice tense with fear.

Jules nodded in agreement. "We need to find Jack. He might be able to help us."

As they swam towards Jack's boat, Jules couldn't help but wonder what would happen next. They had been betrayed by one of their own, and they were up against a powerful enemy with seemingly endless resources.

But she also knew that they couldn't give up. They had to keep fighting, no matter what. Because if they didn't, who would?

As Jules and Alex approached Jack's boat, they were panting heavily, exhausted from their frantic swim. When they reached the vessel, they clambered aboard, gasping for breath.

"What happened down there?" Jack asked, his face etched with concern.

Jules took a deep breath and explained everything that had transpired. "Mia was working with the organizers all along. She set us up and tried to kill us."

Jack's eyes widened with shock. "I can't believe it. That's insane. We have to be careful. They're not playing around."

Jules nodded, her expression serious. "We know that now. But we can't give up. We have to finish this."

Jack looked at her with a mix of admiration and concern. "You're right, Jules. We have to stop them. But we have to be smart about it. They're expecting us now. They'll be ready for us."

Alex nodded in agreement. "But we can't back down. We have to see this through to the end."

Jack rubbed his chin thoughtfully. "Alright then. Here's the plan. We'll take the boat as close as we can to the facility. Then we'll swim in from there. We'll split up into two groups. Jules and Alex, you'll take the west side of the facility. I'll take the east side. We'll try to disable the security systems and find a way in. But be careful. They might have guards posted."

The group nodded in agreement, and they set to work preparing for the final battle.

As they approached the facility, Jules felt a surge of adrenaline coursing through her veins. She couldn't believe they were actually doing this. But she knew that they had to stop the genetic engineering program at any cost.

As they slipped into the water and began to swim towards the facility, Jules felt a sense of unease creeping over her. She couldn't shake the feeling that they were being watched.

Suddenly, she heard a loud, guttural growling sound, and she turned to see a group of massive, genetically-engineered sharks swimming towards them.

"Get ready!" shouted Alex, pulling out his spear gun.

The group braced themselves for the attack, their hearts pounding in their chests.

As the sharks closed in, Jules felt a surge of fear and adrenaline coursing through her veins. She pulled out her own spear gun and aimed it at the nearest shark.

The battle was fierce and deadly. The group fought for their lives against the genetically-engineered beasts, their spears flashing in the water as they tried to fend off the powerful predators.

But even as they fought, Jules couldn't help but feel a sense of awe at the sheer power and beauty of the sharks. They were magnificent creatures, honed to perfection by years of genetic engineering.

But she knew that they had to stop the program. They couldn't let these creatures be used for evil.

As the battle raged on, Jules felt her strength beginning to wane. She had never felt so exhausted in her life. But she knew that she couldn't give up. She had to keep fighting.

Finally, after what felt like an eternity, the last of the sharks lay still, their massive bodies motionless in the water.

The group paused, panting heavily, their faces smeared with blood and sweat. But they knew that they couldn't rest for long. They still had a job to do.

As they swam towards the facility, Jules couldn't help but feel a sense of foreboding. They had won the battle, but the war was far from over.

As they approached the facility, the group's exhaustion gave way to a sense of grim determination. Jules couldn't help but feel a sense of awe at the scale of the operation. The facility was enormous, a sprawling complex of labs and test chambers, all dedicated to the genetic engineering program.

But she knew that they couldn't let it continue. They had to stop it, no matter the cost.

As they climbed out of the water and made their way towards the facility, Jules felt a sense of unease creeping over her. She couldn't shake the feeling that they were being watched.

"Be careful," she whispered to Alex, who nodded in agreement.

They slipped through the shadows, trying to avoid the cameras and guards that patrolled the perimeter. But even as they moved, Jules couldn't help but feel like they were being herded towards their final destination.

Finally, after what felt like hours of sneaking and hiding, they reached the heart of the facility. The air was thick with the stench of chemicals and the hum of machinery.

"We have to find the lab where they're doing the experiments," said Jack. "That's where we'll find the evidence we need to stop them."

The group split up, moving through the maze of labs and test chambers. Jules felt a sense of dread building inside her. What if they didn't find anything? What if they had risked their lives for nothing?

But then, as they reached the final lab, they found what they were looking for.

Mia was there, hunched over a computer console. As they approached, she spun around, a look of fear and anger in her eyes.

"What are you doing here?" she hissed. "You're not supposed to be here."

Jules stepped forward, her voice shaking with anger. "You set us up, Mia. You tried to kill us. Why?"

Mia looked away, her expression haunted. "I didn't have a choice. They were going to kill me. They threatened my family."

Jules felt a wave of pity for the woman. She had been caught up in something far bigger than she could handle.

"But why the genetic engineering program?" asked Alex.

Mia looked at him, a bitter smile on her face. "The true purpose of the program is far more sinister than you could ever imagine. They're not just creating super-soldiers. They're creating something else entirely. Something that could change the world."

Jules felt a chill run down her spine. "What are they creating, Mia?"

But Mia just shook her head, her eyes filled with tears. "I can't say. You have to leave now. It's not safe here."

The group hesitated, unsure of what to do. But then, they heard the sound of footsteps approaching.

"We have to go," said Jack, grabbing Mia's arm. "Now."

As they made their way out of the lab, Jules couldn't shake the feeling that they had only scratched the surface of what was really going on. But for now, they had what they needed. They could use the evidence they had collected to stop the program.

As they made their way back to the boat, the group was quiet, lost in their own thoughts. They had faced death and danger, and they had come out the other side forever changed.

But they knew that they had done the right thing. They had stopped an evil that threatened to consume the world.

The Last Dive

Sarah sat on the deck of the small dive boat, her eyes fixed on the entrance of the underwater cave system. She had been planning this expedition for months, and now the day had finally arrived. With her were four other divers, all experienced and eager to explore the unknown depths of the cave system.

Sarah turned to her group, "Everyone ready? We're about to dive in. Remember, stick together and keep an eye on each other. We don't want anyone getting lost or left behind."

The other divers nodded in agreement, and they quickly checked their gear before jumping into the water. The group descended into the dark abyss, their flashlights illuminating the way as they swam towards the cave entrance.

As they swam deeper into the cave system, the water became colder and darker, and Sarah could feel the tension in the group start to rise. "Okay, everyone, stay calm. This is what we trained for. Let's stick together and keep moving forward."

Suddenly, a powerful current swept through the cave, separating the divers from each other. Sarah fought against the current, struggling to keep her bearings and locate the rest of her group. "Hello? Can anyone hear me?" she called out, her voice echoing off the cave walls.

There was no response, and Sarah knew that she was on her own. She took a deep breath and tried to think logically. She had to find a way out of the cave system, and fast.

As she swam deeper into the cave, she could feel the pressure building in her ears. The darkness was suffocating, and Sarah could hear her heart pounding in her chest. She pushed on, determined to find an exit and reunite with her group.

Finally, after what seemed like hours, Sarah spotted a faint light in the distance. She swam towards it, her heart racing with hope. When she emerged from the cave, she saw the rest of her group waiting on the surface, relieved to see her safe and sound.

"Sarah, are you okay?" one of the divers asked, concern etched on his face.

Sarah nodded, "Yeah, I'm okay. Just got caught in a current, but I'm fine now. Let's regroup and continue exploring the cave system."

The group exchanged a few more words before diving back into the water, eager to continue their exploration. Sarah couldn't help but feel a sense of unease as they swam deeper into the cave system. She couldn't shake the feeling that something was watching them, waiting for the perfect moment to strike.

Sarah followed the rest of the group as they swam deeper into the cave system. The water was getting colder and darker, but they were all determined to see what lay ahead. As they moved forward, Sarah noticed that the cave was becoming narrower and more complex.

Suddenly, Sarah felt a powerful current sweep through the cave. She tried to keep her bearings, but the force of the water was too strong, and she was quickly separated from the rest of the group. She struggled to keep her head above water as the current dragged her deeper into the cave system.

After what felt like an eternity, Sarah finally managed to break free from the current. She looked around and realized that she was completely alone. Panic set in as she realized that she had lost all of her gear in the current, including her flashlight and diving tank.

Sarah took a deep breath and tried to stay calm. She knew that she had to find a way out of the cave system, and fast. She swam blindly through the darkness, using her hands to feel her way around the rocks.

As she swam, Sarah couldn't help but think about the danger that she was in. She was completely alone, without any gear, and the cave system was full of unknown dangers.

Suddenly, she heard a sound in the distance. It sounded like rushing water. She swam towards it, hoping that it was the way out of the cave. As she got closer, the sound grew louder, and she realized that it was a waterfall.

She reached the edge of the waterfall and peered over the edge. The water was rushing down into a deep pool below. She knew that she had no choice but to jump.

Sarah took a deep breath and jumped over the edge, falling into the pool below. She plunged into the water, feeling the force of the waterfall pushing her deeper into the pool.

When she resurfaced, Sarah looked around and saw that she was in a vast underground chamber. The walls were lined with glittering crystals, and the water was a brilliant shade of blue. It was the most beautiful thing that she had ever seen.

As Sarah swam around the chamber, she realized that she had lost all sense of direction. She had no idea which way to go to find her way out of the cave system. She knew that she had to think fast before her situation became even more dangerous.

Sarah swam around the underground chamber, trying to get her bearings. She couldn't believe that she had ended up in such a beautiful place, but she knew that she had to focus on finding a way out. She swam to the edge of the pool and looked up at the walls of the chamber. They were too steep to climb, and there was no obvious exit.

"Okay, Sarah, think," she muttered to herself. "What do you know about caves? There has to be a way out of here."

As she pondered her options, Sarah heard a noise in the distance. It sounded like the fluttering of wings. She swam towards the sound, hoping that it was a bird that could lead her to the exit.

As she got closer, she realized that it wasn't a bird at all. It was a bat, and it was flying straight towards her. Sarah ducked underwater to avoid a collision, but the bat swooped down and landed on her head.

Sarah gasped and thrashed in the water, trying to dislodge the bat. But it refused to budge.

"Hey, get off!" she yelled.

The bat fluttered its wings and squeaked in protest.

"Okay, okay, I won't hurt you," Sarah said, trying to calm the bat down. "But can you show me the way out of here?"

The bat didn't respond, but it didn't fly away either. Sarah took that as a good sign and started swimming in the direction that the bat had come from. She swam through narrow passageways and into dark chambers, all the while keeping an eye on the bat perched on her head.

As they swam, Sarah started to feel a sense of dread. The further they went, the darker it became, and she realized that she had no idea how long she had been swimming. She was lost, alone, and completely in the dark.

She tried to stay calm, but fear was starting to creep in. She couldn't help but think about all of the things that could go wrong. What if she ran out of air? What if she got stuck in a narrow passage? What if she never found her way out?

Just as she was starting to panic, the bat suddenly flew off her head and disappeared into the darkness. Sarah was alone again, and the silence was deafening.

"Come back!" she shouted. "Please, come back!"

But there was no response. Sarah was completely and utterly alone.

Sarah was completely disoriented in the dark cave system, her heart pounding with fear. She had lost track of time and distance, and now she was all alone, with no idea how to get out.

Suddenly, she heard a loud splash in the water. She spun around, scanning the darkness for any sign of danger. And then she saw it - a great white shark, its massive form looming out of the shadows.

Sarah's heart stopped. She had never been so close to a shark before. She had seen them on TV and in documentaries, but this was different. This was real.

The shark began to circle her, its eyes fixed on her with an intense, hungry stare. Sarah could feel her heart pounding in her chest, and she knew that she had to stay calm if she wanted to survive.

She looked around, trying to find a way out of the cave, but there was nowhere to go. She was trapped.

The shark continued to circle her, its jaws snapping with hunger. Sarah tried to stay as still as possible, but her body was trembling with fear.

"Please," she whispered. "Please, just go away."

But the shark didn't listen. It continued to circle, getting closer and closer with each pass.

Sarah knew that she had to do something. She couldn't just sit there and wait for the shark to attack. She had to try to escape.

She took a deep breath and began to swim away from the shark, her heart pounding in her chest. But the shark was too fast. It chased after her, its jaws snapping with hunger.

Sarah could feel the shark's breath on her back, and she knew that she was running out of time. She had to find a way out of the cave, or else she was going to be the shark's next meal.

She swam as fast as she could, dodging and weaving through the narrow passageways of the cave. But the shark was always right behind her, its massive form filling up the small space.

Suddenly, Sarah spotted a small opening in the cave wall. It was just big enough for her to fit through. She swam towards it as fast as she could, praying that she would make it before the shark caught up with her.

She reached the opening and squeezed through, just as the shark's jaws snapped shut behind her. She was safe.

But as she swam away, she could hear the shark thrashing and splashing in the water behind her. It was injured and hungry, and it wasn't going to give up so easily.

Sarah's heart was pounding so hard, she could barely hear anything else. The sound of the shark's thrashing behind her was getting louder, and she knew that she had to keep swimming if she wanted to survive.

She kicked her legs harder, propelling herself through the water with all the strength she could muster. But the shark was fast, and it was gaining on her.

Sarah glanced behind her and saw the massive form of the shark closing in. She could see its sharp teeth glinting in the darkness, and she knew that she had to act fast.

She searched her diving bag for anything that could help her, but she had nothing that could stop a shark. She felt helpless and alone, trapped in the cave with a hungry predator closing in.

Suddenly, an idea came to her. She remembered reading about a technique that divers use to scare off sharks. She took a deep breath and turned around to face the shark.

The shark was just a few feet away now, its jaws gaping open. Sarah held her breath and made herself as big as possible, spreading her arms and legs wide.

"Get away from me!" she shouted at the top of her lungs.

The shark paused for a moment, seeming to consider its next move. And then, to Sarah's surprise, it turned and swam away.

Sarah watched in amazement as the shark disappeared into the darkness. She couldn't believe that it had actually worked. She took a deep breath and swam towards the exit of the cave.

As she emerged into the daylight, she felt a wave of relief wash over her. She had made it out alive. She looked back at the cave, wondering if she would ever go back in again.

As Sarah swam away from the cave, she couldn't shake the feeling that she was being watched. She turned around and saw a massive shape moving in the darkness.

Her heart began to race again as she prepared herself for another attack. But as the shape got closer, she realized that it wasn't a shark at all. It was some kind of massive sea creature.

Sarah had never seen anything like it before. It was at least twice the size of the great white shark she had encountered earlier, with long, powerful fins and a sleek, muscular body.

She watched in amazement as the creature swam towards her, seemingly uninterested in attacking. It circled around her for a moment, and then disappeared back into the darkness.

Sarah was left feeling confused and bewildered. What was that creature? And why had it spared her?

As she swam towards the shore, she couldn't shake the feeling that there was more to this story than she knew. She decided to do some research when she got back to her hotel to see if she could find any information about this mysterious creature.

The next day, Sarah woke up early and headed to the local library. She spent hours poring over books and articles, trying to find any information she could about the creature she had seen.

And then, she found it. A small article in a scientific journal about a previously undiscovered species of deep-sea creature that had been spotted in the area.

Sarah's heart began to race as she read on. The creature was called a Leviathan, and it was a massive, predatory animal that lived in the deep waters off the coast.

According to the article, Leviathans were rarely seen, and their habits and behaviors were largely unknown. But what was clear was that they were incredibly powerful and dangerous, with the ability to take down even the largest of sharks.

As Sarah read on, she realized what had happened the previous day. The great white shark that had been chasing her had been no match for the Leviathan. The creature had sacrificed itself to save her.

Sarah couldn't believe it. She had always thought of the ocean as a dangerous and unforgiving place, full of predators and peril. But now she saw it in a different light.

Sarah sat in the library, stunned by what she had just read. The Leviathan, a creature that could take down a great white shark, had saved her life. She couldn't believe it. As she closed the journal, she realized that she had to tell the rest of the group.

She hurried back to the hotel to find the others, anxious to share her discovery. When she got to the lobby, she saw that everyone was there, waiting for her.

"Sarah! Where have you been? We've been looking for you everywhere!" exclaimed one of her friends.

"I was in the library, doing some research. You won't believe what I found," said Sarah, still catching her breath.

She told them about the Leviathan, and how it had saved her from the great white shark. The group listened in amazement, some of them still skeptical about the existence of such a creature.

As they talked, Sarah realized that she had been lucky to make it out of the cave alive. She couldn't stop thinking about the close encounter she had had with the shark, and the sacrifice the Leviathan had made to save her.

Suddenly, she felt a wave of exhaustion wash over her. She realized that the adrenaline rush she had been feeling since her encounter with the shark had finally worn off. She needed rest.

"I think I need to go lie down," said Sarah, her voice barely above a whisper. "I'm exhausted."

The group immediately sprang into action, helping her to her room and making sure she was comfortable. They could see that she was still shaken from her ordeal and needed time to recover.

The next morning, Sarah woke up feeling better, but still sore from her encounter with the shark. She got dressed and went down to the hotel restaurant for breakfast.

As she was eating, she heard someone calling her name. She turned around to see the rest of the group, who had just arrived.

"Sarah! We've been looking for you. We heard about what happened and we're so glad you're okay," said one of her friends.

Sarah smiled weakly, still feeling a little overwhelmed by everything that had happened. But she was glad to be with her friends again, and to know that they cared about her.

As they talked, Sarah realized that she had been lucky to make it out of the cave alive. She couldn't stop thinking about the close encounter she had had with the shark, and the sacrifice the Leviathan had made to save her.

And then, something caught her eye. She looked up to see a group of people in uniform walking towards them. They were the local coast guard.

"Excuse me, miss," said one of the coast guard officers. "We heard about what happened to you yesterday. We're here to help."

Sarah felt a wave of relief wash over her. She realized that the rest of the group must have contacted the authorities when they realized she was missing.

The coast guard officers helped Sarah to her feet and led her outside to a waiting helicopter. She was flown to the nearest hospital, where she was treated for her injuries and given a clean bill of health.

As she lay in her hospital bed, Sarah couldn't stop thinking about everything that had happened. She had come face to face with a great white shark, been saved by a mysterious Leviathan, and rescued by the local coast guard.

She realized that she had been lucky to survive, and that she would never forget the incredible experience she had had.

After Sarah was released from the hospital, the group gathered in the hotel lobby to discuss what had happened. They were all still in shock, but they knew they had to investigate what had caused the powerful current that had separated them and led to Sarah's near-death experience.

"I think we need to find out what caused that current," said one of Sarah's friends. "It was way too strong to just be a normal tide."

"Yeah, and we need to make sure it doesn't happen again," added another.

The group decided to split up and start asking around about any unusual activity in the area. Sarah was still feeling weak, so she stayed behind at the hotel while the others set out to gather information.

As they talked to locals and scoured the internet, they began to piece together a disturbing picture. A nearby oil rig had suffered an accident a few days ago, which had caused an underwater explosion. The resulting shockwave had created a powerful current that had swept through the area, causing damage to boats and other structures.

The group was shocked. They had no idea that an oil rig was even in the vicinity, let alone that it could cause such devastation.

"We need to go investigate that oil rig," said one of Sarah's friends. "We need to find out what's going on there."

The rest of the group agreed, and they set out to find a way to get to the oil rig. After some searching, they found a local fisherman who was willing to take them out in his boat.

As they approached the oil rig, they could see that something was definitely wrong. There were workers running around in a panic, and smoke was billowing out of one of the towers.

The group docked their boat and approached the workers. They explained that they were there to investigate the cause of the underwater explosion.

The workers were reluctant to talk at first, but the group persisted. Eventually, one of the workers admitted that they had been using outdated equipment to drill for oil, and that had caused the explosion.

"We didn't know what we were doing," said the worker. "We thought we could cut corners, but it all went wrong."

The group was horrified. They realized that the workers' negligence had put their lives in danger, as well as the lives of anyone else in the area.

"We need to report this to the authorities," said one of Sarah's friends. "This is a serious safety issue."

The group left the oil rig and immediately contacted the local coast guard. They reported the workers' negligence and the dangerous situation at the oil rig.

The coast guard arrived on the scene quickly, and they immediately began investigating the situation. The workers were arrested, and the oil rig was shut down until further notice.

As the group sat back in their boat, watching the coast guard take control of the situation, Sarah couldn't help but feel grateful. If they hadn't investigated the cause of the current, they might never have known about the dangerous situation at the oil rig.

"I can't believe we just stopped a potential disaster," said Sarah, still in disbelief.

"That's what friends are for," said one of her friends, smiling.

After the incident at the oil rig, the group knew that they needed to take further action. They had been lucky to survive the dangerous current caused by the explosion, but they didn't want anyone else to be put in the same danger.

"I think we need to take legal action against the oil rig company," said one of Sarah's friends. "They put our lives in danger, and they need to be held accountable for their negligence."

The group agreed, and they began researching their legal options. It wasn't long before they found a lawyer who was willing to take on their case.

The lawyer listened to their story and agreed that they had a strong case. He explained that the oil rig company had a responsibility to ensure the safety of the people in the surrounding area, and they had failed to do so.

"We'll file a lawsuit against the company for damages," said the lawyer. "They need to pay for the harm they've caused."

Sarah felt relieved that they were taking action. She had been feeling helpless after her near-death experience, but now she had a way to fight back.

"I'm so glad we're doing this," she said. "No one should have to go through what we did."

As the lawsuit progressed, Sarah found herself reflecting on her experience. She realized how much she had taken the ocean for granted, and she wanted to do something to protect it.

"I want to become an advocate for ocean conservation," she told her friends. "We need to protect our marine life and make sure that something like this never happens again."

Her friends were supportive of her idea, and they began brainstorming ways to raise awareness about the importance of ocean conservation.

They started by organizing a beach cleanup, where they invited locals to join them in picking up trash from the shoreline. They also reached out to local schools and gave presentations on the dangers of ocean pollution.

Sarah was happy to see the positive impact they were having. She felt like they were making a difference, and she knew that she had found a cause that she was truly passionate about.

As the lawsuit against the oil rig company continued, Sarah and her friends received news that the company had agreed to settle out of court. They would pay damages to the group and make changes to their safety protocols to ensure that nothing like this ever happened again.

Sarah felt like they had won a small victory, but she knew that there was still a long way to go in protecting the ocean and its inhabitants.

"We need to keep fighting for what's right," she said. "We can't let anyone else suffer because of the negligence of others."

Sarah's advocacy work for ocean conservation had started small, but it didn't take long for her story to capture the attention of people around the world. News outlets picked up her story, and soon she was receiving messages of support from people as far away as Japan and Australia.

"I can't believe how much this has blown up," Sarah said to her friends. "I just wanted to do something to help, and now it feels like we have the whole world behind us."

Her friends were proud of Sarah and the work they had done together. They had organized beach cleanups and given presentations to schools, but now they knew they had to take things to the next level.

"We should start a foundation," suggested one of Sarah's friends. "We could use our platform to raise money and awareness for ocean conservation."

Sarah loved the idea and got to work immediately. She contacted lawyers and accountants and began working on the legal structure of the foundation. Meanwhile, her friends helped with marketing and outreach, creating social media pages and designing merchandise to sell.

Within a few months, the foundation was up and running. They held a launch event at a local aquarium, and Sarah was amazed at the number of people who showed up to support them.

"I can't believe this is all happening," she said to her friends. "I never thought I'd be doing something like this."

But Sarah was a natural leader, and her passion for the cause was contagious. She used her platform to spread awareness about the dangers of ocean pollution and overfishing, and she advocated for stronger protections for marine life.

One issue that was particularly close to her heart was shark conservation. After her encounter with the shark, she had come to appreciate the importance of these creatures in the ocean ecosystem.

"Sharks have such a bad reputation," she said to her friends. "But they're actually really important for the health of the ocean. We need to change the way people think about them."

Sarah worked tirelessly to raise awareness about the importance of shark conservation. She organized fundraisers and events, and she even went on a speaking tour to schools around the country.

Her efforts paid off. People began to see sharks in a new light, and Sarah's foundation raised millions of dollars for ocean conservation.

But for Sarah, it was about more than just the money. She had found a greater purpose in life, one that was deeply connected to the ocean and its inhabitants.

"I used to be so afraid of the ocean," she said to her friends. "But now I feel like I'm a part of it. I'm doing everything I can to protect it."

As Sarah looked back on her journey, she realized that her encounter with the shark was not just a terrifying experience, but a turning point in her life. It had led her down a path that she never would have imagined, and it had given her a sense of purpose that she never knew she was missing.

"I'm so grateful for everything that's happened," she said to her friends. "I never thought I'd be here, but I wouldn't want to be anywhere else."

Rogue Wave

Claire paddled out to the break, scanning the horizon for the perfect wave. She had grown up surfing in these waters and knew them like the back of her hand. She could sense the rhythm of the ocean and feel the energy of the waves building beneath her.

As she waited, she struck up a conversation with a fellow surfer who had just paddled out. "Hey, have you been out here long?" she asked.

The surfer smiled. "Long enough to know that these waves are going to be epic today. You ready for some big ones?"

Claire grinned back. "Always ready."

The two chatted for a while, discussing their favorite surf spots and the biggest waves they had ever caught. But as the waves began to build, their conversation trailed off, and they both turned their attention back to the ocean.

Claire spotted a massive wave building in the distance, and she knew it was the one she had been waiting for. She started to paddle furiously, feeling the adrenaline rush through her veins.

As she approached the crest of the wave, she leaped to her feet and rode it all the way to the shore, feeling the wind in her hair and the sun on her face. She let out a whoop of joy and turned back to see her new friend riding a wave behind her.

"Nice one!" he yelled, and she grinned back at him.

They spent the next hour catching wave after wave, pushing themselves to their limits and enjoying every minute of it. The ocean was their playground, and they felt like they could conquer anything.

Finally, as the sun began to set, they paddled back to shore, exhausted but exhilarated.

"That was amazing," Claire said as she pulled her board onto the sand.

The other surfer nodded. "Yeah, it was. Hey, you wanna grab a drink later and talk surf?"

Claire smiled. "Sure, I'd love to. I'll meet you at the shack down the beach in an hour?"

"Sounds good," he said as he walked away, board tucked under his arm.

Claire stood there for a moment, watching him disappear down the beach, before grabbing her bag and heading to her car. As she drove home, she couldn't stop thinking about the incredible waves she had caught that day and the thrill of being out on the ocean.

Claire arrived at the beach shack and saw her new friend, John, sitting at a table with two cold beers waiting for her. She smiled and walked over, grateful for the chance to relax and talk surfing with someone who shared her passion.

"Hey, how was the rest of your day?" John asked as she sat down.

"It was great," she replied, taking a sip of her beer. "Caught some awesome waves out there."

John nodded, grinning. "I saw you catch that big one earlier. It was amazing. You're a hell of a surfer."

Claire blushed. "Thanks. I've been doing it for a while now."

They chatted for a while longer, swapping stories and discussing their favorite surf spots. As they finished their beers, John suddenly looked at his watch.

"Wow, I can't believe it's getting so late. I should probably head out."

Claire nodded, standing up. "Yeah, me too. It's been great talking to you."

They said their goodbyes and Claire made her way back to her car. She felt a sense of contentment wash over her as she drove home, thinking about the amazing day she had just had.

The next day, Claire was back out on the ocean, riding the waves and feeling the rush of adrenaline once again. She had just caught a massive wave and was riding it to the shore when she suddenly felt a shift in the water.

It happened so fast that she barely had time to react. A rogue wave, much larger than anything she had ever seen before, appeared out of nowhere and knocked her off her board. She tumbled beneath the surface of the water, disoriented and alone.

As she struggled to find her bearings, she realized that she was farther from shore than she had ever been before. Panic set in as she realized she was alone in the vast, open ocean.

She tried to paddle back to shore, but the currents were too strong. The more she tried to fight them, the more exhausted she became. She began to feel like she was drowning, her arms and legs burning with fatigue.

As she started to lose hope, she saw a small boat in the distance. It was too far away to reach, but it gave her a glimmer of hope. She started to paddle towards it, focusing all her energy on reaching it.

Finally, after what felt like hours, she reached the boat and was pulled aboard by the crew. They radioed for help and within minutes, a rescue team arrived to take her back to shore.

As she sat on the beach, wrapped in a blanket and surrounded by concerned friends and family, she couldn't help but feel grateful to be alive. She had learned a valuable lesson that day, about the power of the ocean and the importance of respect for its unpredictable nature.

Claire's body went numb as she saw the unmistakable shape of a great white shark approaching her. Her heart raced as she remembered all the stories she had heard about shark attacks.

She tried to stay calm, knowing that panicking would only make the situation worse. She remembered the advice she had been given about sharks - to avoid sudden movements and to try and make herself look as small as possible.

But as the shark drew closer, she realized that it wasn't going to work. She was too exposed in the open water, and the shark was too close for her to make any sudden moves.

She watched in horror as the shark circled around her, its dark eyes fixed on her. It was as if the shark was sizing her up, deciding whether or not she was worth attacking.

Claire's mind raced as she tried to think of a way out of the situation. She knew that fighting the shark was pointless - she was no match for its size and strength.

As the shark continued to circle, she realized that she was going to have to try something else. She remembered the advice she had been given about sharks - to try and make herself appear less like prey.

With that in mind, she tried to swim in a way that was erratic and unpredictable. She kicked her legs and flailed her arms, hoping to confuse the shark and make it think she was not an easy target.

To her relief, it seemed to work. The shark continued to circle her, but it didn't attack. Claire kept swimming, using all her strength to keep moving.

Finally, after what seemed like an eternity, she reached the shore. She collapsed on the sand, panting and shaking with fear.

As she lay there, surrounded by concerned beachgoers, she realized that she had never felt so alive. The experience had been terrifying, but it had also been a powerful reminder of the beauty and danger of the ocean.

Claire lay on the sand for a few minutes, trying to calm down and catch her breath. As she looked out at the ocean, she couldn't help but feel a sense of unease. The shark had come so close to attacking her - she knew she couldn't let her guard down again.

She got up and brushed the sand off her wetsuit, trying to shake off the fear that still lingered in her body. That's when she saw the rock formation in the distance.

It was risky, but she knew she had to try it. The rocks were covered in sharp barnacles and other dangerous sea creatures, but they were also her only hope of escape if another shark came after her.

Without thinking twice, she swam towards the rocks, trying to make as little noise as possible. She knew that sharks were attracted to sound and movement, and she didn't want to draw any unnecessary attention.

As she got closer, she could see the sharp edges of the barnacles jutting out from the rocks. She knew that one wrong move could leave her with a serious injury.

She took a deep breath and began to climb up the rocks, using all her strength to pull herself up. She winced as the barnacles dug into her skin, but she kept going.

Finally, she made it to the top of the rocks. She lay there for a moment, catching her breath and trying to assess her surroundings. From up here, she could see the entire beach, as well as the open ocean beyond.

As she looked out at the water, she saw a dark shape moving in the distance. Her heart raced as she realized it was another shark. She knew she had to get off the rocks and back to the safety of the shore as quickly as possible.

With that in mind, she began to climb down the other side of the rock formation. It was even more difficult than climbing up - the rocks were slick and the barnacles were even sharper than before.

But she didn't give up. She kept climbing, using every bit of strength and determination she had left. Finally, she made it to the bottom of the rocks and started swimming towards the shore as fast as she could.

As she reached the safety of the beach, she collapsed onto the sand once again, gasping for breath. But this time, she felt a sense of triumph. She had faced her fears and come out the other side.

As Claire lay on the sand, catching her breath, she suddenly heard a loud splash in the water. She looked up and saw the great white shark from earlier, swimming straight towards her.

Her heart raced as she realized she was in danger once again. Without a second thought, she swam towards the rock formation she had spotted earlier, hoping to find safety there.

But just as she reached the rocks, the shark lunged at her. She managed to dodge it at the last second, feeling the rush of water as its powerful jaws snapped shut inches from her face.

As she climbed up onto the rocks, she couldn't help but look back at the shark. It was huge, at least ten feet long, with razor-sharp teeth and a hungry look in its eyes.

For a moment, she froze, unable to move as she stared at the beast before her. But then she shook herself out of it and started climbing up the rocks as quickly as she could.

The barnacles dug into her skin, but she pushed through the pain, knowing that she had to get to safety. She could feel the shark circling around the rocks, waiting for its chance to strike.

Finally, she made it to the top of the rocks. She lay there for a moment, panting and shaking with fear. She looked out at the ocean and saw the shark still circling, still waiting for its prey.

But then something strange happened. The shark suddenly turned and swam away, disappearing into the depths of the ocean.

Claire lay there for a few minutes, trying to catch her breath and process what had just happened. She had come face to face with a great white shark and lived to tell the tale.

As she looked out at the ocean, she realized that it was both beautiful and dangerous. She knew she had to respect its power, but she also knew that she couldn't let her fear stop her from exploring its depths.

Claire took a deep breath and sat up, still shaking from the encounter with the great white shark. She looked out at the ocean, hoping that the danger had passed.

But just as she started to relax, she felt something bite her leg. She screamed in pain and looked down to see a smaller shark, about four feet long, clinging to her leg with its razor-sharp teeth.

She tried to shake it off, but the shark held on tight, its jaws clamped down on her flesh. She could feel the blood pouring out of the wound and knew she had to act fast.

With all her strength, she pulled herself away from the shark and kicked it as hard as she could. The shark let go and swam away, leaving her bleeding and scared on the rocks.

Claire looked down at her leg and saw that the wound was deep and bleeding profusely. She knew she had to get back to shore and seek medical attention, but she also knew that she couldn't swim with her injured leg.

She looked around for help, but there was no one else on the beach. She was alone, stranded on the rocks with no way to get back to safety.

She took a deep breath and tried to stay calm, but the pain and fear were overwhelming. She wondered if she would ever make it back to shore, or if she would be another victim of the ocean's deadly creatures.

Claire sat on the rocks, her leg throbbing in pain as she watched the boat in the distance. She waved her arms frantically, hoping that someone would see her and come to her rescue.

As the boat grew closer, she could see that it was a small fishing boat, with a few men on board. She continued to wave, hoping that they would spot her.

Finally, one of the men saw her and pointed her out to the others. They changed course and headed towards her, the engine of the boat roaring loudly in the quiet of the ocean.

Claire felt a wave of relief wash over her as the boat pulled up to the rocks. The men helped her onto the boat and quickly assessed her injury. One of them wrapped a towel tightly around her leg, trying to stop the bleeding.

"Thank you so much," Claire said, her voice shaking with emotion. "I didn't think anyone would find me out here."

"It's our pleasure," one of the men said kindly. "We're just glad we were able to help."

They started the engine and headed back towards shore, the wind whipping through Claire's hair as she looked out at the ocean. She felt a mix of emotions - relief that she was safe, but also a sense of respect and awe for the power of the ocean and its inhabitants.

As they approached the shore, Claire could see the ambulance waiting for her. The men helped her onto a stretcher and lifted her into the back of the ambulance.

As they drove towards the hospital, Claire looked out the window at the ocean. She knew that she would never forget her encounter with the great white shark and the smaller shark that had left her injured and scared.

But she also knew that she couldn't let her fear stop her from exploring the ocean and all of its wonders. She would return one day, stronger and more prepared, ready to face whatever challenges lay ahead.

Claire was rushed into the emergency room as soon as the ambulance arrived at the hospital. The doctors and nurses quickly assessed her injury and prepared her for surgery.

Her family and friends were waiting anxiously in the waiting room, holding onto each other and trying to remain positive. They had all been worried sick about her ever since she had told them about her plans to go diving alone in the ocean.

"I can't believe this happened to her," Claire's sister said, tears streaming down her face. "She's always been so brave and adventurous."

"I know," Claire's mother said, putting a comforting arm around her daughter. "But she'll pull through. She's strong and resilient, just like her father."

As they waited, the hours seemed to stretch on forever. They passed the time by talking about happy memories from their childhood, sharing stories and laughing through their tears.

Finally, after what felt like an eternity, the surgeon came out of the operating room. Everyone jumped up, their hearts pounding with anticipation.

"Is she okay?" Claire's father asked, his voice shaking with emotion.

The surgeon smiled and nodded. "She's going to be just fine. We were able to repair the damage done by the shark and she should make a full recovery."

There were tears of joy and relief as the family hugged each other tightly. They all wanted to rush in and see Claire, but the doctor told them that she needed to rest for a little while longer.

As they settled back into their seats, Claire's brother pulled out his guitar and started to play a gentle melody. The sound filled the room, bringing a sense of peace and calm to everyone there.

Hours passed as they waited for Claire to wake up, but finally, she stirred. Her family rushed to her side, tears of joy streaming down their faces as they hugged her tightly.

"Thank God you're okay," her sister said, her voice choked with emotion.

"I'm sorry," Claire said, tears streaming down her own face. "I should have listened to you guys and not gone out alone."

"It's okay," her mother said, holding her hand tightly. "What's important now is that you're safe and you're going to be okay."

They all sat together for a while, talking quietly and enjoying each other's company. Claire was grateful for their support and love, and she knew that she would never forget this experience.

As she drifted off to sleep, she felt a sense of peace and gratitude wash over her. She knew that she had been given a second chance at life, and she was determined to make the most of it.

Claire's recovery was a slow and painful process. She was forced to take time off from surfing and had to rely on crutches and physical therapy to regain her strength. But with the help of her loved ones, she began to make progress.

At first, she felt frustrated and angry at the world. She had always been so active and independent, and now she felt like she was being held back by her injury.

"Why did this have to happen to me?" she asked her physical therapist one day, tears streaming down her face.

"I don't know," the therapist said kindly. "But what I do know is that you're going to get through this. It's going to be tough, but you're strong enough to do it."

With those words of encouragement, Claire began to work harder than ever. She went to physical therapy every day, pushing herself to the limit even when it hurt.

Her family and friends were there for her every step of the way. They brought her meals, helped her with her exercises, and kept her company when she was feeling down.

"I couldn't have done it without you guys," Claire said one day, as she lay on the couch with her leg propped up. "You've been my rock through all of this."

"We're always going to be here for you," her sister said, smiling at her. "No matter what."

As the days turned into weeks and the weeks turned into months, Claire began to see progress. She was able to walk without crutches, then without a limp, and finally without any pain at all.

And then, one day, she felt ready to get back into the water. She put on her wetsuit and grabbed her surfboard, feeling a sense of excitement and fear in equal measure.

Her family and friends were waiting for her on the beach, cheering her on as she paddled out into the waves. At first, she felt nervous and unsure, but as she caught her first wave, she felt a rush of joy and freedom that she had never felt before.

"I'm back," she shouted, as she rode the wave all the way to the shore.

Her loved ones cheered and clapped, tears of joy streaming down their faces as they watched her. They knew how hard she had worked to get to this point, and they were so proud of her.

As she stood on the shore, looking out at the ocean, Claire knew that she had come full circle. She had faced her fears and overcome them, and she had learned a valuable lesson about the power of the ocean and the importance of respect and caution.

"I'm ready for anything now," she said, a smile spreading across her face. "Bring on the waves!"

Claire felt the sun on her face and the salt in her hair as she paddled out further, searching for the perfect wave. She had missed this feeling so much, and she was determined to make the most of it.

"Looking good out there, Claire!" her brother shouted from the shore.

Claire turned and gave him a thumbs up, feeling a surge of confidence. She had been nervous at first, but now she felt like she was in her element once again.

As she paddled further out, she saw a big wave forming in the distance. Her heart raced as she began to paddle towards it, feeling the rush of adrenaline building inside her.

She could hear her own breaths getting quicker and quicker as she approached the wave, ready to catch it. And then, suddenly, she was airborne, the wind rushing past her as she soared over the water.

For a moment, time seemed to stand still, and Claire felt like she was flying. And then, with a loud crash, she hit the water, tumbling head over heels as she struggled to regain her footing.

But she didn't care. She was laughing and whooping with joy as she rose to the surface, feeling more alive than she had in months.

"That was amazing!" she shouted to her family, who were all cheering and clapping on the shore. "I'm back!"

Over the next few hours, Claire surfed wave after wave, each one bigger and more exhilarating than the last. She felt like she was pushing herself to new limits, testing her body and her mind in ways she had never thought possible.

As the sun began to set, Claire paddled back to the shore, exhausted but happy. She collapsed onto the sand, feeling the warm sun on her skin and the cool breeze in her hair.

"I did it," she said, grinning from ear to ear. "I'm back."

Her family gathered around her, hugging her and congratulating her on her incredible comeback. Claire felt a sense of gratitude wash over her as she looked out at the ocean, realizing that she had been given a second chance to do what she loved most.

"I'll never take this for granted again," she said softly, as the sun dipped below the horizon. "I know now that the ocean is powerful, and that we have to respect it. But I also know that it's a place of beauty and wonder, and that it's worth fighting for."

Her family nodded in agreement, and together they sat on the beach, watching as the stars came out and the waves crashed against the shore.

For Claire, it was a moment of pure joy and contentment. She had overcome her fears and her doubts, and she had emerged stronger and more determined than ever before.

"I can't wait to see what the future holds," she said, closing her eyes and breathing in the salty air. "Bring on the waves."

Blood on the Sand

The family had been planning their vacation for months, and the anticipation was palpable as they drove up to the beach house. Sean, the stepfather, couldn't help but feel a little nervous. He wanted this vacation to bring the family closer together, but he was worried that the tension between him and the kids would ruin everything.

As they settled into the beach house, Myria, the mother, couldn't contain her excitement. "This place is beautiful!" she exclaimed. "Let's go explore!"

Dale, the eldest son, rolled his eyes. "Can we just settle in first?" he grumbled.

Zoey, the younger daughter, elbowed Dale in the ribs. "Come on, let's go see what's around!"

Sean watched as the kids ran off, feeling a pang of sadness. He wanted to be included in their excitement, but he didn't want to overstep his bounds.

Myria put a hand on his shoulder. "Don't worry," she said. "They'll come around."

Sean forced a smile, but he couldn't shake off the feeling of unease. As they explored the area, he couldn't help but notice how Dale and Zoey kept their distance from him. They would talk and laugh with their mother, but when he tried to join in, they would give him short answers and then walk away.

Finally, they made it back to the beach house, and Sean let out a sigh of relief. He was exhausted from the long drive, and he needed some time to himself.

As he sat on the porch, watching the waves crash on the shore, he heard footsteps behind him. He turned to see Zoey standing there, looking at him with a mixture of curiosity and distrust.

"Hey," he said, trying to sound friendly.

Zoey nodded in response, but she didn't say anything.

Sean cleared his throat. "So, do you like it here?"

Zoey shrugged. "It's okay, I guess."

Sean tried to hide his disappointment. "Well, maybe we can find something fun to do together tomorrow. What do you say?"

Zoey looked at him for a moment, then nodded. "Sure."

Sean smiled, feeling a glimmer of hope. Maybe this vacation wouldn't be a disaster after all.

The next morning, the family woke up early, eager to start their day at the beach. They packed their bags with towels, sunscreen, and snacks and headed out to the shore.

As they set up their beach chairs, Myria pulled out a frisbee. "Who's up for some fun in the sun?" she asked.

Dale and Zoey exchanged a look, but Sean decided to join in. As they threw the frisbee back and forth, Sean felt himself letting go of his worries. Maybe this vacation would be a chance for him to bond with the kids after all.

After a while, they decided to go for a swim. The water was warm and inviting, and they all laughed and splashed around. However, as they were swimming, Sean noticed something in the water. He squinted and realized that it was a school of bull sharks.

"Everyone out of the water!" he shouted.

The family scrambled to get out of the water, but the sharks were coming closer. Sean knew that they needed to act fast.

"Grab the frisbee!" he yelled to Myria. "Use it to distract them!"

Myria tossed the frisbee into the water, and the sharks swam after it. The family made it back to shore, shaken but unharmed.

As they caught their breath, Sean couldn't help but think about what could have happened if they hadn't noticed the sharks in time.

"We need to be more careful," he said. "We don't know what else is out there."

Myria nodded, looking just as worried as he was. "We'll be more careful," she promised.

The family spent the rest of the day sunbathing and playing games, but the presence of the bull sharks loomed over them. Sean couldn't shake off the feeling of unease, and he knew that he would need to keep a close eye on the kids.

As they packed up their things and headed back to the beach house, Sean knew that this vacation was going to be anything but relaxing.

Over the next few days, the tension between Sean and the kids continued to escalate. Dale and Zoey seemed to be avoiding him as much as possible, and Sean felt like he couldn't do anything right.

One morning, Sean decided to take the kids out for breakfast. "I thought we could go to that diner we passed the other day," he said, trying to sound cheerful.

Dale rolled his eyes. "Can't we just eat at the beach house?"

Zoey looked at Sean, then at Dale. "Come on, it might be fun," she said.

Sean smiled gratefully at Zoey. "Thanks, Zoey. Let's go."

As they drove to the diner, Sean tried to make small talk, but Dale and Zoey gave him short answers. Sean felt like he was walking on eggshells, not sure what he could say to make things better.

When they got to the diner, they ordered their food and sat down at a booth. The kids were quiet, and Sean couldn't think of anything to say.

Finally, Myria spoke up. "So, what should we do today?"

Dale shrugged. "I don't know. What do you want to do, Mom?"

Myria looked at Sean, then back at the kids. "How about we go to that amusement park we saw yesterday?"

Zoey's face lit up. "Yes! Can we, Dad?"

Sean smiled, happy to see Zoey excited. "Of course. Let's go have some fun."

As they left the diner, Sean felt a glimmer of hope. Maybe this would be the day that everything would turn around.

However, as they were walking through the amusement park, Sean noticed that Dale and Zoey seemed to be avoiding him even more. They would run ahead, talking and laughing with their mother, leaving Sean trailing behind.

Sean felt his frustration growing. He didn't understand why the kids were pushing him away. He just wanted to be a part of their family.

As they were riding a rollercoaster, Sean tried to strike up a conversation with Dale. "So, how's school going?"

Dale gave him a cold stare. "Fine."

Sean sighed, feeling like there was no way to win. He wanted to be a good stepfather, but it seemed like the kids didn't want him around.

When they got back to the beach house, Sean excused himself and went for a walk on the beach. He needed some time to clear his head and figure out what to do.

As he was walking, he heard someone calling his name. He turned to see Myria jogging towards him.

"Sean, what's wrong?" she asked, concern etched on her face.

Sean took a deep breath. "I just don't know what to do. I want to be a good stepfather, but it feels like the kids don't want me around."

Myria put a hand on his arm. "I know it's hard, but we'll figure it out. I'll talk to them, and maybe we can come up with some ways to make things better."

Sean nodded, grateful for Myria's support. Maybe there was hope for their family after all.

As Sean and Myria walked back to the beach house, they found Dale and Zoey already changed into their swimsuits, ready for a dip in the ocean. Sean hesitated for a moment before joining them, still feeling uneasy after the day's events.

"Come on, Sean, it's a beautiful day," Myria said, smiling at him.

Sean took a deep breath and tried to put his worries aside. "You're right. Let's go for a swim."

As they waded into the water, Sean couldn't help but feel a sense of dread. He had heard stories of bull sharks in the area, and the thought of them lurking beneath the surface sent shivers down his spine.

But the kids were having a great time, splashing and playing in the waves. Sean tried to relax and enjoy the moment, but he couldn't shake the feeling of unease.

Suddenly, he saw something moving in the water, a dark shape darting towards them. "Get out of the water!" he shouted, his heart pounding.

But it was too late. A bull shark had already sunk its teeth into Zoey's leg, pulling her under the water. Dale and Myria tried to help, but another shark attacked, biting Dale on the arm.

Sean sprang into action, punching and kicking at the sharks, trying to drive them away. Myria managed to grab Zoey and pull her to safety, but Sean could see that Dale was in trouble. The shark had clamped down on his arm, refusing to let go.

"Get something to hit it with!" Sean yelled, still struggling with the other shark.

Myria ran to the beach house, grabbing a metal pole and rushing back to the water's edge. She swung the pole with all her might, striking the shark on the head and forcing it to release Dale's arm.

Sean pulled Dale to shore, his arm badly mangled and bleeding heavily. Zoey was in shock, her leg torn up by the shark's teeth.

"We have to get them to a hospital," Sean said, his voice shaking. "We have to call for help."

But when they tried to use their phones, they found that there was no signal. They were trapped on the beach, with two injured children and no way to call for help.

"We have to do something," Myria said, looking around frantically.

Sean looked at the kids, both in pain and shock. "We have to stop the bleeding," he said, his mind racing.

Myria nodded, tearing strips of cloth from her shirt and using them to wrap Dale's arm. Sean did the same for Zoey's leg, trying to keep her as comfortable as possible.

As the sun began to set, they huddled together on the beach, trying to keep the kids warm and calm. Sean looked out at the water, watching as the sharks continued to circle, waiting for their next meal.

"We'll make it through this," Myria said, trying to sound reassuring.

Sean nodded, his mind already working on a plan. They couldn't wait for help to arrive. They had to take matters into their own hands.

Sean paced back and forth on the beach, his mind racing with ideas. He knew they needed to find a way to call for help, but their phones weren't working.

"We have to try something," he said, turning to the others. "Maybe there's a radio or something in the house we can use."

Myria nodded. "I'll check."

She ran to the beach house, returning a few minutes later with a small portable radio. Sean quickly turned it on, scanning through the channels.

"Nothing but static," he muttered, frustrated.

Dale groaned in pain, and Zoey whimpered, her leg wrapped in cloth. Sean felt helpless, knowing that they needed medical attention, but there was no way to call for help.

"We can't just sit here," Myria said, her voice shaking.

"What do you suggest?" Sean asked, his tone sharp.

Myria recoiled, hurt by his harsh words. "I don't know, Sean. We have to do something, anything."

Sean sighed, realizing that he was taking his frustration out on Myria and the kids. "I'm sorry," he said, his voice softening. "I just don't know what to do."

"We'll figure something out," Myria said, placing a hand on his shoulder.

They sat in silence for a few minutes, the tension between them palpable. Sean couldn't help but feel like he had let the kids down. He was supposed to be the responsible adult, but he couldn't protect them from the dangers of the ocean.

"We have to try the phones again," Dale said, his voice weak.

Sean nodded, pulling out his phone and dialing 911. But as he feared, there was no signal.

"This is hopeless," Zoey said, tears streaming down her face.

"Don't give up," Myria said, trying to sound encouraging.

But it was hard to stay positive in the face of such overwhelming odds. They were stranded on the beach, with no way to call for help and no idea how long it would be until someone found them.

"I'm scared," Dale said, his eyes closing.

Sean felt a pang of guilt, realizing that he had been so focused on finding a solution that he hadn't paid enough attention to the kids' emotional needs.

"It's okay to be scared," he said, kneeling beside Dale. "But we're going to get through this. Together."

They sat in silence for a few minutes, listening to the sound of the waves crashing against the shore. Sean felt a sense of helplessness wash over him. He had never felt so powerless in his life.

But then he heard a noise, faint at first, but growing louder. It was the sound of a helicopter, coming towards them.

"Over here!" Sean shouted, waving his arms.

The helicopter hovered above them, and Sean could see the rescue crew looking down at them.

"We're saved," he said, tears of relief streaming down his face.

Just then, they noticed something strange. The sharks that had been attacking them were no longer visible in the water. In fact, the water seemed calm and still.

"What's going on?" Zoey asked, her voice trembling.

Dale looked up, his eyes widening. "Look!" he shouted, pointing to a group of dolphins swimming towards them.

The family watched in amazement as the dolphins approached. The creatures seemed to be pushing them towards the shore.

"They're rescuing us," Myria said, tears streaming down her face.

Sean couldn't believe it. It was as if the dolphins knew they were in danger and were helping them to safety.

"Thank you," he whispered, reaching out to touch one of the dolphins as they swam past.

The family felt a glimmer of hope as the dolphins continued to guide them towards the shore. The experience had been terrifying, but it had also shown them the power of nature and the importance of working together.

As they reached the shore, Sean helped Zoey out of the water, while Myria and Dale followed closely behind. They collapsed on the sand, exhausted but grateful to be alive.

"We made it," Dale said, a smile spreading across his face.

Sean hugged him tightly, feeling a sense of pride and relief. "We sure did," he said.

The family sat on the beach, watching as the dolphins swam away into the distance. It was a moment they would never forget, a reminder of the beauty and majesty of the natural world.

"We have a lot to be thankful for," Myria said, breaking the silence.

Sean nodded, looking around at his family. They had been through a traumatic experience, but they had come out the other side stronger and more resilient.

"We'll never forget this," Zoey said, her voice filled with emotion.

The family sat in silence for a few more minutes, watching the sun begin to set over the ocean. It was a peaceful and serene moment, a reminder that even in the darkest of times, there is always hope.

As the family sat on the beach, they were eventually approached by a group of rescuers who had been alerted by the helicopter. They were taken to a hospital where they received treatment for their injuries.

"Myria, are you okay?" Sean asked, as he sat by her bedside.

"I'm fine," she replied, weakly. "Just a few cuts and bruises."

Dale and Zoey were in the next room, also receiving treatment. They had been lucky, but the experience had left them shaken.

As they rested in the hospital, they heard news of the oil spill that had caused the destruction of the ecosystem. The family was shocked and saddened by the news.

"How could this happen?" Zoey asked, tears streaming down her face.

"I don't know," Sean replied. "But we have to do something to help."

The family discussed the issue at length, feeling a sense of responsibility to make a difference. They knew that the dolphins' rescue had become even more significant in light of the disaster.

"We have to spread awareness," Myria said. "We have to let people know what's happening."

The family decided to start a campaign to raise awareness about the effects of the oil spill on the environment. They worked tirelessly, reaching out to people and organizations to gather support for their cause.

In the coming weeks, the family saw an outpouring of support from the community. People came together to help clean up the beaches and raise funds for the affected wildlife.

The family knew that they had made a difference, and it was all thanks to the dolphins that had guided them to safety.

"We owe them everything," Dale said, as he looked out at the ocean. "They saved our lives, and now it's our turn to help them."

The family had come a long way since their traumatic experience. They had been through a lot, but they had emerged stronger and more determined than ever before.

The family spent several days in the hospital, recovering from their injuries and reflecting on the events that had brought them there. As they talked, they began to understand each other better.

"Dad, I'm sorry for being so distant," Zoey said, tears in her eyes. "I didn't realize how much you cared about us."

Sean took her hand, squeezing it gently. "I love you both more than anything," he said. "I want to be a part of your lives, but I also know that I have to respect your feelings."

Dale nodded, looking up from his phone. "Yeah, I think we all need to work on communication," he said. "We can't let things get to a breaking point like they did before."

The family talked for hours, sharing their thoughts and feelings with each other. They realized that they had all been struggling in their own way, but that they were stronger when they worked together.

As they left the hospital, the family felt a renewed sense of purpose. They knew that they had to keep fighting for the environment, but they also knew that they had to fight for each other.

"We're in this together," Myria said, smiling at her family. "And we'll always be here for each other."

The family hugged, feeling a sense of closeness that they had never experienced before. They knew that they still had a lot of work to do, but they were ready for whatever challenges lay ahead.

As they walked along the beach, the family saw the dolphins swimming in the distance. They watched in amazement as the creatures leapt out of the water, a symbol of hope and resilience.

"We have a lot to learn from them," Sean said, his eyes fixed on the dolphins.

The family nodded in agreement, feeling a newfound appreciation for the natural world. They had been through a lot, but they had come out the other side with a new understanding of themselves and each other.

The family decided to stay at the beach for a few more days, savoring their newfound sense of closeness. They spent their time building sandcastles, watching the sunset, and talking about their experiences.

"This has been amazing," Zoey said, as she looked out at the ocean. "I feel like we've grown so much as a family."

Dale nodded, a smile on his face. "Yeah, it's been really great," he said. "I feel like we're all on the same page now."

Sean put his arm around Myria, pulling her close. "I'm just glad we're all here together," he said. "I don't think I could have gone through this without you guys."

The family spent their days swimming, playing games, and lounging in the sun. They laughed and joked, feeling closer and more bonded than ever before.

As they watched the sunset on their final night at the beach, the family knew that they would never forget this experience. They had been through a lot, but they had come out the other side with a deeper appreciation for each other and for the world around them.

"We'll have to come back here someday," Myria said, a hint of sadness in her voice.

Sean nodded, squeezing her hand. "Definitely," he said. "This place will always be special to us."

As the family packed up their belongings and prepared to leave the beach, they knew that they would carry the memories of this trip with them forever. They had been through a lot, but they had emerged stronger and more connected than ever before.

"Together, we can do anything," Dale said, as they walked towards their car.

The family smiled, feeling a sense of optimism and hope for the future. They knew that they still had a lot of work to do, but they also knew that they had each other to rely on.

The family gathered around the bonfire on their last night at the beach, roasting marshmallows and sharing stories. They were reminiscing about their favorite moments of the trip when a group of surfers approached them. The surfers looked like they were in their teens, and they were all wearing wetsuits and carrying surfboards.

"Hey, guys!" one of the surfers called out. "Mind if we join you?"

The family welcomed the surfers and invited them to sit down around the bonfire. The surfers introduced themselves, and two of them, Mychal and Anwyn, caught Sean's attention.

"Mychal... Anwyn?" Sean repeated, his voice cracking with emotion. "Is that you?"

Mychal and Anwyn looked at each other in confusion before turning back to Sean. "Yeah, that's us," Mychal said. "Do you know us?"

Sean's eyes welled up with tears. "I'm your dad," he said, his voice barely above a whisper.

The family was stunned. Mychal and Anwyn looked at Sean with a mixture of surprise and disbelief.

"I've been searching for you guys for years," Sean continued, his voice shaking. "I never thought I would find you."

Mychal and Anwyn looked at each other again, and then at Sean. "We've been looking for you too," Anwyn said. "We wanted to meet you."

The family was overcome with emotion as Sean embraced his long-lost children. They were grateful for the new bond they had discovered and for the unexpected twist that had brought them together.

For the rest of the night, the family and the surfers sat around the bonfire, sharing stories and getting to know each other. Mychal and Anwyn talked about their passion for surfing and their dream of traveling the world. Sean shared stories about his life and his journey to find his children.

As the night wore on, the family knew that their time at the beach was coming to an end. They had experienced so much on this trip, and now, they had a new chapter to look forward to.

"Together, we can do anything," Sean said, looking at his reunited family.

The family smiled, feeling a sense of hope and optimism for the future. They had come to the beach looking for answers, but they had found so much more than that. They had found each other.

Deep Cuts

Maya stood on the deck of the research vessel, taking in the salty sea air and the shimmering blue waters of the Caribbean Sea. She was excited to be starting her latest research project, studying the behavior of bull sharks in their natural habitat. Maya had always been fascinated by sharks, and she had worked hard to become a marine biologist so she could study them up close.

As the boat pulled away from the dock, Maya's mentor and supervisor, Dr. Miller, approached her.

"Are you ready for this, Maya?" he asked with a smile.

"Absolutely," Maya replied eagerly. "I can't wait to get started."

Dr. Miller nodded approvingly. "Good. Remember to stay focused and observe everything around you. We'll be conducting several dives over the next few days, and I expect you to gather as much data as possible."

Maya grinned, knowing that this was exactly what she loved to do. As they reached the designated dive spot, Maya and her team prepared their gear and made their way into the water. The warm tropical waters enveloped her as she descended into the depths, her eyes scanning the surroundings for any signs of shark activity.

As they swam, Dr. Miller called out over the intercom, "Maya, keep an eye out for any interesting behaviors. Take note of any changes in the shark's movements, and be sure to record everything."

"Got it," Maya responded, her focus on the task at hand.

As they continued their dive, Maya spotted a group of bull sharks in the distance. She immediately signaled to her team and they cautiously approached the sharks, observing their behavior and movements.

For the next few hours, Maya and her team conducted several dives, gathering valuable data on the behavior of the bull sharks. Maya was thrilled with the results, knowing that this information could help protect these magnificent creatures and their ecosystem.

As they returned to the surface, Maya couldn't contain her excitement. "Did you see that? The way they swam in formation, it was incredible!" she exclaimed, beaming with pride.

Dr. Miller chuckled, "Yes, Maya, I saw. You've got a real passion for this, and it's clear to see."

Maya smiled, knowing that her dedication to marine biology had led her to this moment.

Maya and her team continued their dives over the next few days, observing the bull sharks and gathering more data. But on the third day, things took a dangerous turn.

Maya was swimming ahead of the group, her eyes focused on a group of bull sharks swimming in the distance. Suddenly, she felt a sharp pain in her leg and looked down to see a bull shark clamped onto her calf. Maya kicked and thrashed, trying to free herself, but the shark wouldn't let go.

"Maya, are you okay?!" Dr. Miller shouted through the intercom, as he and the rest of the team swam over to her.

"No, I'm not okay!" Maya yelled, her voice shaking with fear and pain. "Get it off of me!"

The team quickly sprang into action, trying to pry the shark's jaws open. Finally, with a powerful shove, they were able to free Maya from the shark's grip.

Maya's leg was bleeding profusely, and her arm had been bitten as well. The team quickly brought her to the surface and got her onto the boat, administering first aid and calling for emergency medical assistance.

As Maya was rushed to the hospital, she couldn't help but feel angry and betrayed. She had always respected and admired sharks, but this attack had shattered her perception of them. Maya knew she would never be the same again, physically or mentally.

Months of recovery and rehabilitation followed, with Maya undergoing surgeries and intense physical therapy. She was determined to regain her strength and return to the water, but the memories of the attack continued to haunt her.

One day, as Maya was sitting in her hospital room, she received a call from Captain Morales, a local fisherman she had met on her previous dives.

"Maya, I heard about what happened. I'm so sorry. Is there anything I can do to help?" he asked, concern evident in his voice.

Maya was touched by the gesture. "Actually, yes," she replied. "I want to know everything there is to know about bull sharks in this area. I want to understand why they attacked us."

Captain Morales agreed to help, and over the next few weeks, he shared his knowledge of the local shark population with Maya, giving her a newfound respect for these powerful creatures.

As Maya learned more about bull sharks, she couldn't shake off the anger and fear she felt towards them. She had always believed that understanding and protecting these creatures was crucial, but now all she could think about was revenge.

Maya began to obsess over finding the bull sharks responsible for her attack, convinced that they were still out there, waiting to strike again. She spent countless hours researching and planning, determined to take matters into her own hands.

"Maya, I'm worried about you," Dr. Miller said one day, as he visited her in the hospital. "I understand that you're angry, but you can't let that consume you. Revenge won't bring you peace."

Maya glared at him, her eyes blazing with fury. "You don't understand, Dr. Miller. They nearly killed me. I won't rest until I've taken them down."

Dr. Miller sighed. He knew that Maya's obsession was clouding her judgment, but he also understood the trauma she had experienced. He decided to offer her a compromise.

"Maya, I don't want you to give up on your passion for marine biology. But I also don't want you to make any rash decisions that could put yourself or others in danger," he said. "What if we conduct a study on bull shark behavior and try to find non-lethal ways to protect ourselves from them?"

Maya considered his proposal. She knew that Dr. Miller was right, but the thought of studying bull sharks without taking action against them made her feel helpless.

"Fine," she said begrudgingly. "But I won't rest until I've found the sharks that attacked me."

Over the next few months, Maya and her team conducted a study on bull shark behavior, using drones and underwater cameras to gather data. Maya felt a sense of purpose as she analyzed the footage, determined to find any patterns or weaknesses in the sharks' movements.

But despite the progress they made in their study, Maya's obsession with revenge only grew stronger. She began to spend more and more time alone, poring over the footage and plotting her next move.

One day, as Maya was examining a video of a bull shark swimming near the dive site, she noticed something strange. The shark had a distinctive scar on its dorsal fin, one that she recognized from her own attack.

Maya's heart raced as she realized that this could be the shark that had attacked her. She immediately called Dr. Miller and the rest of the team, insisting that they track down the shark and take action against it.

"Maya, you can't be serious," Dr. Miller said, his voice laced with concern. "We don't even know for sure if this is the same shark. And even if it is, what do you hope to accomplish by killing it?"

Maya was trembling with rage. "I want justice, Dr. Miller. I want these sharks to pay for what they did to me."

Dr. Miller shook his head. "I understand your anger, Maya. But killing these creatures won't solve anything. We need to find a way to coexist with them, to understand and protect them."

Maya felt a surge of frustration. She knew that Dr. Miller was right, but she couldn't let go of her desire for revenge. She began to feel like she was losing herself in her own obsession.

Maya was lost in her thoughts when Dr. Miller's phone rang. He answered the call and began speaking in hushed tones. Maya strained to hear, but she couldn't make out the conversation.

After he hung up, Dr. Miller turned to Maya, his expression grave. "Maya, I have some troubling news. There have been a series of illegal poaching incidents in the area, and it appears that a group of poachers have been targeting bull sharks for their fins."

Maya's eyes widened in shock. "That's horrible. But what does it have to do with me?"

Dr. Miller hesitated before continuing. "Detective Ramirez is investigating the case, and he found evidence that the poachers were using chum and bait to lure the sharks to the area, causing them to become more aggressive and attack. Maya, it's possible that the bull sharks that attacked you were victims of this illegal poaching ring."

Maya's mind was racing. She couldn't believe that humans would stoop so low as to harm innocent creatures for profit. But the more she thought about it, the more it made sense. The sharks that attacked her had been more aggressive than usual, almost as if they were provoked.

"Do you think we can help Detective Ramirez catch these poachers?" Maya asked, her voice filled with determination.

Dr. Miller nodded. "I think it's worth a try. We have footage of the bull sharks from our study, and we might be able to identify the poachers if they were using a certain type of boat or equipment."

Maya was already reaching for her laptop, eager to start analyzing the footage. She felt a sense of purpose that she hadn't felt in months.

Over the next few days, Maya and Dr. Miller worked tirelessly to analyze the footage and compile a list of possible suspects. They handed their findings over to Detective Ramirez, who was impressed by their dedication and expertise.

"Thank you for your help, Dr. Miller, Maya. This is invaluable information," Detective Ramirez said, shaking their hands. "I'll do everything in my power to catch these poachers and put them behind bars."

Maya felt a surge of pride as she watched Detective Ramirez leave. For the first time in a long time, she felt like she was making a real difference in the world.

But even as she worked to catch the poachers, Maya couldn't shake off her anger and fear towards the bull sharks. She still felt like they were her enemies, even though she knew that they were just animals trying to survive.

Maya was determined to help catch the poachers who were harming the bull sharks, but she knew that she needed someone who knew the waters well. That's when she thought of Captain Morales, a local fisherman who was known to be an expert in navigating the Caribbean Sea.

She quickly called him and explained her situation. "Captain Morales, I need your help. I'm trying to catch the poachers who are hurting the bull sharks, and I need someone who knows these waters well. Will you help me?"

There was a pause on the other end of the line before Captain Morales finally spoke. "Miss Maya, I don't know about getting involved in something like this. It's dangerous and unpredictable. Besides, what do you know about fishing and navigating the Caribbean Sea?"

Maya felt her frustration building, but she knew that she needed Captain Morales on her side. "I may not know much about fishing, but I do know how to analyze footage and track patterns. And I need someone like you to help me navigate these waters and find the poachers."

Captain Morales remained silent for a few moments, contemplating Maya's words. Finally, he spoke. "Alright, Miss Maya. I'll meet you at the dock tomorrow morning at sunrise. But you have to promise me that you'll listen to my advice and follow my instructions."

Maya felt a wave of relief wash over her. "Thank you, Captain Morales. I won't let you down."

The next morning, Maya arrived at the dock just as the sun was rising. Captain Morales was already there, preparing his boat for their journey. Maya could see that he was a sturdy man in his mid-fifties, with a gruff demeanor and a weather-beaten face.

"Good morning, Captain Morales," Maya greeted him.

"Good morning, Miss Maya," he replied, not looking up from his work.

As they set out to sea, Captain Morales gave Maya a crash course in fishing and navigating the Caribbean Sea. He showed her how to read the currents, identify different types of fish, and handle the equipment. Maya listened intently, eager to learn everything she could.

After a few hours of searching, they spotted a group of bull sharks swimming near the surface. Captain Morales expertly maneuvered the boat closer to the sharks, while Maya recorded footage of their behavior.

"That's them," Maya said excitedly, pointing to a specific shark with a distinctive fin. "That's the one that attacked me."

Captain Morales nodded grimly. "We have to be careful. Bull sharks are known to be aggressive, and we don't want to get too close."

Maya felt a surge of fear and anger towards the bull shark. But then she reminded herself that they were just animals, and that they were probably reacting to the chum and bait that the poachers were using to lure them.

For the next few hours, Maya and Captain Morales continued their search for the poachers, but they didn't find any leads. As they headed back to shore, Maya couldn't help but feel discouraged.

"I'm sorry we didn't find anything," she said to Captain Morales. "But I appreciate your help."

Captain Morales turned to her with a twinkle in his eye. "Don't be discouraged, Miss Maya. We may not have found the poachers today, but we did gather valuable information. And tomorrow is a new day."

Maya smiled, feeling grateful for Captain Morales' optimism. She realized that she had found a new ally in her quest to protect the bull sharks, and that they would continue their search together.

As they set out on their hunt for the bull sharks, Maya and Captain Morales kept their eyes peeled for any sign of the poachers. Maya was amazed by Captain Morales' expertise in navigating the waters, as he deftly guided the boat through the currents and shoals.

"Captain Morales, how long have you been fishing in these waters?" Maya asked.

"Since I was a boy," he replied with a smile. "My father and grandfather were fishermen, and I learned from them. I've spent my whole life on these seas."

Maya nodded, impressed by his knowledge and experience. She was determined to learn as much as she could from him, and to use her own skills to help catch the poachers.

As they approached a reef, Maya spotted a group of bull sharks swimming in the distance. She pointed them out to Captain Morales, and they both watched as the sharks circled around the boat.

"They're curious," Captain Morales observed. "They can sense something's not right."

Maya nodded, feeling a sense of unease. She had underestimated the intelligence and cunning of the bull sharks, and she knew that they would need to be careful.

Suddenly, Maya spotted a small fishing boat in the distance, with two men aboard. She quickly grabbed her camera and started filming.

"Captain Morales, that must be them!" she exclaimed.

Captain Morales nodded, his face grim. "Stay back, Miss Maya. I'll approach them slowly and try to get a better look."

Maya watched anxiously as Captain Morales maneuvered the boat closer to the poachers. She could see that they were hauling in a large net filled with fish, including several bull sharks.

"Those monsters," she muttered under her breath.

Suddenly, one of the poachers spotted them and started shouting angrily. Maya could see that he was holding a machete, and she felt a surge of fear.

"Captain Morales, we need to get out of here!" she shouted.

But it was too late. The poachers started racing towards them, their boat careening dangerously close.

Captain Morales expertly maneuvered the boat out of their path, but Maya could see that the poachers weren't giving up. They started throwing rocks and other objects at them, their rage and desperation palpable.

Maya could feel her heart racing as they sped away from the poachers. She knew that they were playing a dangerous game, but she also knew that they couldn't give up.

"We need to report them to the authorities," she said, her voice shaking. "We can't let them get away with this."

Captain Morales nodded, his face grim. "I'll take us back to shore, and we'll make the call."

Maya felt a sense of relief as they headed back to the dock. She realized that she had underestimated the risks involved in trying to catch the poachers, but she also knew that she couldn't give up. The bull sharks were counting on her, and she would do everything in her power to protect them.

As they pulled into the dock, Maya's mind was racing. She couldn't shake the image of the poachers throwing rocks at them, and she felt a sense of anger and frustration.

"Captain Morales, we need to make that call now," she said, grabbing her phone.

"Agreed," he replied, his expression serious. "We can't let those poachers continue to wreak havoc on these waters."

Maya dialed the number for the local authorities, and explained the situation to the person who answered. She gave them the location of the poachers and a description of their boat, and urged them to take action.

As they waited for the authorities to arrive, Maya couldn't help but think about the bull sharks. She had risked her life to protect them, but she knew that there was more work to be done.

"Captain Morales, we need to talk to Dr. Miller," she said suddenly. "We need to know the truth about our research."

Captain Morales nodded, his expression grave. "I agree. Let's head back to the lab."

When they arrived at the lab, Maya headed straight to Dr. Miller's office. She knocked on the door, and he invited her in.

"Dr. Miller, we need to talk," she said, her voice trembling.

He looked up from his computer, his expression curious. "What's the matter, Maya?"

She took a deep breath, gathering her thoughts. "Did you authorize the use of chum to attract the sharks?"

Dr. Miller's face paled, and Maya could see a look of guilt in his eyes.

"Yes," he said finally. "I did."

Maya felt a wave of shock and anger wash over her. She had trusted Dr. Miller, and now she realized that their research had put her and her team in danger.

"Why did you do it?" she asked, her voice shaking.

Dr. Miller looked down at his hands, his expression pained. "I thought it would help us gather more data. I didn't realize the risks involved."

Maya felt a sense of devastation as the implications of Dr. Miller's confession sank in. Their research had not only put her and her team in danger, but it had also contributed to the attack on them.

"Dr. Miller, I can't believe this," she said, her voice barely above a whisper. "We were supposed to be studying these sharks, not manipulating them."

He looked up at her, his eyes filled with regret. "I know, Maya. I'm sorry. I didn't realize the risks involved. I just wanted to gather more data."

Maya shook her head, feeling a sense of disillusionment. She had always believed that science was a force for good, but now she realized that it could also be used to harm.

"We need to make this right," she said firmly. "We need to make sure that our research is conducted ethically, and that we're not putting anyone in danger."

Dr. Miller nodded, his expression serious. "I agree. We need to take responsibility for what we've done."

Maya felt a sense of relief as they agreed to work together to make things right. She knew that it wouldn't be easy, but she also knew that they had a responsibility to the sharks, and to the people who depended on these waters for their livelihoods.

Maya's mind was spinning as she left Dr. Miller's office. She couldn't believe what she had just learned - that Dr. Miller's research had not only put her and her team in danger, but it had also enabled the poachers to infiltrate their operations.

She knew that she needed to get to the bottom of this, to find out how the poachers had gained access to their research facility and how they had been able to get so close to the sharks.

She made her way to the lab's security office, where she found the head of security, a stern-looking man named Juan.

"Juan, we need to talk," she said, her voice urgent.

He looked up from his computer, his expression wary. "What's the matter, Maya?"

She took a deep breath, steeling herself. "I think that the poachers were able to infiltrate our research operations because of a breach in security. I need you to help me find out how they did it."

Juan frowned, his brow furrowed in concern. "What makes you think that?"

Maya took a deep breath, her mind racing. "I just spoke to Dr. Miller, and he told me that he authorized the use of chum to attract the sharks. That means that the poachers knew where to find the sharks, and they were able to get close to them because of our research."

Juan's eyes widened in shock. "That's a serious breach in security. I'll look into it right away."

Maya nodded, feeling a sense of relief. She knew that she could trust Juan to get to the bottom of this.

As she waited for Juan to finish his investigation, Maya couldn't help but think about the sharks. They were the reason she had gotten into this line of work in the first place, and she felt a sense of responsibility to protect them.

When Juan finally called her into his office, she was eager to hear what he had discovered.

"Maya, I have some news," he said, his expression grave.

"What did you find out?" she asked, her heart racing.

He handed her a file, and she began to read through it. As she did, her eyes widened in shock.

The file contained evidence linking the poaching ring to their research facility. There were emails between Dr. Miller and the poachers, discussing the use of chum to attract the sharks and the best locations to find them.

Maya felt a wave of anger and disgust wash over her. Dr. Miller's negligence had not only put her and her team in danger, but it had also enabled the poachers to profit from the sharks.

"We need to take action," she said firmly. "We can't let this go on any longer."

Juan nodded, his expression serious. "I'll contact the authorities. We'll make sure that these poachers are brought to justice."

Maya felt a sense of relief wash over her. They had uncovered the truth, and they were taking action to make things right.

As she left Juan's office, she couldn't help but think about what they had learned. The truth was hard to swallow, but it was also a call to action. They had a responsibility to protect the sharks, and they would do whatever it took to make sure that their research was conducted ethically.

Maya spent the next few days working closely with Juan and the authorities to build a case against the poachers. They gathered evidence, conducted interviews, and worked tirelessly to expose the illegal activities that had been taking place.

As she worked, Maya found that her anger and frustration began to give way to a sense of determination. She was no longer focused on revenge or justice for herself and her team, but on making sure that the poachers were held accountable for their actions.

It wasn't easy, but Maya knew that it was the right thing to do. She had always believed that the sharks were the most important thing, and she realized now that the true enemy was not the sharks, but the humans who were exploiting them for profit.

She spent long hours poring over the evidence and making sure that everything was in order. She worked closely with the authorities to ensure that the case was strong enough to hold up in court, and she was determined to see it through to the end.

As the trial approached, Maya felt a sense of nervousness and excitement. She had never been involved in something like this before, and she knew that the outcome would have a profound impact on the future of the sharks and the people who worked to protect them.

On the day of the trial, Maya sat in the courtroom, watching as the poachers were brought in. They looked nervous and afraid, and she couldn't help but feel a sense of satisfaction knowing that they would soon be held accountable for their crimes.

As the trial progressed, Maya listened intently to the testimony and evidence presented. It was clear that the poachers had been operating for years, exploiting the sharks and putting their lives at risk.

Finally, the verdict was delivered. The poachers were found guilty on all charges, and they were sentenced to years in prison. Maya felt a sense of relief wash over her, knowing that justice had been served.

As she left the courthouse, Maya couldn't help but feel a sense of pride. She had worked tirelessly to bring the poachers to justice, and she had done it all for the sharks. She realized now that her true calling was not just to research and study the sharks, but to protect them from those who would exploit them for profit.

As Maya swam in the ocean, surrounded by the magnificent creatures she had worked so hard to protect, she couldn't help but reflect on her journey. She had come a long way from the angry and vengeful person she had been just a few weeks ago.

As she swam, Maya saw a group of sharks swimming together in a tight formation. It was a sight that always filled her with awe, and she watched as they gracefully navigated the water.

Suddenly, Maya felt a gentle bump against her side. She turned to see a small shark nudging her playfully.

"Hey there, little guy," she said with a smile.

As she looked around, Maya realized that she was surrounded by sharks of all sizes and shapes. They were curious and friendly, and she felt a sense of connection to them that she had never felt before.

For a moment, Maya forgot about everything else. She was lost in the beauty and wonder of the ocean and its inhabitants.

But as she continued to swim, Maya couldn't help but think about the poachers who had once threatened these creatures. She thought about the lengths they had gone to for profit and the disregard they had shown for the lives of the sharks.

It was then that Maya realized something important. The poachers were not the only ones who were responsible for the destruction of the environment. Every person who lived on this planet had a role to play in protecting it, and Maya knew that she had to do her part.

She swam back to shore, feeling more determined than ever. She knew that her work was far from over, and that she had to continue fighting for the sharks and the environment.

Maya called the authorities and led them to the poaching ring's operation. With the evidence she had gathered, the authorities were able to arrest the poachers and shut down their operation for good.

In the final scene, Maya was shown standing on the beach, watching as the sun set over the ocean. She reflected on her journey and realized that her obsession with revenge had blinded her to the true beauty and importance of these creatures.

"It's not just about the sharks," she said to herself. "It's about everything. We have to protect everything."

The twist ending served as a powerful commentary on the impact that humans can have on the environment. Maya's journey had taught her that the destruction of the environment was not just the fault of a few individuals, but the responsibility of all people. It was a call to action, a reminder that we all have a role to play in preserving our natural resources for future generations.

Bait

The sun was just beginning to set over the crystal-clear waters surrounding the remote island as the research team arrived. The team of six had traveled from all corners of the globe to be here, excited to begin their groundbreaking research on shark behavior.

Dr. Rebecca Kim, the marine biologist leading the team, scanned the horizon with a sense of awe. "This is it, folks," she said. "Our home for the next few weeks. Let's get to work."

As they unloaded their gear and set up their camp, the team was abuzz with excitement. Dr. John Smith, the shark expert, eagerly discussed the experiment with Dr. Rachel Lee, the behavioral psychologist. Mark Johnson, the data analyst, was more reserved, but couldn't help feeling intrigued by the prospect of using themselves as bait to study shark behavior.

As they settled into their tents for the night, the team discussed the experiment in detail. "It's going to be amazing," Dr. Kim said, her eyes shining. "We'll be able to observe the sharks up close and personal. We'll learn so much about their behavior that we could never learn from afar."

Dr. Smith nodded in agreement. "And with the safety protocols we've put in place, we'll minimize the risks to ourselves and the sharks."

Dr. Lee looked thoughtful. "But what about the ethical implications? Are we really justified in putting ourselves and the sharks in danger for the sake of our research?"

Dr. Kim smiled reassuringly. "We've thought this through, Rachel. We're taking all necessary precautions to ensure the safety of everyone involved. And the knowledge we gain could ultimately lead to better conservation efforts and protect both humans and sharks."

As they drifted off to sleep, each member of the team felt a sense of excitement and anticipation. They knew that what they were about to do was risky, but they were confident that it was worth it.

The next morning, they began their preparations in earnest. They set up a baited area in the shallow waters near the shore and practiced using themselves as bait. Dr. Smith donned a specially designed shark suit and entered the water, attracting a small group of curious sharks.

Mark Johnson monitored the data as the sharks approached and retreated, taking notes on their behavior. Dr. Davis, the veterinarian, observed the sharks from a safe distance, ready to intervene if necessary.

As the day wore on, the team became more confident in their abilities to use themselves as bait. They discussed their findings over dinner, each member of the team contributing their observations and insights.

As they settled into their tents for the night, Dr. Kim turned to the team with a sense of excitement. "Tomorrow, we begin the real experiment," she said. "We're going to learn so much about shark behavior, and I can't wait to see what we discover."

The next day, the team geared up for the real experiment. They entered the water, one by one, with the bait in hand, ready to attract the sharks. Dr. Smith was the first to go in, followed by Dr. Lee, and then Mark Johnson.

As the sharks began to circle, Mark couldn't help feeling uneasy. He had always known that there would be some level of risk involved, but the reality of being so close to these powerful creatures was starting to weigh on him.

"Are you okay, Mark?" Dr. Kim asked, noticing the unease on his face.

Mark hesitated before speaking up. "I'm just starting to have second thoughts about this. What if something goes wrong?"

Dr. Lee chimed in, her voice strained. "I have to admit, I'm starting to question the ethics of this experiment. Are we really justified in putting ourselves and the sharks in danger for the sake of science?"

Dr. Kim's expression turned stern. "We've been over this, Rachel. We've taken all necessary precautions to minimize the risks involved. And the potential benefits of this research are immense."

Dr. Smith added, his attention fixed on the approaching sharks. "Just focus on the data we're gathering. That's the most important thing right now."

As the sharks began to swim closer, tensions rose between the team members. Mark couldn't shake the feeling of unease, and Rachel continued to question the morality of their actions. Dr. Kim and Dr. Smith, however, remained focused on the task at hand.

The experiment continued for several hours, with the team members taking turns as bait and monitoring the sharks' behavior. Mark's anxiety only grew as the day went on, and he found himself starting to withdraw from the group.

At dinner that night, tensions were palpable. Mark was quiet, lost in thought, while Rachel continued to voice her concerns about the experiment's ethics. Dr. Kim and Dr. Smith, meanwhile, were focused on analyzing the data they had collected.

As they settled into their tents for the night, Mark couldn't help but feel conflicted. He knew that the research they were doing had the potential to make a significant impact, but he couldn't shake the feeling that they were taking unnecessary risks.

The next morning, the team was back in the water for another day of the experiment. The tension from the night before still hung heavy in the air, but they were determined to push through and continue with their research.

As they began to bait the sharks, the team worked with a heightened sense of awareness. Mark's unease had only grown since the day before, and Rachel continued to voice her concerns. Dr. Kim and Dr. Smith, however, remained focused on the task at hand.

Suddenly, a shark darted towards the bait and the researcher holding it. In an instant, the shark clamped down on the researcher's arm, dragging them underwater.

Panic set in as the team realized what had happened. Dr. Lee immediately sprang into action, diving into the water to rescue the researcher. With the help of Dr. Kim and Mark, they managed to pull the injured researcher back to the surface.

The team quickly sprang into action, using their medical training to stabilize the victim. Dr. Smith began to assess the severity of the injury while Dr. Kim called for emergency assistance.

As they waited for help to arrive, the team struggled to process what had just happened. Mark was in shock, while Rachel was visibly shaken. Dr. Lee was still in the water, shaking from the adrenaline of the rescue.

Once the emergency team arrived, they rushed the injured researcher to the hospital. The team was left to pick up the pieces and try to make sense of what had just happened.

As they sat around the campfire that night, the reality of their situation began to sink in. They had put themselves and their colleague in grave danger, all for the sake of scientific research.

"We have to stop this experiment," Rachel said firmly. "It's not worth the risks."

Dr. Kim nodded in agreement. "I think she's right. We can't keep putting ourselves in harm's way like this."

Dr. Smith, however, was hesitant. "We've invested so much time and resources into this project. We can't just abandon it now."

"But at what cost?" Mark interjected. "We've already seen what can happen when we push too far. We can't afford to take any more risks."

The team continued to debate the merits of the experiment late into the night, but ultimately, they knew what they had to do. The next morning, they packed up their gear and made the difficult decision to end the experiment.

As they headed back to civilization, the team was left with a mix of emotions. They had come so far and learned so much, but at what cost? They knew that they had to take a hard look at the ethics of their work and consider the consequences of their actions.

The team had just packed up their equipment and were about to leave the island when they heard the sound of a boat approaching. They turned to see a group of tourists disembarking on the beach.

Dr. Kim groaned. "This is the last thing we need right now."

The tourists, a mix of families and adventure-seekers, eagerly approached the researchers, asking about their work with the sharks.

Rachel stepped forward, trying to keep a friendly demeanor. "We're studying the behavior of these sharks and their interactions with other marine life."

The tourists seemed fascinated, but Dr. Lee cut in. "I'm sorry, but we're not taking any visitors at the moment. It's too dangerous."

The tourists looked disappointed, but they didn't push the issue. The team quickly finished packing their gear and boarded their boat, ready to leave the island behind.

As they made their way back to the mainland, the team discussed the potential risks of allowing tourists to observe their work. Mark was especially concerned.

"If something had happened while they were here, it could have been disastrous," he said. "We can't take any chances."

Dr. Smith, however, saw an opportunity. "If we can find a way to make this work, we could raise awareness about the importance of shark conservation. We just need to be careful."

The team agreed to discuss the issue further once they were back at their home base. For now, they were just glad to be leaving the island behind.

As the team approached their home base, they noticed that the weather was starting to take a turn for the worse. Dark clouds were gathering on the horizon, and the wind was picking up.

Dr. Kim looked worried. "I don't like the look of this. We need to secure our equipment before the storm hits."

The team rushed to unload their gear and get everything set up before the storm hit. They knew that if their equipment was damaged, it could set their research back months.

As they finished securing their tents and equipment, the wind started to howl. Rain pounded down on them, and lightning illuminated the sky.

The team huddled in their tents, trying to wait out the storm. The sound of the wind and rain was deafening, and they could feel the ground shaking beneath them.

Suddenly, there was a loud crash, and the team knew that something had gone wrong. They burst out of their tents to find that one of their research boats had been swept away by the storm.

Dr. Smith cursed. "We have to find that boat. It's got our equipment on it."

The team split up, searching through the rain and wind for any sign of the missing boat. After several tense minutes, they found it beached on the shore of a nearby island.

Mark groaned. "This is a disaster. All of our equipment could be ruined."

The team worked quickly to salvage what they could, but the damage was extensive. Cameras and sensors had been smashed, and several pieces of equipment were completely destroyed.

As they sat in their wet and muddy tents, the team knew that the storm had set their research back significantly. They would have to work twice as hard to make up for the lost time.

The team worked tirelessly over the next few days, trying to repair the damage caused by the storm. Tensions were high as they struggled to make up for lost time and get their research back on track.

One afternoon, as the team sat down to discuss their progress, Dr. Lee noticed something odd about Rachel's behavior. She seemed distracted and distant, not fully engaged in the conversation.

"Is everything okay, Rachel?" he asked.

She hesitated for a moment before answering. "I'm fine, just tired."

But Dr. Lee could sense that there was more to it than that. "Are you sure? You seem... off."

Rachel took a deep breath. "I have something to tell you all. Something that I've been keeping secret."

The team looked at her, confused and concerned.

"I've been working with a rival research team," she admitted. "They want me to steal the data we've collected and give it to them."

The team was shocked. "How could you do this to us?" Mark demanded.

Rachel hung her head. "I'm sorry. I didn't know what else to do. They offered me a lot of money, and I was struggling to pay my bills. I never meant for things to go this far."

Dr. Smith was furious. "This is a betrayal of the highest order. You've put our entire research project at risk."

Rachel looked ashamed. "I know. And I'm willing to do whatever it takes to make it right. Please, just give me a chance to make amends."

The team was silent for a moment, unsure of what to do. They had invested so much time and effort into their research, and now it was all at risk.

Finally, Dr. Lee spoke up. "We need to think about this carefully. We can't make any rash decisions. Rachel, you need to leave the island for now. We'll discuss this further once we've had time to think."

Rachel nodded, tears in her eyes. "I understand. I'm sorry."

As she gathered her things and left the island, the team knew that their work had just become even more difficult. They would have to be extra careful now, watching their backs and making sure that their data remained safe.

The team tried to put the incident with Rachel behind them and focus on their research. They continued to bait and observe the sharks, trying to gather as much data as possible before they had to leave the island.

During their last baiting session, the team noticed that the sharks seemed more aggressive than ever before. They circled the bait with greater intensity, snapping their jaws and thrashing in the water.

Dr. Kim looked concerned. "This isn't normal behavior. Something must be causing them to act this way."

Suddenly, one of the sharks lunged out of the water, narrowly missing one of the team members.

"Get out of the water!" Dr. Smith shouted. "Now!"

The team scrambled back onto the boat, heart racing as the sharks continued to thrash in the water.

"What's going on?" Mark demanded.

Dr. Kim looked grim. "I don't know. Maybe the storm stirred up the waters and made them more agitated."

But Dr. Lee had a different theory. "I think there's something else going on here. Something that we're not aware of."

As the team tried to regroup and figure out their next move, the sharks continued to circle the boat, growing more and more aggressive.

"We need to get out of here," Dr. Smith said. "This is too dangerous."

But before they could make a move, the largest shark suddenly charged at the boat, slamming into it with incredible force.

The team was thrown into chaos as they fought for their lives, trying to fend off the attacking sharks with whatever they could find.

As the chaos continued, Dr. Lee realized what was causing the sharks to act this way. "It's Rachel!" he shouted. "She must have tipped off the rival research team, and they've sent someone to sabotage our work!"

The team was stunned. They had been so focused on the sharks that they hadn't even considered the possibility of human interference.

But it was too late to do anything about it now. They were in the midst of a full-blown shark attack, and they had to fight for their survival.

The team fought with all their might, using their research equipment as weapons to fend off the attacking sharks. Eventually, after what felt like an eternity, the sharks began to retreat back into the depths of the ocean.

The team was left shaken and traumatized. They had narrowly escaped death, but they had also lost one of their own. Mark had been killed in the attack, leaving the team devastated and grieving.

As they huddled together on the boat, trying to make sense of what had just happened, Dr. Lee spoke up. "We've made a grave mistake. We never should have brought this many sharks to the island. We never should have put our own lives, and the lives of these creatures, at risk like this."

Dr. Kim nodded in agreement. "We got so caught up in our research that we forgot about the bigger picture. We forgot that there are consequences to our actions."

Dr. Smith looked at the team, her eyes filled with tears. "We have to take responsibility for what happened here. We have to make sure that this never happens again."

The team spent the next few days cleaning up the wreckage and preparing to leave the island. They knew that their research had been a failure, and that they had caused irreparable harm to the ecosystem.

As they boarded the boat to leave, they knew that they would never forget what had happened on that island. They had learned a valuable lesson about the importance of responsible research, and they vowed to carry that lesson with them for the rest of their lives.

As the boat pulled away from the island, the team watched in silence, each lost in their own thoughts. They were relieved to be alive, but they also felt a sense of loss and regret for what they had done.

Suddenly, a helicopter appeared on the horizon, flying low over the water. The team watched in disbelief as it approached their boat and lowered a rope ladder.

A rescue team had arrived, sent by the research organization to check on the team and offer assistance.

"We're here to take you back to civilization," one of the rescue team members shouted over the noise of the helicopter. "Are you all okay?"

The team looked at each other, uncertain of what to do. They had spent months on the island, collecting valuable data on the sharks, and they didn't want to leave it all behind.

Dr. Smith spoke up. "We have a lot of research data that we need to take with us. Is there any way we can bring it with us on the helicopter?"

The rescue team hesitated, looking at each other uncertainly. "We can try," one of them said finally. "But we can't guarantee anything."

The team quickly gathered up their research equipment and data, stuffing it into backpacks and carrying it onto the helicopter. They held their breath as the rescue team secured the equipment and took off, flying back towards civilization.

As they flew over the ocean, the team looked out the window, watching the waves roll by beneath them. They were still in shock from what had happened, but they were also grateful to be alive.

Dr. Kim spoke up, breaking the silence. "We have to make things right. We have to use what we've learned to prevent this from happening again."

The team nodded in agreement, their eyes filled with determination.

As they landed on the mainland and were rushed into medical care, the team knew that they had a long road ahead of them. They had made mistakes, but they were also determined to learn from them and move forward.

As the team recovered from their injuries, they were forced to confront the consequences of their actions. They had caused irreparable harm to the ecosystem and they knew that they were responsible.

Dr. Lee sat in his hospital bed, staring out the window at the city below. "We were so focused on our research that we forgot about the impact it could have," he said, his voice barely above a whisper. "We never should have brought those sharks to the island."

Dr. Smith nodded in agreement. "We were reckless. We put ourselves and the sharks in danger, and it cost Mark his life."

Dr. Kim looked at the team, her expression somber. "We have to take responsibility for what happened. We have to do everything we can to make sure that this never happens again."

The team spent the next several weeks in recovery, each grappling with their own feelings of guilt and remorse. They knew that they had made mistakes, but they were determined to learn from them.

As they began to heal, they started to talk about what they could do to make things right. They knew that they could never undo the damage they had caused, but they could work to prevent it from happening again.

Dr. Lee looked at the team, a determined expression on his face. "We have to make a commitment to ethics and safety. We can't let our passion for research override our responsibility to protect the environment and the creatures that live in it."

The team nodded in agreement, each of them feeling a renewed sense of purpose. They knew that they had a long road ahead of them, but they were ready to take on the challenge.

As they left the hospital and returned to their lives, the team vowed to never forget the lessons they had learned on that island. They would always carry with them the memories of what had happened, and they would use those memories to guide their future research.

Silent Hunter

Maya and Jason peered out of the submersible's small porthole, their eyes wide with excitement and wonder as they descended into the deep-sea trench. The submersible was a state-of-the-art vessel, equipped with all the latest technology to withstand the immense pressure of the deep sea. Maya, a marine biologist, had always been fascinated by the mysteries of the ocean, and being part of a research team that was exploring this uncharted territory was a dream come true.

"Look at that!" Jason exclaimed, pointing to a strange, translucent creature that floated by. "I've never seen anything like it."

Maya grinned. "That's the whole point, Jason. We're here to discover new species and learn more about this incredible ecosystem."

As they continued their descent, Maya and Jason saw even more bizarre creatures - some with tentacles, others with bioluminescent features. But their excitement was short-lived as they noticed a shark that appeared to be following them.

"Is that a great white?" Maya asked, studying the shark's movements.

Jason shook his head. "No, it's too small. Maybe a mako or a tiger shark."

Maya frowned. "It's too persistent. Normal sharks don't usually follow submersibles like this."

As the shark continued to tail them, Maya and Jason grew increasingly nervous. They had encountered sharks before, but this one seemed different, almost purposeful.

"Should we try to scare it off?" Jason asked, eyeing a flare gun.

Maya shook her head. "Let's just keep an eye on it for now. Maybe it'll lose interest."

But the shark didn't lose interest. In fact, as they descended deeper into the trench, it seemed to become more aggressive, darting closer and closer to the submersible.

"I don't like this," Maya muttered, gripping the controls tightly.

Suddenly, the submersible jolted, and Maya and Jason were thrown forward. The shark had bumped into them.

"What the hell?" Jason exclaimed.

Maya's heart was racing as she peered out the porthole. The shark was circling them, seemingly waiting for an opportunity to strike again.

"We need to warn the others," Maya said, reaching for the communication equipment.

But as she pressed the button, all she heard was static. "Damn it," she muttered, trying again.

Still nothing. Maya looked at Jason, her expression grim. "Our equipment must have malfunctioned. We're on our own down here."

Maya and Jason watched as the shark continued to circle their submersible, its movements becoming more erratic with each passing moment.

"There's definitely something off about this shark," Jason said, eyeing the creature warily. "It's not behaving like any shark I've ever seen."

Maya nodded in agreement. "Agreed. We need to figure out what's going on here."

As they pondered their next move, Maya's attention was drawn to the submersible's communication equipment. She tried once again to contact the research station on the surface, hoping to alert them to their situation.

But all she heard was static. Frustrated, Maya tried again, but the result was the same.

"What's going on?" Jason asked, noticing the concern etched on Maya's face.

"The communication equipment seems to be malfunctioning," Maya replied, her voice tinged with worry. "It must be the strong underwater current interfering with the signal."

Jason sighed. "Great. Just what we needed."

As they continued to try to fix the communication equipment, the shark became more aggressive, ramming into the submersible several times.

"We need to get out of here," Maya said, her voice urgent. "This shark is not going to let us go easily."

Jason nodded. "Agreed. But how are we going to do that? Our engines are damaged from the shark's attacks."

Maya's eyes darted around the submersible, searching for a solution. Suddenly, an idea came to her.

"The emergency buoy," she said, pointing to a small, orange object in the corner of the submersible. "We can activate it and hope that someone on the surface sees it."

Jason's eyes widened. "It's worth a shot. Let's do it."

Maya quickly activated the buoy and they watched as it floated to the surface, bobbing up and down in the water.

"Now we just have to hope that someone sees it," Maya said, her voice tense.

As they waited, the shark continued to circle their submersible, its movements becoming more frenzied by the minute.

"I don't like this," Jason muttered, his eyes glued to the shark.

Suddenly, they heard a crackling sound from the communication equipment. Maya rushed to answer it.

"Maya, Jason, can you hear me?" It was their colleague, Dr. Singh, calling from the research station.

"Yes, yes, we can hear you!" Maya exclaimed, relief flooding through her.

"We've received your distress signal," Dr. Singh continued. "We're sending a team down to rescue you. Hang tight."

Maya and Jason looked at each other, their hearts racing with both fear and hope.

"Thank God," Maya whispered.

But as they waited for their rescue, the shark continued to circle them, its movements growing even more frenzied.

As Maya and Jason waited for their rescue, the shark continued to circle them, its movements growing even more frenzied. Suddenly, the submersible jolted as the shark slammed into it, causing them both to stumble.

"What's going on?" Maya shouted, grabbing onto the submersible's controls.

"It's attacking us," Jason replied, his voice tense.

"We need to get out of here," Maya said, her eyes scanning the submersible's damaged engines. "But how?"

Suddenly, Jason's eyes widened. "Look, there's a narrow cave system over there. We can try to hide in there until the rescue team arrives."

Maya nodded, her eyes scanning the cave system. "It's our only chance."

As they approached the cave, the shark followed them, its movements growing more frenzied and aggressive by the second.

"We need to hurry," Jason said, his voice urgent.

But as they entered the narrow cave system, the submersible's movements became more difficult to control. The tight space made it hard to maneuver, and they could feel the shark's attacks growing more frequent and violent.

"This is not good," Maya said, her voice shaking. "We're trapped."

Jason tried to remain calm. "We can't panic. We have to find a way out of here."

But as they tried to navigate the cave system, the shark's attacks became even more frequent and aggressive, causing the submersible to shake and jolt with each impact.

"We're not going to make it," Maya said, her voice trembling.

Jason shook his head. "Don't give up. We can do this."

But as they tried to evade the shark's attacks, they soon realized that they were dealing with a highly intelligent predator that seemed to be able to anticipate their every move.

"It's like it knows what we're going to do before we even do it," Maya said, her voice filled with fear.

"We have to try something different," Jason said, his eyes scanning the cave system for a way out.

Suddenly, Maya's eyes lit up. "The emergency flares. We can use them to distract the shark and buy us some time."

Jason nodded. "Good idea. Let's do it."

As Maya activated the emergency flares, they watched as the shark became distracted by the bright, flashing lights. They used the opportunity to try to navigate their way out of the cave system, but the shark was too quick and too smart for them.

"We're not going to make it," Maya said, her voice filled with despair.

But just as they were about to give up hope, they heard the sound of the rescue team's submersibles approaching.

"We're saved!" Jason exclaimed, relief flooding through him.

As the rescue team approached, the shark retreated, its attacks becoming less frequent and less aggressive.

"We made it," Maya said, tears of relief streaming down her face.

As the rescue team pulled Maya and Jason out of the submersible, they were met by Dr. Chen, a renowned shark expert from the research station on the surface.

"Are you both okay?" she asked, her eyes scanning them for any injuries.

"We're fine, thanks to you," Maya replied, her voice filled with gratitude.

Dr. Chen nodded, a serious look on her face. "We need to figure out what's going on down there. The behavior of that shark is unlike anything we've ever seen before."

Jason nodded. "We've been trying to figure out what it is, but we can't seem to get a good look at it."

Dr. Chen turned to the rescue team. "We need to get back down there and take a closer look. I'll be joining you."

As they descended back into the ocean, Dr. Chen briefed them on the behavior of different types of sharks and how they typically interact with humans. Maya and Jason listened intently, impressed by her knowledge and expertise.

"We need to be careful," Dr. Chen said, her voice serious. "This shark seems to be highly intelligent and very aggressive. It's not behaving like any shark I've ever encountered before."

As they reached the site of the submersible, Dr. Chen immediately began examining the shark's behavior and movements.

"It's definitely not a great white," she said, her eyes scanning the water. "And it's not a tiger shark either. We need to get a closer look."

As they approached the shark, Dr. Chen took detailed notes on its movements and behavior, trying to piece together what was driving it to attack the submersibles.

"It's almost like it's trying to protect something," she said, her voice thoughtful. "But what?"

They continued to observe the shark for several hours, documenting its movements and behavior. Dr. Chen was constantly analyzing the data, trying to uncover any clues as to what was driving the shark's unusual behavior.

Finally, after hours of observation, Dr. Chen turned to Maya and Jason. "I think I have a theory," she said, her eyes bright with excitement.

"What is it?" Maya asked, eager to hear her analysis.

"I think this shark may be defending its territory," Dr. Chen replied. "There could be a hidden underwater cave or some other type of habitat that it's trying to protect."

Maya and Jason exchanged a look. "We did see a narrow cave system," Maya said. "But it was too small for us to explore."

Dr. Chen nodded. "We need to investigate that cave system. It could be the key to understanding this shark's behavior."

As they prepared to descend into the narrow cave system once again, Maya and Jason couldn't help but feel a sense of trepidation. But with Dr. Chen's expertise and guidance, they felt confident that they could uncover the truth behind the mysterious predator.

Maya, Jason, and Dr. Chen squeezed their way through the narrow cave system, the dim light of their flashlights illuminating the rocky walls around them. The water was murky and cold, and the sound of their breathing was the only noise in the otherwise silent cavern.

"This is definitely it," Maya said, pointing to a dark opening in the wall. "This is where we saw the shark disappear into."

Dr. Chen nodded, her eyes scanning the cave. "Be careful. We don't know what could be waiting for us inside."

As they swam deeper into the cave, the water became even colder and the darkness even more complete. Their flashlights barely penetrated the murky water, and they had to rely on touch and sound to navigate the twisting tunnels.

Suddenly, Jason pointed to a faint light up ahead. "What's that?" he asked.

As they swam closer, they saw that the light was coming from a small opening in the ceiling of the cave. They swam up towards it, their hearts pounding with excitement and trepidation.

As they emerged from the opening, they found themselves in a large, underwater cavern. The ceiling was high above them, and the walls were covered in strange, glowing plants and coral.

But what caught their attention the most was the sharks. Dozens of them, all swimming in coordinated patterns around the cavern, their movements synchronized as if they were following some sort of plan.

Dr. Chen watched in amazement as the sharks moved around them, their fins cutting through the water with precise movements.

"These sharks...they're communicating with each other," she said, her voice barely above a whisper. "I've never seen anything like it."

Maya and Jason watched in awe as the sharks continued their synchronized movements. It was like watching a dance, each shark moving in perfect harmony with the others.

Suddenly, one of the sharks broke away from the group and swam towards the submersible. It circled around it, studying it with its advanced sensory abilities.

"It's examining the submersible," Dr. Chen said, her voice tense. "It's like it knows what it is."

The shark continued to circle the submersible, its movements growing more aggressive. Dr. Chen looked on in concern, her mind racing with questions and theories.

"It's not just defending its territory," she said. "It's actively trying to attack the submersible. This behavior is not normal."

Maya and Jason looked at each other, their faces filled with worry. If the shark was able to communicate with other sharks and coordinate attacks, they were in serious danger.

"We need to get out of here," Jason said, his voice urgent. "Now."

Dr. Chen nodded, her face grim. "Agreed. We need to analyze this data and figure out what's going on here."

As they swam back through the cave system, their minds were filled with questions and theories. What was driving this behavior? How were the sharks communicating with each other? And most importantly, how could they protect themselves from such an advanced and dangerous predator?

As the team made their way back to the research vessel, they couldn't stop talking about what they had just witnessed.

"Did you see the way those sharks were moving? It was like they were all connected somehow," Maya said, her eyes wide with amazement.

"I know. It was like they were communicating with each other," Dr. Chen replied. "I've never seen anything like it."

Jason shook his head in disbelief. "I can't believe we just witnessed something like that. And that one shark, the way it was examining the submersible...it was like it was trying to figure us out."

Dr. Chen nodded. "Yes, it was definitely exhibiting some advanced cognitive abilities. We need to figure out what's driving this behavior."

As they climbed back onto the research vessel, the team huddled around the computer screens, pouring over the data they had collected.

"Look at these readings," Dr. Chen said, pointing to a graph on the screen. "These levels of aggression are off the charts. Whatever is driving this behavior, it's powerful."

Maya leaned in closer. "And look at these bioluminescent creatures. They're everywhere in the cave system. Do you think they have something to do with it?"

Dr. Chen nodded thoughtfully. "It's possible. The shark seemed to be guarding something important. We need to investigate further."

The team suited up and made their way back to the cave system. As they swam deeper into the caverns, they were surrounded by a dazzling array of bioluminescent creatures. Strange fish with glowing eyes, glowing coral formations, and glowing jellyfish drifted by them.

Suddenly, they saw movement up ahead. Dozens of sharks were swimming in a tight formation, their fins cutting through the water with precision.

"They're protecting something," Dr. Chen whispered. "We need to be careful."

As they approached the sharks, they saw that they were clustered around a large, glowing rock formation. The rock was covered in strange markings, almost like ancient hieroglyphics.

Dr. Chen swam closer to the rock, examining the markings with a flashlight. "This is incredible," she said. "These markings are unlike anything I've ever seen before. It's almost like they're a map or some sort of code."

Maya and Jason swam closer, their eyes widening with excitement. "Do you think this is what the sharks are protecting?" Maya asked.

Dr. Chen nodded. "It's definitely a possibility. We need to take some samples and bring them back to the lab for analysis."

As the team began collecting samples, they noticed movement out of the corner of their eyes. More sharks were gathering around them, their movements growing more aggressive.

"We need to get out of here," Jason said, his voice tense. "Now."

The team quickly gathered their samples and made their way back to the research vessel. As they climbed aboard, they were filled with excitement and wonder.

"We may have just discovered something incredible," Dr. Chen said, her voice filled with awe. "This could change everything we know about these creatures and their behaviors."

The team huddled around the samples they had collected, eagerly discussing their findings. "These markings are incredible," Dr. Chen said, pointing to the hieroglyphics on the rock. "I've never seen anything like it. We need to study this further."

"I agree," Maya said, examining the samples through a microscope. "But we need to be careful. We don't know what kind of creatures are lurking around here."

As if on cue, they heard a low growling sound coming from the depths of the cave system. They looked at each other, fear creeping into their hearts.

"What was that?" Jason asked, his voice barely above a whisper.

"I don't know," Dr. Chen said, her eyes scanning the darkness. "But we need to be prepared for anything."

Suddenly, they saw movement out of the corner of their eyes. A school of deep-sea creatures was swimming toward them, their razor-sharp teeth glinting in the dim light.

"Get ready!" Dr. Chen shouted, drawing her harpoon gun. "We need to defend ourselves."

The creatures attacked with a ferocity that the team had never seen before. They were faster and stronger than any other deep-sea creature they had encountered. Maya fired her stun gun, but it had no effect on the creatures. Dr. Chen fired her harpoon gun, but it only seemed to enrage them.

Jason was the first to suffer a significant injury. One of the creatures latched onto his arm, its teeth sinking deep into his flesh. He cried out in pain, struggling to break free.

"Help me!" he shouted, his voice filled with panic.

Maya and Dr. Chen rushed to his side, firing their weapons at the creatures. But there were too many of them, and they seemed to be working together in a way that was unprecedented.

As the team fought for their lives, they realized that they were hopelessly outmatched. They had no choice but to retreat and regroup.

"Swim for the exit!" Dr. Chen shouted, her voice filled with urgency. "We need to get out of here now!"

The team swam as fast as they could, but the creatures were relentless. They nipped at their heels, tearing at their gear, and trying to drag them down into the depths.

As they neared the exit, Dr. Chen fired a flare gun, illuminating the cave system with a burst of light. The creatures recoiled, blinded by the sudden brightness. The team seized the opportunity and made a run for it.

They burst out of the cave system, gasping for air. Jason's arm was bleeding profusely, and Maya had a deep gash on her leg.

"We need to get back to the research vessel," Dr. Chen said, her voice shaking. "We need medical attention."

As they swam back to the vessel, the team realized that they had underestimated the dangers of the deep. The creatures they had encountered were more vicious and more intelligent than they had ever imagined.

"We need to be more careful," Maya said, wincing in pain. "We can't let our guard down for even a second."

Dr. Chen nodded, her face grim. "We have a lot to learn about the creatures that inhabit these depths. But we can't let this setback stop us. We need to keep exploring, keep learning, no matter the cost."

As the research vessel came into view, the team swam towards it, their injuries throbbing with pain. They had barely made it out of the cave system alive, and the thought of returning to the depths filled them with dread.

Dr. Chen quickly radioed the vessel, requesting medical attention. The crew on board sprang into action, lowering a medical kit into the water and preparing the necessary equipment.

As the team received treatment, they discussed the encounter they had just had. "Those creatures were unlike anything I've ever seen," Maya said, wincing as the doctor stitched up her leg. "They were working together, almost as if they were communicating."

"I know," Dr. Chen said, her voice grim. "And it's not just the creatures we have to worry about. There are other teams down here, rival researchers who will stop at nothing to protect their secrets."

"What do you mean?" Jason asked, his face pale from loss of blood.

Dr. Chen took a deep breath. "I've been doing some digging, and I think I've uncovered something. There's a rival research team that has been experimenting with genetic modification. They've been trying to create creatures that are better adapted to the deep sea, but they've also been using these creatures to protect their research."

"What kind of creatures?" Maya asked, her curiosity piqued.

Dr. Chen hesitated for a moment before answering. "Sharks," she said finally. "They've been genetically modifying sharks to enhance their abilities, and then releasing them into the deep. These sharks are incredibly strong, incredibly fast, and incredibly smart. They've been attacking anyone who gets too close to their research sites."

The team sat in stunned silence, trying to process what they had just heard. "So that's what attacked us in the cave system," Jason said, his voice barely above a whisper.

Dr. Chen nodded. "It's clear that these sharks are being used to protect something down here. Something important enough that a rival research team would go to these lengths to keep it hidden."

"But what could be so important?" Maya asked, her eyes wide with wonder.

Dr. Chen shrugged. "I don't know. But we're going to find out. We came down here to explore, to learn about the secrets of the deep sea. And we're not going to let a few genetically modified sharks stop us."

The team looked at each other, a newfound determination in their eyes. They had faced danger before, but this was something else entirely. They were up against a rival research team with unknown resources, and a pack of genetically modified sharks that would stop at nothing to protect their secrets.

But they were scientists, explorers, adventurers. And they were not going to back down.

The team spent the next few days gathering as much information as they could about the rival research team and their experiments. They pored over scientific journals, interviewed other researchers in the area, and scoured the internet for any clues.

Finally, they pieced together enough information to make a plan. They knew that the rival team's research station was located deep underwater, and that the only way to get there was to dive down to the ocean floor and follow a narrow cave system.

They also knew that the Silent Hunter, as they had come to call the genetically modified shark, would be waiting for them.

The team geared up for the dive, making sure to bring plenty of oxygen tanks and a variety of underwater weapons. As they descended into the deep, they could feel the weight of the water pressing in on them, the darkness of the abyss surrounding them.

The cave system was treacherous, filled with sharp rocks and narrow passages. But the team pushed on, determined to reach their destination.

As they approached the research station, they saw the Silent Hunter waiting for them, its massive form looming in the darkness.

"Remember what we learned about its behavior," Dr. Chen reminded the team. "It's smart, but it also has predictable patterns. We can use that to our advantage."

The team spread out, each member taking a different position. They knew that the Silent Hunter was used to attacking from behind, so they set up a trap, luring it into a narrow passage where they would have the advantage.

The plan worked perfectly. As the Silent Hunter charged towards them, the team fired a barrage of weapons, stunning the shark and leaving it disoriented.

They made a break for it, swimming as fast as they could towards the surface. But the Silent Hunter was not so easily defeated. It regained its bearings and gave chase, its massive form barreling towards them.

The team swam frantically, trying to outrun the beast. But it was gaining on them, its jaws opening wide as it prepared to strike.

Just as they thought all was lost, Maya had an idea. She remembered something she had read about shark behavior, about how they were sensitive to certain frequencies of sound.

She quickly grabbed a device from her bag, activating it and sending out a high-pitched sound that only the Silent Hunter could hear.

The effect was immediate. The shark recoiled, its sensitive ears overwhelmed by the sound. It turned and swam away, disappearing into the darkness.

The team let out a collective sigh of relief, swimming the rest of the way to the surface.

As they emerged from the water, they were greeted by the crew of the research vessel, who had been monitoring their progress the whole time.

"You did it!" the captain exclaimed. "You actually took on the Silent Hunter and won!"

The team smiled, tired but triumphant. They had faced their fears, their rival research team, and a genetically modified shark, and had come out on top.

Dr. Chen turned to the team, a proud smile on her face. "You know what this means, don't you?" she said.

The team looked at her quizzically.

"It means that we have uncovered something truly remarkable down here," she said. "Something that could change the course of scientific discovery for years to come."

The team nodded, still catching their breath from the intense encounter they had just had.

"But for now," Dr. Chen said, clapping her hands together. "Let's get back to the lab and start analyzing this data. There's still so much we don't know about the deep sea."

As the team made their way back to the lab, they couldn't help but feel a sense of awe and gratitude for the power of the ocean. They had just come face to face with a genetically modified shark, and they had survived.

"I can't believe we actually did it," Maya said, still trying to catch her breath. "We took on the Silent Hunter and won."

"It was a team effort," Dr. Chen replied. "We couldn't have done it without each other."

As they arrived back at the lab, the team immediately got to work analyzing the data they had collected. They poured over the samples they had taken, discussing their findings and brainstorming new avenues of research.

But there was something different about their approach now. They had a newfound respect for the ocean and the creatures that lived in it. They knew that their work had the potential to unlock new discoveries, but they also recognized the importance of doing so responsibly.

"We need to make sure that we're not just exploiting the ocean for our own gain," Maya said. "We need to be mindful of the impact that our research could have on the environment."

Dr. Chen nodded in agreement. "We have a responsibility to protect the ocean and its inhabitants," she said. "We can't forget that."

The team worked late into the night, fueled by a renewed sense of purpose. They discussed ways to minimize their impact on the environment, brainstormed new methods of sustainable research, and pledged to always put the well-being of the ocean first.

As the sun began to rise outside, the team finally called it a night. They were exhausted, but also invigorated by their experience.

"I think we're going to be okay," Maya said, as they left the lab and headed back to their living quarters. "As long as we remember why we're doing this, and always keep the ocean's best interests at heart."

Dr. Chen smiled. "I couldn't agree more," she said. "We have a responsibility to the ocean and to each other. And I have a feeling that we're going to do great things together."

The team nodded, feeling a sense of camaraderie and purpose that they had never felt before. They had faced their fears and come out on the other side, stronger and more determined than ever.

Devil's Teeth

Alex stepped off the bus and took a deep breath of the salty sea air. She looked around at the quaint town, filled with charming little shops and restaurants, but her eyes were drawn to the beach. She could see a small crowd gathered around something in the distance. As she approached, she heard their murmurs and gasps.

"Another one," a woman whispered.

Alex edged closer, trying to see what was going on. She heard a man say, "It's the shark, I'm telling you. The same one that's been terrorizing us for weeks now."

Alex's heart sank. She had heard about the shark attacks, but had hoped they were just rumors. She had been hired as a marine biologist to study the local marine life, but now her focus shifted to finding a way to stop the shark.

As she walked towards her new workplace, she bumped into a rugged-looking man with a fishing net slung over his shoulder.

"Watch where you're going," he grumbled.

"I'm sorry," Alex said. "I'm new here. My name is Alex."

"Sam," he replied. "You're the new marine biologist, right?"

"Yes, that's me. I heard about the shark attacks. Do you know anything about them?"

Sam snorted. "I know plenty. My brother was killed by that damn shark. The authorities ain't doing nothing about it, either."

Alex's heart went out to Sam. "I'm sorry for your loss. I'm going to do everything I can to stop that shark."

Sam looked at her skeptically. "Good luck with that. You're going to need it."

Alex didn't let Sam's cynicism deter her. She spent the rest of the day at her new workplace, gathering as much information as she could about the shark attacks. She talked to the locals, took pictures of the bite marks on the victims, and studied the patterns of the attacks.

As she was leaving for the day, she saw Sam again. "Hey, Sam. Do you have a minute?"

Sam grunted in response.

"I was wondering if you could take me out on your boat. I want to see the ocean up close and get a better idea of what we're dealing with."

Sam hesitated for a moment, then said, "Alright. Meet me at the dock at sunrise."

Alex nodded, feeling a sense of excitement and trepidation. She was determined to find a way to stop the shark, but she knew it wouldn't be easy.

The next morning, Alex arrived at the dock at sunrise, feeling a mix of nerves and excitement. Sam was already there, preparing his boat for the journey out to sea.

"Ready to go?" he asked.

Alex nodded, and they set off, the sun rising over the horizon as they made their way out to the open ocean. Sam maneuvered the boat expertly, scanning the water for any sign of the shark.

They had been out for a couple of hours when they spotted something in the distance. At first, Alex couldn't make out what it was, but as they drew closer, she saw a dark shape moving just beneath the surface of the water.

"That's it," Sam said grimly.

Alex's heart raced as she watched the shark move closer to the boat. She had seen sharks before, but this one seemed much larger and more aggressive than any she had ever encountered.

Suddenly, there was a commotion in the water. A group of people had gathered on the shore, shouting and pointing towards the ocean. Alex and Sam looked over to see a swimmer flailing in the water, screaming for help.

Without hesitation, Sam turned the boat towards the swimmer, and they sped towards him as fast as they could. But they were too late. The shark had already reached the swimmer, and they watched in horror as it dragged him under the water.

Alex felt sick to her stomach as they pulled the lifeless body onto the boat. She knew then that this shark was a true danger to the town, and she was more determined than ever to find a way to stop it.

Back on shore, the town was in a state of panic. The local authorities were scrambling to come up with a plan to deal with the shark, but Alex knew they needed more information before they could take any action.

She spent the next few days studying the shark's behavior, analyzing the patterns of its attacks and its movements in the water. She talked to experts in the field, and even reached out to other marine biologists around the world for their input.

Slowly but surely, Alex began to piece together a plan to stop the shark. It wasn't going to be easy, but she was determined to see it through.

As Alex delved deeper into her research, she began to uncover a troubling truth: the town's mayor, Thompson, was more concerned with protecting the tourism industry than stopping the shark. She had heard rumors of corruption, but she never imagined it could be this bad.

Alex tried to confront Thompson about her findings, but he brushed her off.

"I assure you, Ms. Johnson, we are doing everything we can to stop this shark. Our priority is the safety of our citizens and visitors," he said smoothly.

But Alex could tell he was lying. She could see the greed in his eyes, and the way he constantly looked over his shoulder, as if he had something to hide.

Determined to get to the bottom of things, Alex turned to Sheriff Lopez for help. But he was torn between his duty to protect the town and his loyalty to the mayor.

"Look, Alex, I know you're trying to help, but you need to be careful. Thompson has a lot of power around here, and he's not afraid to use it," Lopez warned her.

But Alex refused to back down. She continued to investigate, gathering more and more evidence of Thompson's corruption. And as she did, she noticed a change in the way the townspeople looked at her.

At first, they had been grateful for her help in trying to stop the shark. But now, as word of her investigation spread, they began to turn on her. They accused her of trying to ruin the town's economy, of being a troublemaker.

It all came to a head one afternoon, when Alex was walking down the street and was confronted by a group of angry locals.

"We don't want you here anymore," one of them shouted. "You're causing more harm than good."

Alex tried to reason with them, but they wouldn't listen. And then, suddenly, Sheriff Lopez appeared, his face dark with anger.

"Everyone, disperse!" he shouted, drawing his gun. "Ms. Johnson is here on official business, and if anyone interferes with that, they'll have to deal with me."

The crowd scattered, and Alex felt a surge of relief. But she knew the fight was far from over. Thompson and his cronies would stop at nothing to protect their interests, and she was just a lone marine biologist trying to do the right thing.

As Alex struggled to overcome the corruption in the town, she realized that it was up to her and Sam to take matters into their own hands. Together, they set out on a dangerous journey to find the shark and devise a plan to stop it.

The weather was harsh, with strong winds and heavy rain, making it difficult to navigate the boat. But Alex and Sam were determined to press on.

After several hours, they finally spotted the shark in the distance. Alex's heart raced as they moved closer, trying to stay hidden from the creature's view.

"We need to get a closer look," Sam whispered.

Alex nodded, her eyes fixed on the shark. As they drew closer, they noticed something odd. The shark was not swimming alone. It was accompanied by several smaller sharks, all following it in a sort of pack.

"We need to be careful," Alex said, her voice low. "These other sharks could be a problem."

They continued to follow the group, keeping their distance as they observed their behavior. It was clear that the large shark was the leader, and the others followed its every move.

Sam and Alex spent the next few hours carefully studying the pack, trying to find a weakness they could exploit. But they soon discovered that this was no ordinary shark. It was much smarter and more cunning than they had anticipated.

As they tried to get closer, they were attacked by other predators, including a group of vicious sea lions. Sam maneuvered the boat expertly, but it was clear that they were in for a difficult fight.

"We need to regroup," Alex said, her voice urgent. "We can't take on this many predators at once."

They retreated to a nearby island, using the time to come up with a new plan. It was clear that they needed to separate the large shark from the rest of the pack, but they weren't sure how to do it.

As they huddled together, trying to stay warm in the cold rain, Alex felt a sense of determination wash over her. They had come too far to give up now.

"We'll find a way," she said, looking at Sam with a determined glint in her eye. "We'll stop this shark, no matter what it takes."

Alex and Sam spent the night on the island, huddled together for warmth as the rain poured down around them. As they waited for morning, they talked about their plan and how they could separate the large shark from the rest of the pack.

As they spoke, Alex couldn't help but feel a growing attraction to Sam. He was so confident and skilled, and his passion for marine biology was contagious. But she knew that now was not the time for romance. They had a job to do, and lives were at stake.

The next morning, they set out once again, determined to find a way to stop the shark. But as they worked, they couldn't help but steal glances at each other, their attraction growing stronger with each passing moment.

As they sailed, Sheriff Lopez watched them from afar, suspicion growing in his mind. He had always been wary of outsiders, and the fact that they seemed to be spending so much time together only added to his suspicions.

He began to dig into their pasts, looking for any information that could prove they were up to no good. But try as he might, he couldn't find anything concrete.

Meanwhile, Alex and Sam continued their hunt for the shark, their feelings for each other growing stronger by the day. But they both knew that now was not the time for romance. There was still work to be done, and they couldn't afford to let their feelings get in the way.

As they worked, they faced more and more obstacles. The weather grew worse, and they were attacked by more predators. But they never gave up hope. They knew that they were getting closer to their goal, and that they would eventually find a way to stop the shark.

One night, as they sat around the campfire, Alex found herself unable to resist any longer. She leaned in close to Sam and whispered, "I know we can't act on it now, but I just wanted you to know that I have feelings for you."

Sam smiled and took her hand. "I feel the same way," he said. "But for now, let's focus on stopping this shark. We can talk about this more once it's all over."

They shared a quiet moment together, the fire crackling in the background. And as they looked out into the dark ocean, they knew that they would do whatever it took to protect the town.

Little did they know that Sheriff Lopez was watching them, suspicion growing stronger with each passing day.

As they continued their hunt for the shark, Alex and Sam couldn't shake the feeling that Sheriff Lopez was watching them. They knew that they needed to gain his trust if they were going to have any chance of stopping the creature.

One day, they decided to approach him and offer to work together. It was a risky move, but they knew it was the only way to get the sheriff on their side.

To their surprise, Sheriff Lopez was more than willing to listen. He had been watching them for days and had come to the same conclusion as Alex and Sam: that the shark was the real threat to the town.

They sat down together and discussed their options, eventually coming up with a plan to lure the shark into a trap. It was a risky move, but they knew it was their best chance to stop the creature.

As they worked, they talked about their differences and tried to find common ground. It wasn't easy, but they all knew that the safety of the town was more important than their personal issues.

Alex and Sam spent long hours preparing the trap, studying the shark's behavior and trying to anticipate its movements. Sheriff Lopez provided the resources they needed, including a team of divers and a specialized boat.

It was a tense few days as they waited for the shark to make its next move. But finally, the creature appeared on their radar, heading straight for the trap.

They sprang into action, using all their skills and expertise to lure the shark into the trap. It was a dangerous game, and they all knew that one mistake could mean disaster.

But they were determined to succeed, and in the end, their plan worked. The shark was trapped, and they were able to safely transport it to a nearby research facility.

As they watched the creature swim away, Alex and Sam couldn't help but feel a sense of relief. They had done it. They had stopped the shark and saved the town.

But their thoughts soon turned to the future. They knew that there were more threats out there, and that they would need to work together to protect the town from whatever came next.

As Alex and Sam celebrated their victory over the shark, they received an unexpected call. It was from a retired marine biologist who had dealt with the same species of shark before.

He explained that he had been monitoring their progress and was impressed with their work. He offered to help them modify their plan and capture the shark once and for all.

Alex and Sam were surprised but grateful for the offer. They knew that this expert knowledge could make all the difference in their fight against the shark.

They met with the retired marine biologist, who introduced himself as Dr. Carter. He had spent years studying this particular species of shark and knew its behavior patterns inside and out.

Together, they worked to modify their plan, taking into account Dr. Carter's expertise. They knew that the shark was a formidable opponent, and they needed all the help they could get.

As they implemented their new plan, they encountered some unexpected obstacles. The shark was more intelligent than they had anticipated, and it seemed to be one step ahead of them at every turn.

But with Dr. Carter's help, they were able to adapt quickly and make the necessary changes. They worked tirelessly, day and night, determined to capture the creature and prevent any more attacks on the town.

Finally, their hard work paid off. They were able to lure the shark into a trap, and with Dr. Carter's guidance, they were able to safely transport it to a nearby research facility.

As they watched the shark swim away, Alex, Sam, and Dr. Carter shared a sense of accomplishment. They had worked together to achieve what seemed impossible, and they had come out victorious.

But their work wasn't over yet. They knew that there were always more threats lurking beneath the surface of the ocean, and they would need to be ready to face them head-on.

As they parted ways, they promised to stay in touch and continue working together to protect the ocean and the creatures that called it home.

As Alex, Sam, and Dr. Carter parted ways, they knew that their fight against the shark was far from over. They continued to monitor the situation closely, studying the behavior of the shark and analyzing their previous encounters with it.

One day, they received a disturbing report. The shark had returned to the waters surrounding the town, and it was more aggressive than ever before.

They knew that they needed to act quickly, and they began to plan their final showdown with the creature. They were determined to end its reign of terror once and for all.

They worked tirelessly, gathering their equipment and reviewing their plan. They knew that this was their last chance to stop the shark, and they needed to be prepared for anything.

As they set out to sea, they could feel the tension in the air. They were all nervous, but they knew that they needed to remain focused and work together if they were going to succeed.

It wasn't long before they spotted the shark. It was larger than they remembered, and it seemed to be more aggressive than ever before.

They sprang into action, using all their skills and knowledge to outsmart the creature. They worked together seamlessly, each member of the team playing their part to perfection.

As the battle raged on, it became clear that the shark was not going down without a fight. It was strong and resilient, and it seemed to be able to anticipate their every move.

But Alex, Sam, and Dr. Carter refused to give up. They continued to fight, even as the odds seemed to be against them.

Finally, they got their chance. The shark made a fatal mistake, and they were able to deliver the final blow. It was over.

As they watched the creature sink to the bottom of the ocean, Alex, Sam, and Dr. Carter shared a sense of relief. They had done it. They had defeated the shark and saved the town once and for all.

But as they made their way back to shore, they knew that their work was not yet done. There would always be threats lurking beneath the surface of the ocean, and they would need to be ready to face them head-on.

But for now, they allowed themselves a moment of celebration. They had worked together to achieve what seemed impossible, and they had come out victorious.

As Alex, Sam, and Dr. Carter returned to shore, they were met with cheers and applause. The town had been eagerly awaiting news of their victory, and they were overjoyed to hear that the shark had been defeated.

Alex and Sam smiled at each other, their relief palpable. They knew that they had been through a lot together, and they were grateful to have each other's support.

As they made their way through the crowd, they were approached by a reporter from the local newspaper. "Can you tell us what it was like to finally defeat the shark?" the reporter asked.

"It was a long and difficult battle," Alex replied, "but we were determined to do whatever it took to protect the town and its residents."

Sam added, "We couldn't have done it without the help of Dr. Carter. His knowledge and expertise were invaluable."

Dr. Carter smiled modestly, "It was a team effort. We all worked together to achieve our goal."

As the celebration continued, Alex and Sam found themselves drawn to each other. They had been through so much together, and they realized that they had developed strong feelings for each other.

"Sam, there's something I need to tell you," Alex said, looking into her eyes. "I know we've been through a lot together, but I can't help the way I feel about you."

Sam smiled, "I feel the same way, Alex. I didn't want to say anything before because I didn't want to complicate things, but I can't ignore my feelings anymore."

They hugged each other tightly, both feeling a sense of relief that their feelings were finally out in the open.

Meanwhile, Sheriff Lopez had been watching the celebrations from a distance. He knew that he had played a small role in the defeat of the shark, but he also knew that his time as sheriff was coming to an end.

As the crowds began to disperse, he made his way over to Alex and Sam. "I need to talk to you both," he said.

They followed him to a quiet corner of the beach, where he explained his decision to resign from his position as sheriff.

"I've seen too much corruption in this town," he said, his voice heavy with emotion. "I can't continue to turn a blind eye to it. I want to join the fight against corruption, and I need your help."

Alex and Sam nodded, understanding the gravity of the situation. They knew that the road ahead would not be easy, but they were ready to do whatever it took to bring about change in their town.

As they parted ways, they made a promise to each other. They would continue to work together, to protect their town, and to fight for what was right.

The next morning, Alex and Sam woke up early to start their day. They walked along the beach, watching the sunrise and discussing their plans for the future.

"I can't believe we're staying here," Sam said, smiling. "But I think it's the right decision. We can make a difference in this town."

Alex nodded in agreement. "And we have the support of Dr. Carter and the new sheriff. We can work together to create a better future for Devil's Teeth."

As they walked back to their hotel, they noticed that there was a small crowd gathering near the pier. Curious, they made their way over to see what was happening.

They saw that the retired marine biologist, Dr. Carter, was giving a talk to the crowd. He was discussing the importance of responsible tourism and how the town needed to change its ways.

"We can't keep relying on the sharks to bring in tourists," he said. "We need to promote the natural beauty of this town and protect it for future generations."

Alex and Sam listened intently, impressed by Dr. Carter's passion for the cause. After the talk, they approached him to offer their help.

"We want to help promote responsible tourism," Sam said. "And we want to make sure that the town is safe for visitors and locals alike."

Dr. Carter smiled, "I'm glad to have your support. We can make a real difference here."

Meanwhile, Sheriff Lopez had been working hard to investigate the corruption in the town. He had uncovered evidence of illegal activities and was determined to bring those responsible to justice.

He called Alex and Sam to his office to discuss his findings. "I've found evidence that some of the town officials have been involved in illegal activities," he said. "I need your help to gather more evidence and build a case against them."

Alex and Sam nodded, "We're in. We want to help bring about change in this town."

Over the next few weeks, Alex, Sam, Dr. Carter, and Sheriff Lopez worked tirelessly to promote responsible tourism and investigate the corruption in the town.

They met with business owners, held town hall meetings, and launched a campaign to clean up the beach. They also worked with the local police department to increase safety measures and crack down on illegal activities.

Their efforts paid off. The town began to see an increase in responsible tourism, and the residents felt safer and more secure.

As the sun set on another day, Alex and Sam sat on the beach, watching the waves roll in. They smiled at each other, knowing that they had made a real difference in the town.

"This is a new beginning for Devil's Teeth," Alex said, taking Sam's hand. "And I'm glad we're a part of it."

Sam nodded, "Me too. It feels good to know that we're making a difference."

As they walked back to their hotel, they knew that there was still work to be done. But they were ready for whatever challenges lay ahead.

Fool's Gold

Jack was sitting at a bar in Miami, nursing a drink and trying to forget about the recent failure of his last treasure hunt. He was just about to call it a night when a man in a fedora approached him.

"Excuse me, are you Jack?" the stranger asked.

Jack looked him up and down warily. "Who's asking?"

The man took a seat beside him. "My name's Frank. I heard you're in the treasure hunting business."

"I am," Jack said, eyeing him suspiciously.

Frank leaned in closer. "I know where you can find a Spanish galleon that sank off the coast of Florida. And it's not just any old galleon - this one was carrying a shipment of gold and jewels worth millions."

Jack raised an eyebrow. "And what makes you think I'm interested?"

Frank grinned. "I know your reputation, Jack. You're one of the best in the business. And I also know that you're not afraid to take risks."

Jack hesitated. He'd been burned by false leads before, and he wasn't sure he wanted to risk his time and money on another wild goose chase.

"How do I know you're telling the truth?" he asked.

Frank shrugged. "You don't. But if you're interested, I can sell you the location for a fair price."

Jack shook his head. "I don't pay for information. If you want to help me out, give me the location and I'll cut you in on the profits if I find anything."

Frank considered this for a moment before nodding. "Fair enough. The galleon is said to have sunk off the coast of a remote island about 100 miles south of here. It's a treacherous area, but if anyone can find it, I believe it's you."

Jack thanked him and finished his drink. As he left the bar, he couldn't help but feel a sense of excitement building within him. The idea of discovering a lost treasure was too tantalizing to ignore.

Jack couldn't do this alone. He needed a crew he could trust to help him find the Spanish galleon. The first person he thought of was his friend and partner, Ben.

Ben was a grizzled old sea dog with years of experience in treasure hunting. Jack knew he could rely on him to have his back, no matter what.

He called Ben up and explained the situation to him. "I've got a lead on a Spanish galleon that sunk off the coast of Florida. I need your help to find it."

Ben didn't hesitate. "You know I'm always up for a good treasure hunt, Jack. When do we leave?"

Jack grinned. "As soon as possible."

They met up the next day to discuss their plan of action. Ben brought in his own team of divers, including his nephew Mark and his friend Tony. Together, they made a formidable team.

But Jack knew they needed more than just divers to find the galleon. That's when he remembered a marine biologist he had met a few years ago named Sarah. She was an expert on tiger sharks, which were known to inhabit the area where the galleon was supposed to have sunk.

He called her up and explained the situation. To his surprise, she was eager to join the expedition. "I've always wanted to explore that area," she said. "And who knows? We might even make some new scientific discoveries along the way."

Jack was pleased to have her on board. "Great, we'll need all the help we can get."

Over the next few days, they gathered their equipment and made the necessary preparations. Jack and Ben spent countless hours poring over maps and historical records, trying to pinpoint the exact location of the galleon.

Sarah spent her time studying the behavior of tiger sharks and developing a plan to protect the divers from potential attacks. She also brought along some specialized equipment, including a hydrophone to track the movements of the sharks.

Finally, the day of the expedition arrived. They loaded up their boat with all their gear and set out into the open sea. Jack felt a sense of excitement and apprehension as they sailed closer and closer to their destination.

The crew sailed for several hours, battling rough seas and strong currents, but finally, they reached the remote island where the galleon was believed to have sunk.

Jack scanned the horizon, searching for any signs of the shipwreck. "According to the maps, the galleon should be around here somewhere."

Sarah pulled out her hydrophone and listened intently. "I'm not picking up any shark activity in the area, but that could change at any moment."

Ben turned to Jack. "We'll need to be careful when we dive. The currents can be treacherous, and there could be all sorts of obstacles down there."

Jack nodded. "Agreed. Let's get our gear ready and make a plan."

They spent the next few hours preparing for the dive, checking their equipment and going over their plan. Jack and Ben would lead the dive, while Sarah would stay on the boat to monitor the hydrophone and keep an eye out for any potential threats.

Finally, they were ready to go. Jack and Ben suited up and took the plunge into the water. As they descended deeper and deeper, the world around them became dark and murky.

But then, Jack saw something glinting in the distance. He swam closer and realized it was a piece of gold, half-buried in the sand. He looked around and saw more treasures scattered around the area.

"Ben, I think we found it!" he called out.

Ben swam over to him, and together they explored the area, marveling at the treasures they found. There were gold coins, jewels, and other priceless artifacts. It was like stepping back in time to the heyday of the Spanish Empire.

As they made their way back to the boat, Jack couldn't help but feel a sense of triumph. They had done it - they had found the lost Spanish galleon and its treasures.

But as they approached the boat, they heard a loud hissing sound. Sarah's voice crackled over the radio. "Guys, we have a problem. There's a tiger shark heading your way."

Jack and Ben quickly swam to the boat, where Sarah was frantically scanning the water with her hydrophone.

"Where is it?" Jack asked, his heart racing.

"It's getting closer. I estimate it's about 50 meters away," Sarah replied.

Ben grabbed a spear gun and got ready to defend himself. "We'll have to scare it off. Get the flares ready."

Jack and Sarah quickly handed Ben a handful of flares, which he lit one by one and tossed into the water. The bright lights and loud noises were enough to scare off the tiger shark, and it swam away.

Jack breathed a sigh of relief. "Thanks, Sarah. That was a close one."

Sarah nodded. "No problem. I'm just glad everyone's okay."

They got back to the task at hand, which was searching for more treasures from the galleon. They split up and began to explore the area, searching for any clues that might lead them to the shipwreck.

But they quickly ran into trouble. The currents were much stronger than they had anticipated, and the underwater terrain was treacherous. They swam through narrow caves and crevices, their flashlights barely illuminating the way.

At one point, Ben got stuck in a narrow passage and had to be freed by Mark and Tony. "Thanks, lads. That was a close one," he said, catching his breath.

But the team persevered. They dove deeper and deeper, searching every nook and cranny for any sign of the galleon. And finally, after hours of searching, they found what they were looking for.

Jack spotted a glint of gold in the distance and swam towards it. As he got closer, he realized that it was a piece of the galleon's hull, still intact after all these years.

"Ben, Sarah, come take a look at this," he called out.

They swam over and saw the hull for themselves, marveling at the sight. It was an incredible discovery, one that would change their lives forever.

As they continued to explore the area, Maya spotted something unusual on the ocean floor. She swam closer, her heart racing with excitement.

"Guys, come over here!" she called out to the others.

They swam over to her and saw what she had discovered - a small statue, covered in seaweed and coral.

"Wow, Maya, this is amazing," Jack said, examining the statue closely. "It looks like it could be from the same time period as the galleon."

Sarah nodded. "This could be a significant clue. It could lead us straight to the wreck."

As they were admiring the statue, they suddenly heard a loud thumping sound. They turned around and saw a group of sharks approaching them, attracted by the commotion.

"Guys, we need to get out of here," Ben said, his voice tense with fear.

But before they could swim away, the sharks attacked. The crew frantically tried to fend them off with their spears and flares, but they were outnumbered.

Maya was separated from the group and found herself face to face with a massive tiger shark. She tried to swim away, but it was too fast. The shark lunged at her, its jaws snapping shut.

But at the last second, Maya thrust the statue into the shark's mouth, using it as a makeshift weapon. The shark recoiled in pain, and Maya swam away as fast as she could.

When she reached the safety of the boat, the others were waiting for her, their faces etched with worry.

"Are you okay?" Jack asked, helping her out of the water.

Maya nodded, still shaking with fear. "I'm okay. I just...I don't know how we're going to get past those sharks."

But Sarah had an idea. "We need to use the sharks to our advantage. We can use their sense of smell to lead us straight to the galleon."

The crew quickly got to work, attaching a piece of bait to a long rope and tossing it into the water. The sharks immediately swarmed towards it, their powerful sense of smell leading them straight to the source.

Using the sharks as a guide, the crew followed them through the treacherous underwater terrain, their hearts racing with excitement and fear.

And finally, after what felt like an eternity, they saw it - the wreckage of the Spanish galleon, lying on the ocean floor.

As the crew approached the wreckage of the galleon, they could feel their excitement mounting. This was it - the moment they had been waiting for.

But as they began to explore the area, they noticed something strange. The sharks in the area seemed to be more aggressive than usual, circling closer and closer to the crew.

"We need to be careful," Sarah warned. "These sharks are more aggressive than we thought."

But the crew was too caught up in their excitement to pay much attention to Sarah's warning. They swam deeper and deeper, exploring the wreckage and searching for treasure.

That's when it happened - one of the crew members, Tony, was attacked by a massive tiger shark. The others could hear his screams echoing through the water as he fought to fend off the shark.

"Tony, hold on, we're coming!" Jack shouted, swimming towards him as fast as he could.

But it was too late. By the time they reached Tony, the shark had already dealt a fatal blow. The crew was devastated, their joy turning to sorrow and anger.

"We have to get out of here," Ben said, his voice shaking with emotion. "This place is too dangerous."

But Jack wasn't ready to give up yet. "No, we can't give up now. We have to keep going. For Tony."

The crew hesitated, but Jack's determination was contagious. They took a deep breath and continued their search, their eyes scanning the wreckage for any sign of treasure.

But the memory of Tony's death hung over them like a dark cloud, and they couldn't shake the feeling that they were being watched.

"We need to take precautions," Sarah said, her voice firm. "We can't let another one of us get hurt."

The crew nodded, and they quickly got to work setting up a system of ropes and barriers to protect themselves from the sharks. They worked through the night, their fingers numb and their bodies aching, but they knew it was worth it.

Finally, as the sun began to rise, they emerged from the water, exhausted but triumphant.

"We did it," Jack said, his voice filled with pride. "We found the galleon."

But the memory of Tony's death lingered, a reminder of the dangers that lay beneath the surface of the sea.

As the crew took a break on the deck of their boat, Sarah couldn't shake the feeling that there was something more to the shark attacks.

"I've been studying these sharks for years," she said, her brow furrowed in thought. "And I can't help but feel like there's something different about them. Something that's making them more aggressive."

The others listened intently as Sarah continued.

"I think there's a specific scent that's attracting these sharks. Something that's drawing them to us," she said, her voice growing more animated with each word. "And if we can figure out what that scent is, we could use it to our advantage."

The crew looked at each other, intrigued by Sarah's theory.

"What do you suggest we do?" Jack asked, his eyes gleaming with excitement.

Sarah thought for a moment before responding. "We need to start experimenting. We can try using different scents to see if we can attract or repel the sharks. And if we can figure out what they're after, we could use it to lure them away from us."

The crew quickly got to work, gathering materials and setting up an experiment. They used pieces of meat and other items to test different scents, watching as the sharks reacted to each one.

And finally, they found it - the scent that seemed to attract the sharks. It was a combination of seaweed and algae, mixed with a specific type of fish.

"We've got it!" Sarah exclaimed, her face lighting up with excitement. "This is what the sharks are after."

The crew looked at each other, their eyes filled with determination. They knew that they had found the key to unlocking the secrets of the ocean.

With renewed energy, they dove back into the water, using the scent to guide them as they searched for the galleon. And this time, they were prepared for any shark attacks that came their way.

As they swam deeper and deeper, their hearts racing with excitement, they knew that they were on the brink of discovering something incredible.

The crew worked tirelessly, following the scent they had discovered, until they reached a cluster of rocks that they believed could be hiding the wreckage of the galleon.

"We have to be careful," Sarah warned, her eyes scanning the area for any sign of danger. "The scent might attract more sharks than we can handle."

But Jack was undeterred. "We've come too far to turn back now. We have to take the risk."

The crew quickly got to work, setting up a trap for the sharks using the scent they had discovered. They used a piece of meat as bait, hoping that it would lure the sharks away from them.

As they waited for the sharks to take the bait, the crew couldn't help but feel a sense of excitement. They knew that they were on the verge of a great discovery.

But then, something strange happened. The sharks didn't just take the bait - they began to circle around the crew, getting closer and closer with each passing moment.

"We need to get out of here," Sarah said, her voice rising in panic. "This is a trap, and we're the ones who are caught."

The crew tried to swim away, but the sharks seemed to be everywhere. They were surrounded, with no way out.

"We have to fight back," Jack said, his voice firm. "We can't let them take us down without a fight."

The crew rallied, using whatever they had at their disposal to fend off the sharks. They kicked and punched, using their equipment as weapons, fighting with every ounce of strength they had.

But it was no use. The sharks were too numerous, too powerful. And as the crew began to tire, their fate seemed to be sealed.

Just when it seemed like all hope was lost, a miracle happened. A pod of dolphins appeared out of nowhere, swimming towards the crew with lightning-fast speed.

The dolphins began to attack the sharks, using their sharp beaks to injure them and drive them away. The crew watched in amazement as the dolphins fought off the sharks, freeing them from their trap.

"We're saved!" Ben shouted, his voice filled with relief.

The crew swam towards the dolphins, thanking them for their help. And as they made their way back to the surface, they knew that they had witnessed something incredible - the power of the ocean, and the creatures that inhabit it.

As the crew recovered from their harrowing encounter with the sharks, they knew that they couldn't give up. They had come too far, risked too much, to turn back now.

"We have to keep going," Jack said, his voice resolute. "We can't let those sharks stop us from finding the galleon."

The crew nodded in agreement, steeling themselves for what lay ahead. They knew that the journey would be dangerous, but they were determined to see it through.

As they swam deeper into the ocean, the crew was on high alert, scanning the area for any sign of danger. And then, they saw them - a pack of tiger sharks, swimming towards them with deadly intent.

"We have to fight them off," Sarah said, her voice filled with urgency.

The crew quickly got into formation, using their knowledge of shark behavior to outsmart the predators. They kicked and punched, using their equipment to fend off the sharks, but the sharks were relentless, attacking them from all sides.

"We need a plan," Ben said, his voice rising above the chaos. "We can't keep fighting them like this forever."

Sarah quickly came up with an idea. "We can use the scent that we discovered to attract the sharks away from us," she said. "If we can lead them away, we can make our escape."

The crew quickly got to work, using the scent to lure the sharks away from them. And as the sharks followed the scent, the crew made their escape, swimming towards the galleon.

But their victory was short-lived. Just as they were about to reach the galleon, the sharks returned, more aggressive than ever before.

"We have to fight them off again," Jack said, his voice filled with determination.

The crew rallied, using everything they had learned to fight off the sharks. But the sharks were too numerous, too powerful. And as the crew began to tire, they knew that they were in trouble.

And then, tragedy struck. One of the crew members, Alex, was attacked by the sharks. The crew watched in horror as he fought for his life, his blood staining the water around him.

"We have to save him!" Sarah shouted, her voice filled with desperation.

The crew quickly came to Alex's aid, using everything they had to fend off the sharks. And as they fought, they could see the glimmer of hope - a chance to save their friend.

But it was too late. Alex succumbed to his injuries, his lifeless body sinking into the depths of the ocean.

The crew was devastated, their hearts heavy with grief. But they knew that they had to press on, to honor Alex's memory by completing their mission.

With renewed determination, they made their way towards the galleon, their eyes fixed on the prize that lay ahead.

As the crew finally reached the galleon, they couldn't help but feel a sense of emptiness. The price they paid for this treasure was too high, and the loss of their friend Alex still weighed heavily on their hearts.

Ben was the first to speak, his voice somber. "This isn't what we were expecting," he said, gesturing towards the old, rusted treasure chest lying on the deck. "After everything we've been through, this is all we have to show for it."

The crew gathered around the chest, staring at it in disappointment. They had risked everything for this, and it was not the treasure they had dreamed of finding.

Sarah spoke up, her voice filled with sorrow. "We lost a friend, but we gained knowledge," she said, gesturing towards the sea. "We know now that the ocean is a dangerous place, and we can't take it for granted."

Jack nodded in agreement, his gaze fixed on the chest. "We may not have found the treasure we were hoping for, but we gained something much more valuable," he said. "We gained the knowledge that we can't let our desire for treasure blind us to the dangers around us."

The crew spent the next few days going through the galleon, salvaging what they could. They found old coins, broken pieces of jewelry, and a few rusted swords, but nothing of real value. They gathered what they could and prepared to leave.

As they made their way back to shore, the crew was quiet, lost in their own thoughts. They had been through so much, and the treasure they had risked everything for was not what they expected. But they had gained something much more valuable - the knowledge that they could not let their desire for treasure blind them to the dangers of the ocean.

When they reached the shore, they were greeted by a group of reporters, eager to hear their story. The crew shared their harrowing tale, warning others of the dangers of the ocean and urging them to take precautions.

As they left the beach, the crew walked in silence, each lost in their own thoughts. They had gained something much more valuable than treasure - they had gained knowledge and experience. And they knew that they would never forget the lessons they had learned.

The Deep End

Maya, Jack, Alex, Sarah, and Tyler were hanging out at the beach, enjoying the sun and the waves crashing against the shore. Maya, the natural leader of the group, suggested they go for a swim to a nearby island.

"What do you guys say we swim to that island over there?" Maya asked, pointing to a small island in the distance.

"Are you serious? That's a long swim," Jack said nervously, remembering his past encounter with a shark.

"Oh come on, Jack. Don't be a wimp," Alex teased, trying to lighten the mood.

"I'm in," Tyler said, already starting to take off his shirt.

Sarah looked hesitant, but she didn't want to be left out. "I guess I could give it a try," she said softly.

Maya smiled, pleased that her friends were willing to go along with her idea. "Great! Let's get ready to go."

They all quickly changed into their swimsuits and made their way to the water. Maya led the way, with Jack trailing nervously behind. Alex was cracking jokes, trying to keep everyone's spirits up. Tyler was already swimming ahead, eager to get started. And Sarah was silently observing, taking in the scene around her.

As they swam, they chatted and laughed, enjoying each other's company. Maya kept a close eye on everyone, making sure they were all okay. Jack was still visibly anxious, but Maya encouraged him to keep going.

After a while, they began to realize that the current was stronger than they thought, and it was pushing them further out to sea.

"This is getting pretty intense," Tyler said, his voice slightly strained.

"Yeah, maybe we should turn back," Jack said, starting to panic.

"No way! We're almost there," Maya said, her competitive spirit kicking in. "Just keep swimming, guys."

As they continued to swim, the waves grew bigger and stronger. The wind picked up, making it harder to stay on course. Jack's anxiety was at an all-time high.

"I don't think I can do this," he said, his voice shaking. "What if there are sharks out here?"

"Relax, Jack. We're in the middle of the day. Sharks don't usually come out during this time," Sarah reassured him.

Maya added, "Plus, we're all together. Sharks are less likely to attack a group of people."

Tyler chimed in, "Yeah, man. We got your back."

Slowly, Jack's nerves started to settle, and he continued to swim. They were making progress, but it was slow going. The current was pushing them further and further from the shore, and they could feel their energy levels dwindling.

"This is getting harder than I thought," Alex said, panting.

Maya agreed, "Yeah, I think we need to conserve our energy. Let's take a break and float for a bit."

They all stopped swimming and floated in the water, looking up at the blue sky above them. The cool water was refreshing on their skin, and they took deep breaths, trying to regain their energy.

Suddenly, Sarah let out a scream, causing everyone to panic.

"What is it?!" Maya asked, her voice urgent.

"I...I think I saw something in the water," Sarah said, her voice trembling.

"What? What did you see?" Jack asked, his fear returning.

"I'm not sure. It was big and dark. It could have just been a shadow," Sarah said, trying to convince herself.

Maya decided it was better to be safe than sorry. "Okay, everyone, let's stick together and keep moving. We can't let fear hold us back. We've come too far to give up now."

The group took a deep breath and continued to swim. It was slow progress, but they were making their way towards the island. As they got closer, they could see the sandy shore and the palm trees swaying in the breeze. They were almost there.

The group was getting closer and closer to the island when they suddenly heard a loud splash behind them. They turned to see a dorsal fin circling around them.

"What is that?" Tyler asked, his voice shaking.

"It's probably just a dolphin," Maya said, trying to calm everyone down.

But as the fin got closer, they could see that it was not a dolphin. It was a great white shark.

"Get out of the water! Now!" Maya shouted.

But it was too late. The shark attacked Tyler, biting him in the leg. Tyler let out a scream, and the others were frozen with fear.

"Swim! Swim to the island!" Maya yelled, pushing the others towards the shore.

They swam as fast as they could, but the shark was still circling around them, waiting for its next target. It attacked Sarah next, biting her arm. Maya tried to distract the shark by splashing around, but it was too focused on its prey.

"Jack, come on! We have to get out of the water!" Maya said, grabbing his arm.

Jack was frozen with fear, watching as the shark attacked his friends.

"Come on, Jack! We have to go!" Maya shouted, pulling him towards the shore.

They made it to the island, but the shark was still circling around them in the water.

"We have to do something," Maya said, looking around for a way to defend themselves.

"We can use our fins as weapons," Alex suggested, taking off his fins and handing them to the others.

The group used their fins to fend off the shark, taking turns distracting it and attacking it with their fins. It was a fierce battle, but eventually, they managed to scare the shark away.

They collapsed onto the sand, panting and exhausted.

"I can't believe we just survived a shark attack," Jack said, still in shock.

Maya looked around at her friends, grateful that they were all okay. They had survived the attack together, and it had brought them even closer.

Maya took charge of the group, assessing their injuries and trying to figure out what to do next. Tyler's leg was badly injured, and Sarah's arm was bleeding profusely.

"We need to find a way to stop the bleeding," Maya said, searching through their backpacks for first aid supplies.

"We're stranded here. What if nobody comes to rescue us?" Alex said, his voice filled with worry.

"We can't think like that. We need to stay positive and do everything we can to survive," Maya replied, trying to keep everyone calm.

Jack looked around at their surroundings. The island was small, with only a few palm trees and some rocks. There was no sign of civilization anywhere.

"What are we going to do for food and water?" he asked.

Maya thought for a moment. "We can try to collect rainwater and find some fruit from the trees. It's not ideal, but it's better than nothing."

The group worked together to gather rainwater and search for fruit. They found some coconuts and were able to crack them open for their juice. It wasn't much, but it would sustain them for a little while.

As the days passed, their injuries began to heal, but they were still stranded on the island. They tried to signal for help by building a fire and waving their arms, but nobody came.

"I can't believe we're still stuck here," Sarah said, tears in her eyes.

"We have to keep trying," Maya said, putting a comforting hand on Sarah's shoulder.

One day, Maya spotted a boat in the distance. "Over there! I see a boat!" she shouted, jumping up and down.

The group waved their arms and shouted for help, and the boat eventually spotted them. They were rescued and taken back to civilization, where they received medical attention and reunited with their families.

As they hugged each other, Maya realized how much the experience had changed them. They had gone through something traumatic together, and it had made them closer than ever.

After being rescued from the island, the group was eager to put their ordeal behind them and move on with their lives. However, Maya couldn't shake the feeling that there was something they had missed on the island.

"I keep thinking about the island. What if we missed something?" she said to the group over lunch one day.

"Like what?" Tyler asked, still nursing his injured leg.

"I don't know. Maybe there were other people there, or something else we didn't see," Maya replied.

The group looked at each other, unsure of what to say. They had been so focused on surviving and getting rescued that they hadn't really explored the island.

"I think we should go back and check it out," Maya said, determination in her voice.

The others were hesitant, but eventually, they agreed to go back to the island. Maya had done some research and found a boat that could take them there.

As they approached the island, Maya's heart was pounding with excitement and fear. She didn't know what they would find, but she was determined to find out.

As they stepped onto the shore, Maya noticed something strange. There were footprints in the sand, leading away from the beach.

"Guys, look at this," she said, pointing to the footprints.

The group followed the footprints, which led them to a small campsite. There were tents set up, a fire pit, and even some cooking utensils.

"Someone's been here recently," Maya said, looking around.

They searched the campsite and found a notebook with some writing in it. It was written in a language they didn't recognize, but there were sketches of strange symbols and diagrams.

"What is this?" Alex asked, holding up the notebook.

"I don't know, but it looks like someone was studying something here," Maya replied, flipping through the pages.

As they continued to explore the island, they found more evidence of human activity. There were strange structures built out of driftwood and rocks, and even more notebooks with writing and sketches.

"I think we stumbled onto something bigger than we thought," Maya said, her eyes widening.

The group was excited and scared at the same time. They didn't know what they had found, but they knew it was important.

As the group continued to explore the island, their excitement quickly turned to fear when they heard a familiar sound – the sound of a shark's fin slicing through the water.

"Everyone, get out of the water!" Maya shouted, her heart racing.

They scrambled out of the water and onto the shore, watching as the shark circled them.

"We have to do something!" Tyler said, picking up a rock and throwing it at the shark.

The rock hit the shark, but it didn't seem to do much. The shark continued to circle them, getting closer and closer.

"We need to work together to fight it off," Maya said, looking around for anything they could use as a weapon.

They found some sticks and rocks and began to swing them at the shark, trying to keep it at bay.

The shark lunged at Tyler, and Maya quickly grabbed a stick and jabbed it in the shark's side. The shark let out a loud shriek and swam away.

The group was shaken but relieved that they had survived the attack. They knew they couldn't stay on the island any longer – they needed to come up with a plan to get off.

"We need to find a way to signal for help," Maya said, looking around for anything they could use.

They found some old flares in one of the abandoned campsites and decided to use them to signal for help.

As they set off the flares, they noticed something strange in the distance – a faint light, flickering in the darkness.

"What's that?" Sarah asked, squinting her eyes.

"I don't know, but it might be a boat," Maya said, her heart pounding with hope.

The group ran towards the light, hoping that it was a rescue boat. As they got closer, they realized that it was indeed a boat – but it wasn't a rescue boat.

It was a group of men, armed and dangerous, heading towards them.

The group froze in fear as they watched the armed men approaching them. Maya quickly grabbed the flare gun and fired a warning shot into the air.

"What do you want?" she shouted, trying to sound confident.

One of the men stepped forward, his face hidden by a hood.

"We're not here to hurt you. We're looking for something," he said, his voice deep and gravelly.

"What are you looking for?" Maya asked, her hand shaking.

"That's none of your concern," the man replied, taking a step closer.

The group took a step back, but Maya stood her ground.

"We don't want any trouble. We just want to get off this island and go home," she said.

The man looked at her for a moment, then nodded.

"Fine. We'll leave you alone for now. But if you find anything, let us know," he said, turning and walking back to his boat.

The group watched as the men sailed away, relief flooding through them.

"We have to get off this island now," Maya said, her voice shaking.

They quickly got to work, gathering materials to build a raft. They found some old logs and driftwood and used vines to tie them together.

It took several days of hard work, but they finally finished the raft. They loaded it up with the few supplies they had left and pushed it into the water.

The raft was wobbly and unstable, and they knew they had a long journey ahead of them. But they were determined to get back to civilization.

As they sailed away from the island, they faced new challenges. They had to find food and water to survive, and they had to navigate through treacherous waters.

But they worked together, taking turns paddling and keeping watch. They caught fish and collected rainwater, and they were able to keep going.

Days turned into weeks, and they finally spotted land on the horizon. They paddled towards it, hope flooding through them.

As they got closer, they realized that they had made it – they had survived.

The group cheered as they spotted land on the horizon. They had made it through the dangerous waters and had finally reached safety.

But their joy was short-lived as they heard a familiar sound – the sound of a shark's fin slicing through the water.

"Oh no, not again!" Tyler exclaimed, fear creeping back into his voice.

Maya quickly sprang into action, her mind racing as she tried to come up with a plan.

"We need to distract the shark so that you guys can swim to shore," she said, her voice determined.

"What about you?" Sarah asked, her eyes wide with fear.

"I'll distract the shark," Maya said, taking a deep breath. "I'll swim in the opposite direction, and hopefully, it will follow me instead of you guys."

The group protested, but Maya was resolute. She knew it was a risky plan, but she was willing to put herself in danger to save her friends.

"Get to shore as quickly as you can," she said, her voice shaking slightly. "I'll meet you there."

The group reluctantly agreed, and they quickly swam towards shore while Maya swam in the opposite direction.

The shark quickly spotted Maya and began to swim towards her, its jaws gaping open.

Maya swam as fast as she could, her heart pounding in her chest. She could feel the shark getting closer and closer, its teeth almost brushing against her feet.

Just when it seemed like all hope was lost, Maya spotted a large rock in the distance. She quickly swam towards it and climbed up onto it, hoping that the shark wouldn't be able to follow.

The shark circled the rock, trying to find a way to get to Maya. Maya could feel its hot breath on her face, and she knew she had to act fast.

She reached into her pocket and pulled out a small mirror she had found on the island. She angled it towards the shark, hoping to blind it temporarily.

The plan worked – the shark was temporarily blinded, and Maya quickly jumped back into the water and swam towards shore.

The group cheered as they saw Maya swim towards them, and they quickly pulled her onto the shore.

"You're a hero," Tyler said, hugging Maya tightly.

Maya smiled, relief flooding through her. They had made it through the ordeal together, and they had all survived.

As the group sat in the hospital room, they were surrounded by doctors and nurses who were examining their injuries.

Tyler had deep bite marks on his leg, and Sarah had a broken arm. Maya had several scratches and bruises, but she was otherwise okay.

The group was silent, lost in their own thoughts as they processed the events of the past few weeks.

"I can't believe we made it," Maya said, breaking the silence. "I thought we were going to die out there."

Tyler nodded, his face pale. "I still can't believe we were attacked by a shark. It's like something out of a horror movie."

Sarah shuddered, her arm in a sling. "I never want to go near the ocean again. I'm scarred for life."

The group fell into a somber silence, each lost in their own thoughts. They had been through an experience that had changed them forever.

As the days passed, the group began to work through their trauma. They attended therapy sessions and talked to each other about their fears and anxieties.

Maya was particularly affected by the experience. She had put herself in danger to save her friends, and she couldn't shake the feeling that it was all her fault.

"I should have been more careful," she said to Tyler one day. "I put us all in danger."

Tyler shook his head, his eyes kind. "You saved our lives, Maya. We wouldn't be here if it weren't for you."

Maya smiled weakly, grateful for his words. Slowly but surely, she began to work through her guilt and fear.

As the weeks turned into months, the group began to heal. They went back to their normal lives, but they were forever changed by the experience.

They had survived an ordeal that had tested their strength and resilience, and they had come out the other side stronger.

As the group continued to work through their trauma, they couldn't shake the feeling that they needed to do something to prevent others from experiencing what they had gone through.

"We have to warn other people about the shark," Sarah said, her voice determined. "We can't let anyone else get hurt."

The group nodded in agreement, and they began to brainstorm ideas for how to warn others.

"We could put up signs on the beach," Tyler suggested. "Or we could talk to the lifeguards and get them to warn people."

Maya shook her head. "We need to do something more. Something that will really get people's attention."

The group fell into a thoughtful silence, each lost in their own ideas. After a few minutes, Maya spoke up.

"I've got it," she said, a smile spreading across her face. "We can make a video and post it online. We can show people the reality of what can happen if they're not careful."

The group nodded in agreement, and they got to work. They filmed footage of the shark in the water, and they interviewed each other about their experience.

"We thought we were invincible," Sarah said in the video, her voice trembling. "But we were wrong. We almost lost our lives because we weren't careful."

The video went viral, and it was shared all over social media. People were shocked by the footage, and they began to take the threat of sharks more seriously.

The group received countless messages from people who had seen the video and were grateful for the warning. They had made a real difference, and they knew that they had prevented others from being hurt.

As the weeks turned into months, the group began to heal even more. They had found a sense of purpose in helping others, and they had become closer than ever before.

"We really went through something together," Tyler said one day, looking at Maya and Sarah. "We'll always have each other's backs."

Maya and Sarah smiled, grateful for their friendship. They had been through an experience that had tested their strength and resilience, but they had come out the other side stronger and more united than ever before.

Chumming the Waters

The sun had just risen above the horizon, casting a golden glow over the calm waters of the ocean. Jack and Sarah were already on the dock, loading their fishing gear onto their boat.

"Good morning, Jack," said Tom, another fisherman who had just arrived at the dock. "You going out to catch that marlin today?"

"You bet, Tom," replied Jack with a grin. "I've been after that big fish for months now. I think today's the day I finally catch it."

"I hope so," said Sarah, smiling at her husband's enthusiasm. "But be careful, Jack. The ocean can be unpredictable."

Jack waved off Sarah's concern. "I've been fishing these waters for years, Sarah. I know what I'm doing."

As they set out to sea, Jack couldn't help but feel a sense of anticipation. He had always loved the thrill of the catch, and the thought of finally catching that elusive marlin had been consuming him for months.

But as the day wore on and the sun climbed higher in the sky, Jack's excitement began to fade. He had been fishing for hours without catching anything, and his frustration was mounting.

"I don't understand it," he muttered to himself. "I've tried everything. I should have caught something by now."

Sarah looked at him sympathetically. "It's okay, Jack. Fishing isn't always easy. Sometimes you just have to keep trying."

But Jack was determined. He pulled out a bucket of chum and began to scatter it over the side of the boat.

"What are you doing?" asked Sarah, looking worried.

"I'm chumming the waters," replied Jack. "It'll attract more fish."

Tom looked at Jack with concern. "Be careful, Jack. Chumming can attract sharks too."

Jack waved off Tom's warning. "I've been fishing these waters for years. I know what I'm doing."

The chum quickly attracted a school of small fish, and Jack's spirits lifted as he reeled them in. But then he noticed something in the distance - a dark shape moving quickly towards the boat.

"Tom, what is that?" he asked, pointing.

Tom's face went pale. "Sharks," he said quietly. "Lots of them."

The next morning, Jack and Sarah woke up early to prepare for their fishing trip. They loaded up the boat with all their supplies and equipment, double-checking everything to make sure they had everything they needed.

"You ready for this, Jack?" asked Sarah as she lifted a cooler onto the boat.

"You bet," said Jack, grinning. "I've been waiting for this day for months."

Sarah smiled at his enthusiasm, but couldn't help feeling a little worried. "Just be careful, okay? The ocean can be dangerous."

"I know, Sarah," said Jack, putting his arm around her. "But I've been fishing these waters for years. I know how to handle myself."

As they set out to sea, Sarah couldn't help but feel a little nervous. She watched as Jack prepared his fishing gear and set up the chum bucket.

"Are you sure it's safe to chum the waters?" she asked tentatively.

Jack rolled his eyes. "Yes, Sarah. I've done it plenty of times before. It's perfectly safe."

Tom, who had joined them on the boat, looked concerned. "I don't know, Jack. There have been a lot of shark sightings in this area lately."

Jack waved off Tom's warning. "I've got this under control, Tom. Don't worry about it."

Sarah tried to push her worries aside and focus on the excitement of the potential catch. She helped Jack bait his hooks and watched as he cast his line into the water.

As they waited for a bite, Jack opened up a cooler and pulled out a couple of beers. "Here, Sarah," he said, handing her one. "Cheers to catching that big marlin."

Sarah clinked her bottle against his. "Cheers."

But as the day wore on and they still hadn't caught anything, Sarah's worries began to grow. She watched nervously as Jack scattered more chum into the water.

"Jack, are you sure this is a good idea?" she asked, her voice shaking a little.

Jack looked at her, a little annoyed. "Yes, Sarah. I'm sure. Chumming attracts more fish. It's a common technique."

Tom cleared his throat. "It's also a common technique for attracting sharks."

Jack scoffed. "I know what I'm doing, Tom. Don't worry about it."

But Sarah couldn't shake the feeling of unease. She looked out over the water, watching as the waves lapped against the side of the boat.

"Maybe we should head back," she said quietly.

Jack looked at her, his face falling. "What? No way. We haven't caught anything yet. We can't give up now."

Sarah bit her lip, feeling torn between her love for her husband and her concern for his safety. "I just don't want anything to happen to you, Jack."

Jack put his arm around her. "I'll be fine, Sarah. I promise. Let's just give it a little while longer, okay?"

As the day wore on, Jack became increasingly confident in his decision to use chum. "See, Sarah, I told you it would work," he said triumphantly as he pulled in a small fish.

Sarah forced a smile, but she couldn't shake the feeling of unease. She watched as Jack tossed the fish back into the water and scattered more chum into the waves.

Tom cleared his throat. "I don't like this, Jack. We should head back."

Jack scoffed. "Come on, Tom. We're just getting started. We'll catch that marlin yet."

Sarah looked out over the water, feeling a sense of foreboding. She watched as the chum spread out across the waves, attracting more and more fish.

Suddenly, Jack's line went taut. "I've got one!" he shouted, reeling in his catch.

Sarah watched nervously as Jack pulled in a large fish. "Be careful, Jack!" she warned.

But Jack was too caught up in the thrill of the catch to listen. He yanked on the line, pulling the fish towards the boat.

As the fish came closer, Sarah gasped in horror. It wasn't a marlin, but a large shark.

"Jack, it's a shark!" she screamed.

Jack grinned, completely unfazed. "Looks like we caught a bigger fish than we bargained for," he said, pulling the shark onto the boat.

Tom looked sick. "We need to let it go, Jack. It's not safe."

But Jack was already measuring the shark, his eyes gleaming with excitement. "This is a great catch, guys. We're going to make headlines with this one."

Sarah felt sick to her stomach as Jack posed for pictures with the shark, completely oblivious to the danger he was in.

As they headed back to shore, Sarah couldn't help but feel relieved that they had made it through the day without any major injuries. But she knew that they had been lucky, and that it was only a matter of time before their luck ran out.

As they headed back out to sea the next day, Jack couldn't help but keep an eye on the water. He had noticed a few sharks in the distance the day before, but he had thought they were harmless.

Sarah watched him closely. "Are you okay, Jack?" she asked.

"I'm fine," he said, forcing a smile. "Just keeping an eye out for those marlin."

Tom spoke up. "Jack, I really think we need to be careful with the chum. It's attracting a lot of sharks."

Jack sighed. "Tom, we've been over this. The chum is working. We just need to be careful."

Sarah looked at Tom. "What do you mean, Tom? Are the sharks dangerous?"

Tom nodded. "Yeah, they're dangerous. Chumming the waters like this is just asking for trouble."

Jack shrugged. "We'll be fine. We just need to keep an eye out."

As they continued to fish, Jack couldn't shake the feeling of unease. He watched as more and more sharks began to circle the boat, attracted by the chum.

Suddenly, one of the sharks lunged at a fish on Jack's line, nearly pulling him overboard.

"Jack!" Sarah shouted, grabbing onto him to keep him from falling in.

Tom rushed over to help. "I told you, Jack! We need to stop this!"

Jack pulled his line back in, panting heavily. "Okay, okay. Maybe we should stop with the chum."

Sarah breathed a sigh of relief. "Thank goodness. I was getting worried."

Tom nodded. "Yeah, we need to be careful out here. The ocean is unpredictable."

As they began to pack up their gear and head back to shore, Jack couldn't help but feel a sense of dread. He had always thought he was invincible out on the water, but he was beginning to realize just how dangerous it could be.

The next day, Jack was determined to catch a marlin. He had promised himself that he wouldn't use the chum again, but as the hours went by, he grew impatient.

"Come on, guys, let's try the chum again. It worked before, didn't it?" Jack said, eyeing the empty bucket.

Sarah shook her head. "Jack, we agreed that it was too dangerous."

Tom chimed in. "I have to agree with Sarah. We shouldn't take any more risks."

But Jack was getting desperate. "Just one more time. I promise I'll be careful."

Reluctantly, Tom filled the bucket with chum and tossed it overboard. Almost immediately, the water began to roil with activity as the sharks circled the boat.

Sarah watched nervously as the sharks came closer and closer. "Jack, we need to stop this. We're attracting too many sharks."

Jack nodded, suddenly realizing the danger they were in. He grabbed the rope attached to the chum bucket and tried to pull it up, but it was too heavy.

"Guys, help me pull this up!" Jack shouted.

Together, the three of them strained to pull the chum bucket up, but it was no use. The sharks had caught the scent and were circling the boat, their fins slicing through the water like knives.

Sarah screamed as one of the sharks leaped out of the water, its jaws snapping just inches from the boat.

"Jack, we need to get out of here!" Tom shouted.

Jack nodded, frantically trying to start the boat's engine. But it wouldn't turn over.

Sarah could feel her heart pounding in her chest as the sharks continued to circle the boat. "What are we going to do?"

Just then, one of the sharks lunged at the boat, its razor-sharp teeth sinking into the wooden hull. Jack shouted as he tried to fend it off with a paddle, but it was no use.

"We're under attack!" Sarah screamed.

The boat shook as another shark bit into the hull. Jack could feel the water rising and knew they needed to act fast.

"Sarah, grab onto this!" he shouted, tossing her a life preserver.

She caught it and quickly put it on, her hands shaking with fear.

"Jack, what do we do?" she cried.

"We need to get off this boat before it sinks," he said, grabbing a piece of debris and helping her onto it.

As they drifted away from the sinking boat, Jack scanned the water for any signs of the other sharks.

"We need to keep our wits about us," he said, trying to remain calm. "We're going to make it out of this."

But Sarah could see the fear in his eyes. "Jack, what if we don't make it?"

He put a hand on her shoulder. "We will. We just need to stay alert and keep moving."

As they drifted, they could hear the sound of the sharks circling in the water around them. Jack tried to paddle with his hands, but it was slow going.

"We need to find something to use as a paddle," he said, scanning the debris around them.

Sarah pointed to a piece of wood floating nearby. "What about that?"

Jack grabbed it and began to paddle, trying to steer them away from the sharks. But they were getting closer.

Suddenly, one of the sharks lunged at them, its jaws snapping just inches from Sarah's feet.

She screamed and nearly fell off the debris, but Jack grabbed onto her and pulled her back up.

"We can't let them get us," he said, gritting his teeth. "We have to fight back."

As the sharks continued to circle, Jack looked around for anything he could use as a weapon. He spotted a broken oar floating nearby and quickly grabbed it.

"Sarah, stay behind me," he said, brandishing the oar.

Together, they fended off the sharks as best they could, their hearts pounding with fear.

But the sharks kept coming, their jaws snapping and teeth gleaming in the sunlight.

"We need help," Sarah cried, tears streaming down her face.

Just then, they heard the sound of a helicopter overhead. Jack waved his arms frantically, hoping to catch their attention.

"Over here! Help us!" he shouted.

The sound of the helicopter grew louder as it approached, and Jack and Sarah waved their arms even more frantically. Suddenly, the chopper appeared overhead, hovering just above them.

A rescue diver jumped out of the helicopter and swam over to them, a look of concern on his face. "Are you okay?" he asked.

"We need help. We were attacked by sharks," Jack said, his voice shaking.

The diver quickly assessed the situation and radioed for backup. Within minutes, a second helicopter arrived on the scene, carrying a group of survivors from another boat that had been attacked by the same group of sharks.

"Thank God you're here," Jack said, relief flooding through him.

The survivors introduced themselves as Michael, Lisa, and Ben. They had been out on a fishing trip when their boat was attacked, just like Jack and Sarah.

"We managed to fight off the sharks with our fishing rods, but our boat sank," Michael explained.

"We were drifting on a piece of debris when we saw your boat being attacked," Lisa added.

Ben looked at Jack and Sarah. "We saw you guys fighting off the sharks. You're lucky to be alive."

Jack nodded, still in shock from the experience. "We're just glad to be alive."

The group quickly assessed their situation and realized they needed to stick together if they were going to survive.

"We need to find some kind of shelter," Michael said. "And we need to keep our wits about us."

Together, they worked to build a makeshift raft out of the debris floating around them. They tied it together with ropes and used their paddles to steer it away from the sharks.

As they drifted, they saw more and more debris from the other boats that had been attacked. But they stayed focused on their goal of finding shelter and staying alive.

Hours turned into days as they floated on the open sea, fending off the occasional shark attack and searching for land.

But finally, they spotted a small island in the distance. With renewed hope, they paddled towards it as fast as they could.

As they approached the island, they could see that it was covered in dense jungle. But they didn't care. They had found shelter and a chance to survive.

As they approached the island, the sun began to set, casting an orange glow across the sky.

"We need to find a way to secure our raft," Lisa said, pointing to the shore.

They paddled towards a small cove, where they found a place to tie up their raft.

"We need to set up camp here for the night," Michael said, looking around.

Jack scanned the area, trying to assess the dangers. "We need to be careful. There could be all sorts of dangers on this island."

As they set up their makeshift camp, they heard the sound of the sharks in the distance. It was a haunting sound that sent chills down their spines.

"We need to stay hidden tonight," Ben said, looking out towards the open sea.

But as the night fell, the sharks became more aggressive. They could hear them circling around the cove, waiting for their chance to attack.

"We need to hide underwater," Jack said, taking charge. "We can't risk being seen by those sharks."

The group quickly submerged, holding their breath as they hid under the water. They could see the sharks circling above, their teeth gleaming in the moonlight.

Jack could feel his lungs burning as he tried to hold his breath. He knew he had to find a way to reach the surface before it was too late.

He motioned to the group, signaling that he was going to swim for the surface. They nodded, understanding the risk.

Jack kicked his legs as hard as he could, trying to reach the surface. But his lungs were on fire, and he knew he couldn't hold his breath much longer.

Just as he reached the surface, a shark lunged at him, its jaws snapping just inches from his face.

He quickly dove back down, swimming towards the group.

"We need to find a way to avoid the sharks," Jack said, gasping for air.

The group huddled together, trying to come up with a plan. But they knew they were running out of time.

"We need to find a way to distract them," Michael said. "If we can create some sort of commotion, they might swim away."

They quickly began to splash the water, making as much noise as they could. It worked, and the sharks swam away, searching for easier prey.

As they surfaced, Jack breathed a sigh of relief. "We made it," he said, looking around at the other survivors.

But they knew their journey was far from over. They had to find a way to stay alive on this island, with no food or water and the constant threat of shark attacks.

As the sun rose the next morning, the group set out to explore the island, searching for sources of food and water.

They trekked through the dense jungle, avoiding dangerous creatures and trying to stay out of sight from any passing sharks.

But as they walked along the shoreline, Jack felt a sharp pain in his leg. He looked down to see a deep gash, blood streaming down his leg.

"It's a shark bite," Sarah said, examining the wound. "We need to get him to a hospital."

The group immediately went into action, using their fishing line to create a makeshift stretcher. They carefully lifted Jack onto it and began carrying him towards the shore.

As they walked, the pain in Jack's leg became unbearable. He gritted his teeth, trying to fight through it.

"We're going to get you help," Sarah said, trying to reassure him.

Finally, they reached the shore, where they spotted a fishing boat in the distance.

"Help!" Michael shouted, waving his arms frantically. "We need help!"

The fishing boat approached, and the crew quickly assessed the situation.

"We'll take you to the hospital," the captain said, motioning for them to climb aboard.

They carefully lifted Jack onto the boat, trying to minimize the pain. Sarah climbed on board after him, holding his hand tightly.

As the boat sped towards the nearest hospital, Jack felt his eyes closing. He was losing consciousness, his body weakened from the loss of blood.

But as they reached the hospital, he could hear the sound of doctors and nurses rushing towards them.

"We've got a shark bite victim!" the captain shouted, motioning towards Jack.

The medical team quickly went into action, rushing Jack into surgery.

Sarah watched as they worked to save his life, tears streaming down her face. She knew how close they had come to losing him.

Finally, the surgery was over, and the doctors emerged with good news. Jack was going to be okay.

As he slowly opened his eyes, he saw Sarah sitting next to him, holding his hand.

"We made it," she said, a smile spreading across her face.

Jack smiled weakly, grateful to be alive. They had survived an impossible ordeal, and he knew they would never forget the bravery and perseverance it took to make it out alive.

As Jack lay in the hospital bed, his mind raced with thoughts about the ordeal they had just been through. He couldn't believe how close they had come to losing their lives.

He turned to Sarah, who was sitting beside him, and spoke quietly. "I never should have chummed the waters," he said, shaking his head. "I should have listened to Tom's warning."

Sarah nodded, squeezing his hand. "We were lucky to make it out alive," she said. "We should never underestimate the power of the ocean again."

Jack closed his eyes, trying to shake off the memories of the shark attack. He knew he had made a mistake, and he vowed to never take unnecessary risks again.

"I was foolish," he said, opening his eyes. "I put all of us in danger because of my pride."

Sarah shook her head. "It's not just you," she said. "We all took the risk together. We all have to take responsibility for what happened."

Jack nodded, understanding her point. He knew that they had all made mistakes, and that they had all learned a valuable lesson from their experience.

"I just hope we can use this experience to help others," he said. "To warn them about the dangers of the ocean, and to make sure they don't make the same mistakes we did."

Sarah smiled at him. "We will," she said. "We'll make sure that everyone knows the risks and the importance of listening to experienced fishermen like Tom."

Jack closed his eyes, feeling a sense of relief wash over him. He knew that he had come close to losing everything, but he also knew that he had gained a new perspective on life.

As he drifted off to sleep, he thought about the power of the ocean, and the need to respect it. He knew that he would never forget the lessons he had learned on that fateful fishing trip.

Shark Alley

As the small boat approaches the island, the group of tourists can feel the excitement and anticipation building in the air. Jake leans over the railing, scanning the water for any sign of the great white sharks he knows are waiting for them.

"Can you believe we're really doing this?" he says to Maria, who is nervously gripping the railing beside him.

Maria gives a weak smile. "I don't know, Jake. It all seems a bit crazy to me."

"Don't worry, babe," Jake reassures her. "Tom's been doing these tours for years. He knows what he's doing."

As they step off the boat onto the rocky shore, they are greeted by Tom, a weathered man with a rugged look and an air of confidence.

"Welcome to Shark Alley," he says, a hint of amusement in his voice as he sees the mixture of excitement and fear on the tourists' faces.

Sarah, a young and enthusiastic marine biologist, joins Tom in greeting the group. "I'm Sarah, and I'll be leading the research aspect of the tour," she says, gesturing to the various scientific equipment on the boat.

Jake eagerly steps forward. "So, how close are we going to get to the sharks?"

Tom chuckles. "As close as you're willing to go, my friend. But don't worry, we've got a sturdy cage to keep you safe."

Maria looks at the cage apprehensively. "How strong is it?"

Tom reassures her. "It's built to withstand the force of a great white shark attack. You'll be safe inside."

As the group boards the boat, they are introduced to the other tourists. There is a family with a young child, a retired couple, and a thrill-seeker like Jake. The excitement and nervous energy on the boat are palpable as they set off into the deep, murky waters.

Sarah begins to explain the research they will be conducting, but Jake interrupts her with a grin. "Let's cut to the chase. When do we get to see some sharks?"

The other tourists laugh nervously, but Tom cuts in. "Patience, Jake. We'll get there soon enough."

As the boat approaches the designated spot, the excitement on the boat reaches a fever pitch. The tourists watch in awe as Tom and his crew lower the shark cage into the water.

"Alright, who's ready to go first?" Tom asks, a mischievous glint in his eye.

Jake eagerly volunteers to go first and quickly gets into his wetsuit and fins. He's practically bouncing with excitement as he climbs into the cage and straps himself in.

Maria watches nervously from the boat as the cage is lowered into the water. She starts to back out, but the thrill-seeker, who introduces himself as Mike, grabs her arm. "Come on, don't be a chicken. You don't want to miss this."

Tom nods reassuringly. "The cage is perfectly safe. You'll be amazed at what you see."

Maria takes a deep breath and reluctantly puts on her wetsuit. As she climbs into the cage, her heart is pounding with fear and anticipation.

The water is cold and murky, and the only sound is the muffled hum of the engine and the bubbles from the divers' regulators. But as soon as Jake and Maria's heads go below the surface, they are met with a breathtaking sight.

The water is teeming with life - schools of fish darting around the cage, sea turtles gliding by, and in the distance, the shadowy form of a great white shark.

Jake points excitedly as the shark gets closer. "Look, it's coming right at us!"

Maria grips the bars of the cage, her heart racing. "Is it going to attack us?"

Tom shakes his head. "No, it's just curious. It won't bother us as long as we don't provoke it."

Mike leans over the side of the cage, snapping pictures with his waterproof camera. "This is insane. I can't believe we're this close to a great white."

The shark circles around the cage, eyeing the divers with a detached curiosity. Maria can feel her fear starting to fade, replaced by a sense of awe and wonder.

As the dive comes to an end, the tourists clamber back onto the boat, exhilarated and buzzing with excitement. Jake can hardly contain himself. "That was incredible! I can't wait to do it again."

Maria smiles, feeling a newfound sense of courage. "Yeah, me too."

As they head back to the island, Sarah starts to download the data from the equipment they used during the dive. "We got some amazing footage of the sharks. This is going to be great for our research."

Tom nods in agreement. "And it's great for business too. I have a feeling this tour is going to be a big hit."

As the tourists and crew on the boat were basking in the excitement of their recent shark cage dive, dark clouds began to gather on the horizon, obscuring the sun and signaling the arrival of an impending storm. Within minutes, the wind began to pick up, causing the boat to rock back and forth on the waves.

Tom quickly sprang into action, barking orders to his crew to secure the equipment and prepare for the storm. "Everyone, hold on tight! This is going to be a bumpy ride!"

Jake clung to the side of the boat, his excitement replaced by fear as he watched the waves grow larger and more violent. Maria grabbed onto his arm, trying to steady herself as the boat tossed and turned.

Suddenly, a bolt of lightning struck nearby, illuminating the dark clouds and sending a shiver down everyone's spine. The crew scrambled to get the cage back onto the boat before the storm hit in full force, but it was too late.

A huge wave crashed against the boat, sending the cage and the tourists plummeting into the water. Maria gasped as she was plunged into the cold, murky depths, struggling to keep her head above water as the waves buffeted her body.

She could hear screams and splashing all around her as the other tourists struggled to stay afloat. The crew members on the boat were desperately trying to reel them in, but the rough waves made it nearly impossible.

As if the situation couldn't get any worse, the scent of blood began to fill the water, drawing in the sharks that had been circling nearby. Maria could see their shadowy forms darting through the water, their jaws gaping open as they lunged towards the struggling tourists.

"Get back in the cage!" Tom yelled, his voice barely audible over the howling wind and crashing waves. "It's your only chance!"

The tourists quickly swam towards the cage, clinging to the bars as the sharks circled closer and closer. Jake's heart was pounding in his chest as he watched a shark swim past him, its jaws snapping just inches away.

Maria clung to the cage, her body shaking with fear and cold. She could feel the sting of saltwater in her eyes, making it difficult to see what was happening around her. Suddenly, there was a jolt, and she realized that the cage had become detached from the boat and was now adrift in the open ocean.

"We're stranded!" Mike shouted, his voice hoarse with fear. "We're going to die out here!"

Tom shook his head, his eyes scanning the horizon for any sign of help. "We're not going to die. We just need to hold on until the storm passes."

But as the minutes turned into hours, Maria began to lose hope. The storm showed no sign of abating, and the sharks were growing bolder, drawn in by the scent of blood and the thrashing of the tourists' limbs.

Maria could feel the adrenaline coursing through her veins as she clung to the bars of the cage, watching in terror as the sharks circled closer and closer. "We have to do something!" she cried out, her voice hoarse from screaming.

Jake nodded, his face pale with fear. "But what can we do? We're stuck in this cage, and the sharks are trying to break through the bars."

One of the other tourists, a middle-aged woman with short blonde hair, spoke up. "Maybe we should try to signal for help. We could use our cell phones or a flare gun if we have one."

Mike shook his head, his eyes scanning the water for any sign of rescue. "It's no use. The storm is too intense, and no one will be able to find us out here."

As if on cue, another bolt of lightning struck nearby, illuminating the dark water and the circling sharks. Maria could feel her heart pounding in her chest, and she could sense the panic rising in the other tourists as well.

"We can't just sit here and wait to die," she said, her voice shaking. "There has to be something we can do."

Tom, who had been quiet for most of the ordeal, suddenly spoke up. "I have an idea, but it's risky. We could try to swim back to the boat and use it as a shield against the sharks."

The other tourists looked at him in disbelief. "Are you crazy? The waves are too rough, and the sharks will tear us apart!"

Tom shook his head. "It's our only chance. We can't just sit here and wait for rescue. We have to take action."

Jake nodded, his face determined. "Let's do it. We'll swim back to the boat and use it as a shield. Together, we can fight off the sharks."

The other tourists hesitated, unsure of whether they should follow Jake's lead. But as the sharks continued to attack the cage, they realized that they had no other choice.

They took a deep breath and braced themselves for the cold water, then plunged into the ocean, swimming as fast as they could towards the boat. The waves were rough, and the sharks were still circling, but they pushed on, driven by the fear of what would happen if they stayed in the cage.

As they reached the boat, they grabbed onto the side, pulling themselves up onto the deck. The sharks followed them, their jaws snapping at their heels, but the tourists were determined to fight back.

Using whatever they could find on the boat as weapons, they lashed out at the sharks, striking them with oars and fishing nets. The sharks were fierce, but the tourists were determined, and they fought back with everything they had.

For what felt like hours, they battled the sharks, their bodies battered and bruised from the relentless assault. But in the end, they emerged victorious, driving the sharks away and securing their safety.

As they collapsed on the deck, panting and exhausted, Tom looked at the group with pride. "You did it. You fought back against the odds and survived. You're all heroes."

Maria looked at the others, feeling a sense of camaraderie that she had never experienced before. "We're in this together. No matter what happens, we'll always have each other."

The tourists huddled together on the deck of the boat, still shaken from their harrowing encounter with the sharks. Tom was bandaging a deep cut on Maria's arm, while Jake and the blonde woman were scanning the water for any sign of rescue.

Suddenly, one of the tourists gasped, pointing towards the water. "Look! The thrill-seeker is trying to escape!"

Everyone turned to see the thrill-seeker, a young man in his twenties with a thrill-seeking mentality, attempting to climb out of the cage and swim to the surface. The other tourists shouted for him to stop, but he was too caught up in the excitement of the moment to listen.

As he swam towards the surface, the water around him began to roil, and suddenly a large shark lunged out of the water, its jaws closing around the thrill-seeker's leg. The tourists screamed in horror as the shark dragged him under, blood clouding the water.

For a few moments, no one moved or spoke, stunned by what they had just witnessed. Finally, Jake spoke up, his voice trembling. "We have to do something. We can't just sit here and wait to die like he did."

The blonde woman nodded, her face pale. "He thought he was invincible. But we know better now. We have to do everything in our power to survive."

Maria looked around at the group, seeing the fear and determination in their eyes. "We can't give up. We have to fight back, just like we did before."

Tom nodded, his jaw set. "We'll find a way out of this. We'll survive, no matter what it takes."

The tourists huddled together, their bodies battered and bruised, but their spirits unbroken. They knew that they were facing incredible odds, but they were determined to survive, no matter what.

As the tourists huddled together on the deck of the boat, Sarah sat in the corner, surrounded by books and research papers. She had been studying the sharks' behavior for hours, trying to find any clues that could help them survive.

Jake approached her, his face grim. "Sarah, any luck with your research?"

Sarah looked up from her books and rubbed her tired eyes. "Not much, I'm afraid. I've been studying their movements and vocalizations, trying to understand their behavior. But it's hard to make sense of it all."

Maria chimed in, her voice soft. "Do you think there's any way we could communicate with them? Maybe make them understand that we're not a threat?"

Sarah shook her head. "I'm not sure. From what I've seen, they seem to view us as prey. But I'm not giving up hope yet. There has to be something we can do."

Tom walked over, holding a makeshift spear in his hand. "I don't know about all this studying, but I do know one thing. We need to defend ourselves. And if that means fighting back, then so be it."

The tourists nodded in agreement, their faces grim. They knew that they were facing a difficult situation, but they refused to give up.

Sarah went back to her research, determined to find a way to survive. She pored over charts and diagrams, trying to understand the sharks' behavior. As she studied, she began to notice a pattern in their movements.

"They seem to be following a specific path," she said, pointing to a chart on the table. "If we can figure out where they're going, we might be able to avoid them altogether."

Jake looked at the chart, nodding in agreement. "That's a good idea. But how do we figure out where they're going?"

Sarah thought for a moment, then spoke. "We need to observe them more closely. Maybe we can see something we haven't noticed before."

The tourists agreed, and they spent the next few hours watching the sharks' movements, trying to piece together their behavior.

As the sun began to set, Sarah stood up, a determined look on her face. "I think I've figured it out. The sharks seem to be following a specific scent trail. If we can mask our scent, we might be able to avoid them."

The tourists looked at each other, a glimmer of hope in their eyes. Maybe there was a way to survive after all.

The tourists listened to Sarah's plan, feeling a glimmer of hope. But Maria's face grew pale, her eyes darting around nervously.

"I don't know if I can handle this much longer," she whispered, her voice shaking. "I keep seeing sharks everywhere, even when there aren't any."

Jake put a comforting arm around her, his eyes filled with concern. "You're going to be okay, Maria. We're going to get through this together."

But as the hours ticked by, Maria's fear continued to grow. She started to see visions of sharks attacking her, their jaws snapping shut around her body.

The other tourists tried to comfort her, but nothing seemed to help. She was becoming increasingly overwhelmed by the situation, and her hallucinations were only getting worse.

Sarah noticed Maria's distress and walked over to her. "Maria, are you okay? Do you need medical attention?"

Maria shook her head, her eyes wild. "I don't know what's happening to me. I can't seem to control my fear."

Sarah put a hand on her shoulder, her voice gentle. "It's okay to be scared. We all are. But we have to try to keep it under control. Otherwise, we won't be able to make rational decisions."

Maria nodded, tears streaming down her face. "I'm trying, but it's so hard. I keep seeing those sharks everywhere."

Jake hugged her tightly, his voice soothing. "We'll get through this, Maria. We'll find a way to survive, no matter what it takes."

But even as he spoke, Maria could feel the fear gnawing at her insides. She knew that she needed to get a grip on herself, but she didn't know if she could.

As the night wore on, Maria struggled to keep her fear under control. She tried to focus on Sarah's research, hoping that it would give her something to hold on to. But even as she read through the data, she could feel the fear creeping back in.

As Maria struggled with her fear, Jake and Tom huddled together, trying to come up with a plan to distract the sharks and lead them away from the cage.

"We need to do something to get their attention away from us," Jake said, his voice low. "Otherwise, they're going to keep circling us until we're too weak to fight back."

Tom nodded in agreement, his eyes scanning the water. "But what can we use as bait? We don't have anything on board that would be appealing to them."

Jake thought for a moment, then spoke. "What about the chum? We could use that to create a scent trail, leading them away from us."

Tom looked skeptical. "But won't that just make them more aggressive? They'll be attracted to the scent, and then we'll have even more sharks to deal with."

Jake chewed on his lower lip, considering the options. "Maybe if we use a decoy of some sort. Something that looks like prey, but isn't actually alive."

Tom nodded slowly, his expression thoughtful. "I think I see what you're getting at. We could use something like a fake seal or sea lion. The sharks would be drawn to it, thinking they had an easy meal, and then we could lead them away from the cage."

Jake's face lit up with excitement. "Yes, that's exactly what I was thinking. We can rig up a decoy using some of the equipment we have on board. It won't be perfect, but it might be enough to distract them for a while."

The two men set to work, using their ingenuity and resourcefulness to construct a fake seal out of old wetsuits, rope, and other materials they found on board. They covered it in the chum, hoping that the scent would be enough to draw the sharks away from the cage.

As they lowered the decoy into the water, they held their breath, watching anxiously as the sharks started to circle it. For a few moments, it seemed like their plan was working.

But then, the sharks began to grow more aggressive, lashing out at the fake seal with their powerful jaws. The tourists watched in horror as the decoy was torn apart, the chum scattering into the water.

Jake and Tom looked at each other, their faces grim. It seemed like their plan had backfired, and now they were in even more danger than before.

Jake and Tom looked at each other, their faces grim. It seemed like their plan had backfired, and now they were in even more danger than before.

As the tourists watched in horror, the sharks began to attack the cage again with renewed vigor. Maria screamed as a shark slammed into the cage, shaking it violently.

Just when it seemed like all hope was lost, a rescue team finally arrived on the scene. The tourists cheered as they saw the boats approaching, their lights piercing the darkness.

But as the rescue team got closer, they could see that the situation was even worse than they had imagined. Sharks were still circling the cage, and some of the tourists were injured or worse.

The rescue team sprang into action, working quickly to get the tourists to safety. But as they tried to lift the cage out of the water, the sharks grew more aggressive, attacking the rescue boats and causing chaos.

In the chaos, some of the tourists were left behind, their screams echoing in the night. Maria was among them, her fear overwhelming her as the sharks continued to attack.

Jake and Tom stayed behind, trying to fend off the sharks as best they could. But it soon became clear that they were outnumbered and outmatched.

As they watched the rescue boats pull away, Jake and Tom knew that they were facing a fight for survival. They huddled together, trying to come up with a plan.

"We need to find a way to distract the sharks," Jake said, his voice urgent. "Otherwise, they're going to keep attacking us until we're too weak to fight back."

Tom nodded, his eyes scanning the water. "But how can we do that? We don't have anything left to use as bait."

Jake's eyes narrowed, his mind racing. Then, he spotted something in the distance - a fishing boat, its lights flickering in the darkness.

"Tom, I think I see a boat over there," he said, pointing. "Maybe they have some bait or something we can use to distract the sharks."

Tom looked skeptical, but he was willing to try anything at this point. They swam over to the boat, their hearts pounding with fear.

As they climbed aboard, they saw that the boat was empty - the crew had probably fled when they heard the commotion. But Jake spotted a cooler in the corner, and he quickly opened it up.

Inside, he found a few pieces of fish, still relatively fresh. He grabbed them and swam back to the cage, Tom following close behind.

The sharks were still circling, their eyes fixed on the cage. But as Jake tossed the pieces of fish into the water, they suddenly lost interest in the cage, turning their attention to the new prey.

Jake and Tom watched in relief as the sharks swam away, their fears finally abating. They knew that they had been lucky to survive, and they were grateful for the rescue team that had managed to save some of their fellow tourists.

As they climbed aboard the rescue boat, they knew that they would never forget the terror they had experienced in the water that night. But they also knew that they had a newfound appreciation for the power of nature, and the importance of always being prepared for the unexpected.

As the survivors of the shark attack were pulled to safety, they were met by a team of paramedics who rushed to their aid. The tourists were in a state of shock and disbelief, still trying to come to terms with the horror they had just experienced.

Sarah, still clutching her research notebook, was among the first to speak. "We have to do something," she said, her voice trembling. "We can't just let this happen again."

The paramedic nodded sympathetically, but there was little he could say to comfort her. "We'll do everything we can to make sure you all get the help you need," he said.

As the survivors were taken to the hospital for treatment, they were left to grapple with the aftermath of the attack. Many of them had lost friends and family members in the chaos, and they were struggling to come to terms with their grief.

Maria and Jake, once so close, now found themselves unable to connect. They had both been traumatized by the attack, and the memory of what had happened seemed to loom over their relationship.

"I just can't stop thinking about it," Maria said, her eyes brimming with tears. "Every time I close my eyes, I see those sharks attacking the cage."

Jake nodded sympathetically, but he was lost in his own thoughts. He couldn't help but feel guilty for the role he had played in the disaster. "I never should have gone along with that stupid plan," he muttered.

Maria reached out to him, trying to offer comfort. "It's not your fault," she said. "We all made mistakes. We were all just trying to have an adventure."

Jake knew that she was right, but it was hard to shake the feeling of guilt that had settled in his chest. He couldn't help but wonder what he could have done differently to prevent the tragedy from happening.

Meanwhile, Sarah threw herself into her research, determined to find a way to prevent future shark attacks. She spent long hours pouring over her notes, looking for patterns and insights that might help her better understand the behavior of great whites.

As she worked, she couldn't help but think of the people who had been lost in the attack. She knew that she couldn't bring them back, but she was determined to honor their memory by doing everything in her power to prevent similar tragedies from occurring in the future.

In the weeks and months that followed, the survivors slowly began to pick up the pieces of their shattered lives. They went to therapy, talked to each other, and tried to find ways to move forward.

For Maria and Jake, it was a slow and difficult process. But as they worked through their trauma together, they slowly began to rebuild their relationship, finding comfort in the fact that they had survived the ordeal together.

And for Sarah, the tragedy had sparked a new sense of purpose. She continued her research, determined to make a difference in the world and to prevent others from experiencing the same horror that she had seen.

The Mercy Kill

John and Jack had been planning this trip for months. They were both experienced sailors and had taken many trips together in the past. They were excited to embark on another adventure, hoping to explore new waters and make new memories.

As they set sail on a clear day, they joked and chatted about their plans for the trip. They talked about the fish they wanted to catch, the islands they wanted to visit, and the stories they wanted to share with each other.

But their luck ran out quickly. Within hours, the sky turned dark, and the wind began to howl. The sea grew rough, and the waves pounded against their boat. John and Jack scrambled to secure their gear and batten down the hatches, but it was too late.

A huge wave crashed against the boat, sending it rolling over onto its side. John and Jack were thrown into the water, gasping for air and struggling to stay afloat. They frantically looked for each other in the chaos, trying to grab onto something to stay alive.

"John! Jack! Where are you?" yelled John, searching for his friend in the water.

"I'm here, John! Hold on!" Jack yelled back, clinging onto a piece of debris.

John finally spotted Jack, who was holding onto a piece of the boat's mast. He quickly swam over to him and helped him climb onto the debris.

"Are you okay?" John asked, panting heavily.

"My leg... it's broken," Jack replied, wincing in pain.

John saw that Jack's leg was twisted at an odd angle, and he knew that they were in trouble. They were stranded in the middle of the ocean, with no rescue in sight and no way to call for help.

"We need to stay together and try to stay alive until help comes," John said, trying to sound confident.

But deep down, he knew that they were in a dire situation. They were alone, injured, and at the mercy of the elements. The storm raged on, and they drifted farther and farther away from land.

The sun had set, and the darkness made it difficult for John to see anything. He knew that they needed to stay awake and alert, but exhaustion was setting in. Jack's leg was swollen and infected, and he was becoming delirious from the pain and fever.

"We need to keep talking and stay awake," John said, trying to keep Jack alert.

"I don't think I can do it, John. I'm so tired," Jack said, his voice weak and shaky.

Suddenly, they heard a loud noise in the distance. John strained his ears to listen, and he heard the sound of a ship's horn.

"Jack, did you hear that? I think it's a ship!" John said, excitedly.

They both strained their eyes to look for the ship, but they couldn't see anything in the darkness. But the sound of the ship's horn grew louder and more distinct, and John felt a glimmer of hope.

"Help! Over here! We're here!" John shouted at the top of his lungs.

They continued to shout and wave their arms, hoping that someone would see them. After what felt like an eternity, they finally saw the silhouette of a ship in the distance. The ship was moving towards them, but the waves were still high, making it difficult for the ship to approach them.

John and Jack continued to shout and wave their arms, trying to get the ship's attention. Finally, they saw a small boat being lowered from the ship, and a group of sailors rowing towards them.

"We're saved! We're saved!" John shouted, tears of relief streaming down his face.

The sailors helped John and Jack onto the boat, and they were taken aboard the ship. They were met with kindness and concern from the crew, who gave them food and water and tended to Jack's injuries.

"I can't believe it. We're alive," Jack said, his voice shaking with emotion.

"I know. It's a miracle," John said, his eyes glistening with tears.

John and Jack were overwhelmed with gratitude and relief. They knew that they had been given a second chance at life, and they were determined to make the most of it.

John and Jack were relieved to be rescued from the open sea, but their troubles were far from over. Jack's leg injury was worse than they thought, and it was clear that he needed medical attention.

The ship's doctor examined Jack's leg, and he determined that it was broken in several places. He carefully set the bone and applied a cast, but he warned Jack that he would need to rest and take it easy for the next few weeks.

"You'll need to stay off that leg for at least a month, Jack. I've given you some pain medication, but you'll need to rest as much as possible," the doctor said, looking at Jack with concern.

John watched as Jack winced in pain, his face pale and sweaty. He felt helpless, knowing that there was nothing he could do to ease Jack's suffering.

"I'm sorry, Jack. I should have been more careful during the storm," John said, his voice filled with regret.

"It's not your fault, John. We were both caught off guard. It was just bad luck," Jack said, trying to sound reassuring.

But John couldn't shake the feeling of guilt. He knew that Jack was suffering because of his mistake, and he felt responsible for Jack's pain.

Days turned into weeks, and Jack's condition did not improve. In fact, it seemed to be getting worse. His leg was swollen and red, and he was running a fever. The ship's doctor examined him again and determined that his wound had become infected.

"I'm sorry, Jack. We're going to have to amputate your leg," the doctor said, his voice solemn.

John and Jack were both shocked by the news. They had hoped that Jack's leg would heal on its own, but now it seemed like amputation was the only option.

"I don't know if I can do it, John. I don't know if I can go on with just one leg," Jack said, tears streaming down his face.

John put a comforting arm around Jack's shoulder. "We'll get through this together, Jack. I'll be here for you, every step of the way."

As the ship sailed on, John and Jack were left to rest in a small cabin. Jack's condition continued to worsen, and the doctor made the decision to amputate his leg. It was a difficult and painful procedure, but the doctor did everything he could to make it as painless as possible.

Days after the surgery, John was helping Jack rest when he noticed a dark shape circling in the water around them. At first, he thought it was a trick of the light, but as the shape got closer, he realized with horror that they were being stalked by sharks.

"Jack, wake up! We have to get out of here!" John said urgently, shaking his friend awake.

Jack groggily opened his eyes and saw the sharks circling around them. His face went pale with fear.

"What do we do, John? We're trapped!" Jack said, his voice shaking.

John quickly looked around the cabin, trying to find anything that could be used as a weapon. He spotted a metal pipe and grabbed it, hoping it would be enough to fend off the sharks.

As the sharks got closer, John swung the pipe at them, trying to drive them away. But it was a losing battle. The sharks were persistent and kept coming back, circling closer and closer to the two men.

"We have to get out of here, John! We can't fight them off forever!" Jack yelled, his panic rising.

John knew that Jack was right. They couldn't stay in the cabin forever, but he didn't know what else to do. He swung the pipe again, but it was knocked out of his hand by one of the sharks.

Just when it seemed like all hope was lost, the ship's crew came to the rescue. They had spotted the sharks circling the cabin and had rowed out to help John and Jack. With their help, John and Jack were quickly brought aboard the ship, safe from the sharks.

"We owe you our lives," John said, tears streaming down his face.

"It's all in a day's work," one of the sailors said with a grin.

John and Jack were grateful to be alive, but the experience left them shaken. They knew that they were lucky to have survived, and they were determined to make the most of their second chance at life.

As John and Jack recovered from their ordeal with the sharks, Jack's condition continued to worsen. He was in constant pain and became delirious, unable to defend himself from any danger. John watched in agony as his friend's condition deteriorated.

The ship's doctor did everything he could, but Jack's body was weak and unable to fight off the infection. John knew that Jack was dying, and he felt helpless to do anything about it.

One day, as they were resting in the cabin, John noticed a group of sharks circling the ship once again. His heart sank as he realized that they were in danger once again. But this time, Jack was in no condition to defend himself.

John knew that he had to make a difficult decision. He could stay with Jack and risk both their lives, or he could kill Jack to distract the sharks and save himself. The thought of leaving Jack to die was unbearable, but John knew that it might be their only chance of survival.

He looked at Jack, who was lying in a feverish sleep, his breaths shallow and labored. John's heart broke as he thought about what he had to do.

"I'm sorry, Jack," John whispered, tears streaming down his face. "I have to do this."

He took a deep breath and picked up a heavy tool, ready to strike Jack and use him as bait for the sharks. But just as he was about to strike, something inside him snapped.

"No. I can't do it," John said, dropping the tool to the ground. "I won't leave you here to die alone."

He stayed by Jack's side, holding his hand and whispering comforting words. The sharks circled closer and closer, but John didn't move. He was determined to stay with his friend until the very end.

In the end, the ship's crew came to their rescue once again, driving off the sharks and pulling John and Jack to safety. Jack was taken to the ship's infirmary, but it was too late. He had passed away during the attack.

John was devastated by the loss of his friend, but he knew that he had made the right decision. He had stayed with Jack until the end, refusing to abandon him to the sharks.

As the ship sailed on towards their destination, John grieved for Jack but also felt a sense of gratitude. He was grateful to have known Jack and to have had the chance to stand by his side, even in the face of death.

John sat alone in the cabin, staring blankly at the wall. The guilt and trauma weighed heavily on him, and he couldn't shake the feeling that he had made the wrong decision.

He couldn't stop thinking about what he had almost done. The image of Jack's face, pale and lifeless, haunted him day and night. He wondered if he could have done something differently, something that would have saved both their lives.

"I should have found another way," John said aloud, his voice cracking with emotion. "I should have been able to save him."

But no matter how hard he tried to rationalize his decision, the guilt remained. He felt like a murderer, like he had taken Jack's life with his own hands.

As the days passed, John withdrew further and further into himself. He didn't talk to anyone, didn't eat or sleep. He just sat there, lost in his own thoughts.

One day, the ship's captain came to see him. He had heard about what had happened and wanted to check on John.

"How are you holding up?" the captain asked, his voice gentle.

John didn't respond. He just sat there, staring at the wall.

"John, I know this is hard," the captain continued. "But you did the right thing. You stayed with Jack until the end, and that's what counts."

John shook his head. "No. I should have found another way. I should have been able to save him."

The captain sat down next to him. "John, listen to me. You did everything you could. You were there for Jack when he needed you, and that's what matters. You can't change what happened, but you can honor Jack's memory by living your life to the fullest."

John looked at the captain, his eyes filled with tears. "I don't know if I can do that. I don't know if I can ever forgive myself."

The captain put a hand on John's shoulder. "You will, in time. It won't be easy, but you'll get through this. And remember, we're all here for you."

John didn't say anything, but he felt a small glimmer of hope. Maybe, just maybe, he could find a way to move on from the guilt and trauma that had consumed him.

Days turned into weeks, and John's guilt and trauma continued to consume him. He knew he couldn't go on like this forever, and so he decided to seek help. He made an appointment with the ship's counselor, hoping that talking to someone would help him make sense of what had happened.

The counselor's office was small and cozy, with a comfortable armchair and a desk covered in books. John sat nervously in the armchair, his hands shaking.

"Hi, John. I'm Dr. Patel," the counselor said, extending her hand.

John shook her hand, trying to keep his emotions in check. "Nice to meet you."

"So, tell me, what brings you here today?" Dr. Patel asked, settling into her own chair.

John took a deep breath. "I'm here because I'm struggling with some things. I was in a situation recently where I had to make a difficult decision, and I'm not sure if I made the right one."

Dr. Patel nodded. "Can you tell me more about this situation?"

John hesitated for a moment, reliving the events in his mind. "My friend and I were stranded at sea, and we were attacked by sharks. My friend was dying, and I had to make a decision to either stay with him and risk both our lives, or kill him to distract the sharks and save myself."

Dr. Patel listened intently, her face impassive. "And what did you decide to do?"

"I decided to stay with him," John said, his voice barely above a whisper. "But I still feel like I made the wrong decision. I should have been able to save him."

Dr. Patel leaned forward, her eyes kind. "John, you did everything you could. You stayed with your friend until the end, and that's a brave thing to do. You couldn't have known what was going to happen."

John shook his head. "But I feel like I killed him. Like I had blood on my hands."

Dr. Patel nodded. "It's common to feel that way in situations like this. But the reality is, you did what you had to do to survive. And that doesn't make you a bad person."

John looked at her, his eyes filled with tears. "But how do I move on from this? How do I stop feeling so guilty?"

Dr. Patel smiled gently. "That's where therapy comes in. We'll work together to help you process your feelings and find ways to cope with the trauma you've experienced."

Over the next few weeks, John met with Dr. Patel regularly. They talked about what had happened, how John was feeling, and what he could do to move forward. They practiced mindfulness exercises, deep breathing, and visualization techniques to help John manage his anxiety and guilt.

Slowly but surely, John began to feel like himself again. He still grieved for his friend, but he no longer felt overwhelmed by guilt and trauma. With the help of therapy, he had found a way to move on from the past and embrace the present.

After several weeks of therapy, John felt like he was in a better place emotionally. But there was still one person he hadn't spoken to about what had happened: his close friend, Emily.

Emily and John had been friends for years, and they had grown even closer during their time on the boat. But John had never told her about what had happened with his other friend.

One day, John decided it was time to confide in Emily. They met up for coffee, and John took a deep breath before starting.

"Emily, there's something I need to tell you. It's about what happened on the boat."

Emily listened intently as John recounted the events that had led to his friend's death. She didn't interrupt or judge him, just let him talk.

"I've been struggling with it ever since. I feel so guilty, like I could have done more to save him."

Emily put a hand on John's shoulder. "John, you did everything you could. You stayed with him until the end. That's a testament to your character."

John looked at her, tears in his eyes. "But I still feel like I killed him."

Emily shook her head. "No, John. The sharks killed him. You did what you had to do to survive. And I'm sure your friend would have wanted you to live."

John sighed, feeling a weight lifted off his shoulders. "Thank you, Emily. I really needed to hear that."

From that moment on, John felt like a weight had been lifted off his shoulders. He and Emily talked more about what had happened, and he realized that having someone to confide in was a powerful thing.

Their friendship deepened as a result of this shared experience. They became even closer, spending more time together and relying on each other for support.

John knew that what had happened on the boat would always be a part of him, but with the help of therapy and the support of his friends, he felt like he could move forward with his life.

After months of therapy and support from Emily and his other friends, John thought he had put the tragedy behind him. But one day, a police officer knocked on his door with a warrant for his arrest.

John was charged with murder for killing Jack on the boat. He was stunned. How could this be happening? He had already gone through so much pain and trauma, and now he had to relive it all again.

John hired a lawyer and prepared for the trial, but he still felt like he was living in a nightmare. Emily was by his side the whole time, helping him to stay strong.

"I can't believe this is happening," John said, his voice shaking.

"I know," Emily replied, placing a comforting hand on his back. "But we'll get through it together. You didn't do anything wrong, John. You were just trying to survive."

The trial began a few weeks later, and it was emotional and difficult for everyone involved. The prosecutor painted John as a cold-blooded killer who had intentionally left Jack to die.

John's lawyer argued that he had acted out of self-defense, that he had no other choice but to fight off the sharks in order to save himself and Emily.

Emily was called to the witness stand, and she recounted the events of that day. She spoke about how scared they were and how they had done everything they could to save Jack.

At the end of the trial, the jury took a long time to deliberate. John felt sick to his stomach, unable to eat or sleep.

Finally, the verdict was announced. John was acquitted of all charges.

He felt a wave of relief wash over him, and he turned to Emily, tears in his eyes. "Thank you," he whispered. "I couldn't have done it without you."

Emily hugged him tightly. "Of course, John. I'll always be here for you."

From that day on, John felt like he had finally been given closure. The trial was over, and he could finally start to move on with his life. He knew that he would never forget what had happened on the boat, but he also knew that he had people in his life who would always be there to support him.

After the trial, John struggled to find a sense of normalcy. He tried to go back to work, but found it difficult to concentrate. He spent a lot of time at home, thinking about what had happened and how he could move on.

Emily continued to be there for him, listening to him whenever he needed to talk. But John knew that he couldn't rely on her forever. He needed to find a way to cope with his trauma and guilt on his own.

He started seeing his therapist more frequently, and they worked on strategies for managing his anxiety and negative thoughts. John also began to reconnect with old friends, people he had lost touch with over the years.

One night, he went out for drinks with his college roommate, Tom. They talked about old times and caught up on each other's lives.

Tom noticed that John seemed distant, and he asked him what was wrong.

John took a deep breath. "I was involved in something... really terrible. I don't know if I can talk about it."

Tom nodded. "You don't have to if you don't want to. But I want you to know that I'm here for you, no matter what."

That simple statement meant the world to John. He felt like he had been carrying a heavy burden for so long, and finally someone else was offering to help him carry it.

Over the next few weeks, John began to open up more to his old friends. He told them about what had happened on the boat, and how he had been charged with murder.

To his surprise, his friends were supportive and understanding. They didn't judge him or ask him difficult questions. They just listened and offered their love and support.

Slowly but surely, John began to find meaning in his experience. He started to see that his trauma had given him a new perspective on life. He appreciated the little things more, and he didn't take anything for granted.

He also realized that he wanted to use his experience to help others. He started volunteering at a local shelter, offering support to people who had gone through similar traumas.

John knew that he could never forget what had happened on the boat, but he also knew that he could learn to live with his guilt and trauma. He had a long way to go, but he was taking small steps every day towards a brighter future.

The Red Tide

Kai emerged from the water, his board under his arm, and walked back up the beach. His long blonde hair was matted to his face, and his wetsuit clung to his muscular frame. He stopped and looked out at the ocean, taking a deep breath of salty air. It was a perfect day for surfing.

As he turned to head back to his truck, he noticed a sign on the beach that read "Contaminated Water: No Swimming." He paused, looking around to see if anyone else was heeding the warning. But the water was still dotted with surfers, and the waves were too good to pass up.

"Ah, screw it," Kai muttered to himself. "I'm sure it's fine." He threw his board in the back of his truck and drove off, excited to hit the waves.

As he parked near the beach and got out of his truck, he noticed a woman in a lab coat watching him. She was carrying a clipboard and seemed to be taking notes.

"Hey, what's up?" Kai called out to her.

The woman looked up, startled. "Oh, sorry, I didn't mean to stare. I'm Dr. Maya Patel. I'm a marine biologist studying the local ecosystem."

Kai grinned. "Oh, cool. I'm Kai. Professional surfer, lover of the ocean."

Dr. Patel smiled back, but there was a hint of concern in her eyes. "Kai, I hate to be the one to say this, but the water is contaminated. It's not safe to be in there."

Kai shrugged. "Yeah, I saw the sign. But I'm not too worried. I've surfed in worse water before."

Dr. Patel shook her head. "Please be careful. We still don't know what kind of toxins are in the water or how they'll affect the local ecosystem."

Kai grinned again. "Don't worry, doc. I'll be just fine." And with that, he grabbed his board and headed out to the waves.

As he paddled out, he couldn't help but feel a thrill of excitement. The waves were perfect, and he was in his element. But as he waited for the next set, he noticed something strange in the water. It was a reddish-brown tint, and there seemed to be a weird smell coming off of it.

Kai shrugged it off and caught the next wave, riding it all the way to the shore. He was exhilarated, but as he emerged from the water, he noticed a small cut on his foot. It was bleeding, and he realized that the water must have been more contaminated than he thought.

Kai looked down at his foot and cursed under his breath. The cut wasn't deep, but it was bleeding enough to be concerning. He knew he should get it checked out, but he couldn't resist the waves.

As he walked back up the beach, he noticed Dr. Patel still there, scribbling away on her clipboard. He walked up to her, trying to hide the concern on his face.

"Hey, doc," he said, trying to sound casual. "You see any of those toxins you were talking about?"

Dr. Patel looked up from her clipboard and frowned. "Kai, are you okay? You're bleeding."

Kai shrugged. "Just a small cut. Happens all the time when you're surfing."

Dr. Patel shook her head. "Please, let me take a look. We don't know what kind of contaminants are in the water. It could be dangerous."

Kai hesitated for a moment before finally relenting. He sat down on the beach, and Dr. Patel began to examine his foot.

"It doesn't look too bad," she said, wiping away the blood with a cloth. "But you should still get it checked out by a doctor."

Kai nodded, feeling a twinge of embarrassment. "Yeah, I know. I'll go see one later."

Dr. Patel finished cleaning the wound and stood up, looking out at the ocean. "Kai, I have to admit, I was skeptical of your claims about the contaminated water and the creatures it's producing. But after seeing your cut and the strange tint in the water, I think you might be onto something."

Kai's face lit up. "Really? You believe me?"

Dr. Patel nodded. "Yes, I do. And I think we need to work together to figure out what's happening here."

Kai grinned. "Awesome. Let's do it."

And with that, the two of them set off to study the contaminated water and the creatures it was producing. Over the next few weeks, they collected samples of the water and the strange creatures that were washing up on the shore. They ran countless tests in Dr. Patel's lab, trying to figure out what was causing the contamination and how it was affecting the local ecosystem.

As they worked, Kai and Dr. Patel developed a close relationship. They spent long hours in the lab, bouncing ideas off of each other and discussing their findings. Kai was impressed by Dr. Patel's intelligence and dedication, and he found himself falling for her as they worked side by side.

But despite their progress, they were still stumped by the contamination. They couldn't figure out where it was coming from or how to stop it. And as they worked, they began to realize just how serious the situation was. The contaminated water was affecting not just the local marine life, but also the health of the people who lived near the coast.

As they sat in Dr. Patel's lab, Kai and Dr. Patel poured over their data, trying to find a breakthrough in their investigation. Kai rubbed his tired eyes, feeling the weight of the situation pressing down on him.

"We've tested everything we can think of," he said, frustration creeping into his voice. "How are we going to find out where this contamination is coming from?"

Dr. Patel shook her head. "I don't know, Kai. But we can't give up now. Too many people's lives are at risk."

Kai nodded, determination returning to his face. "You're right. We have to keep going."

The next day, Kai decided to go undercover to investigate the source of the contamination. He donned a wetsuit and swam out to the site where the contamination was the most concentrated. As he dove deeper into the water, he saw something glinting in the sand.

He reached out and grabbed it, pulling it up to the surface. It was a metal cylinder, rusted and battered. He swam back to shore, heart pounding with excitement. This could be the evidence they needed to take down the company responsible for the contamination.

When he got back to Dr. Patel's lab, he showed her the cylinder. She immediately recognized it as a container used to transport toxic waste.

"This is it," she said, her voice shaking with anger. "This is the proof we need to bring down that company."

Kai grinned. "So what's our next move?"

Dr. Patel leaned in close to him. "We're going to have to be very careful. This company has a lot of money and influence. We need to make sure we have all our ducks in a row before we make any moves."

Over the next few weeks, Kai and Dr. Patel worked tirelessly to gather more evidence against the company. They discovered that the corporation had been illegally dumping toxic waste into the ocean for years, and that they had been hiding their activities from the authorities.

But they knew that they needed more than just evidence. They needed to make sure that the company was held accountable for their actions. So, they decided to take their evidence to the media.

Kai and Dr. Patel held a press conference, presenting their findings to the public. They showed pictures of the contaminated water, the strange creatures it was producing, and the metal cylinder Kai had found.

The response was immediate. People were outraged that a corporation had been putting their health at risk for years. The media picked up the story, and soon, the company was facing a major public relations crisis.

Kai and Dr. Patel watched from the sidelines as the company's CEO was forced to step down and the corporation was hit with heavy fines. They felt a sense of relief knowing that they had made a difference, but also a sense of sadness for all the damage that had been done.

As they walked out of the press conference, Dr. Patel turned to Kai. "I'm proud of you, Kai. You took a stand for what was right, even when it was difficult."

Kai smiled at her. "I couldn't have done it without you. We make a pretty good team, don't we?"

Dr. Patel's smile grew wider. "Yes, we do. But our work isn't done yet. We need to make sure that this never happens again."

Kai nodded. "Agreed. Let's get started."

As Kai and Dr. Patel continued their work, they couldn't help but notice the strange creatures that were emerging from the contaminated water. The creatures were unlike anything they had ever seen before, and they seemed to be evolving at an alarming rate.

Kai pointed to one of the creatures that had crawled onto the shore. "What is that thing?"

Dr. Patel shook her head. "I don't know. It doesn't look like anything that should exist in nature."

As they watched, more and more of the creatures emerged from the water. They had strange appendages and multiple eyes, and they seemed to be getting bigger and stronger with each passing day.

"We have to do something about these creatures," Kai said. "They're a danger to the public."

Dr. Patel nodded. "I agree. But we have to be careful. These creatures are mutating at an alarming rate. We don't know what they're capable of."

Over the next few days, the situation became more dire. People were being attacked and injured by the mutated creatures, and it seemed like there was no end in sight.

Kai and Dr. Patel worked around the clock to find a solution. They consulted with marine biologists, toxicologists, and other experts, but no one had ever seen anything like these creatures before.

Then one day, a breakthrough came. Dr. Patel discovered that the creatures were feeding on a particular type of algae that was only found in the contaminated water.

"We have to eliminate the source of the algae," she said.

Kai nodded. "But how do we do that?"

Dr. Patel thought for a moment. "We can use a chemical that will neutralize the algae without harming the rest of the ecosystem. It's risky, but it's our best chance."

Kai agreed, and they immediately set to work. They worked with a team of experts to develop the chemical and to ensure that it would only affect the algae.

Finally, the day of the operation arrived. Kai and Dr. Patel donned protective gear and headed out to the site of the contamination. They administered the chemical, and within hours, the algae began to die off.

Over the next few days, they watched as the mutated creatures began to disappear. The situation began to stabilize, and people were no longer being attacked by the creatures.

As they walked back to their lab, Kai turned to Dr. Patel. "That was one of the craziest things I've ever seen."

Dr. Patel smiled. "Yes, it was. But we did it. We saved lives and made a difference."

Kai nodded. "I just hope that nothing like this ever happens again."

Dr. Patel put a hand on his shoulder. "We can't predict the future, but we can be prepared. And we will be."

Kai and Dr. Patel returned to their lab, feeling a sense of relief but also a growing unease. They knew that the contaminated water was only one part of the problem, and that the corporation responsible for the toxic waste would do everything in its power to cover up its tracks.

"We need to start gathering evidence," Kai said as they sat down at their desks. "We can't let them get away with this."

Dr. Patel nodded. "I agree. But we have to be careful. This company is powerful and influential. They could ruin our careers and our lives if we're not careful."

Kai leaned back in his chair. "I know. But we can't just sit back and do nothing. We have to fight for what's right."

Dr. Patel smiled. "I'm with you, Kai. Let's do this."

Over the next few weeks, they worked tirelessly, gathering documents, interviewing witnesses, and piecing together a trail of evidence that led directly to the corporation. They knew they were onto something big when they found evidence of bribes being paid to local officials to turn a blind eye to the illegal dumping.

But the corporation wasn't going to go down without a fight. They began to pressure witnesses to recant their statements, and even went so far as to destroy some of the evidence that Kai and Dr. Patel had gathered.

"This is getting out of control," Kai said, frustrated. "We're going to lose everything if we don't put a stop to this."

Dr. Patel nodded. "I know. But we have to keep going. We're so close to exposing the truth."

As they worked late into the night, they heard a knock on the door. When they opened it, they were surprised to see a man in a suit standing there.

"Can I help you?" Dr. Patel asked.

The man smiled. "I'm here to make you an offer."

Kai and Dr. Patel exchanged a look.

"What kind of offer?" Kai asked.

The man stepped forward. "I represent the corporation responsible for the toxic waste. We know that you've been gathering evidence against us, and we want to make sure that information doesn't see the light of day."

He pulled out an envelope and handed it to Kai.

"Inside that envelope is a lot of money. More than you could ever make in a lifetime. All you have to do is forget about the evidence and walk away."

Kai and Dr. Patel looked at each other, their minds racing.

"We'll never take your money," Dr. Patel said, her voice firm.

The man shrugged. "Suit yourself. But know that we have powerful friends. If you continue down this path, you'll regret it."

With that, he turned and walked away.

Kai and Dr. Patel watched him go, feeling a sense of dread wash over them.

"What are we going to do?" Kai asked.

Dr. Patel took a deep breath. "We're going to keep going. We're going to expose the truth, no matter what it takes."

Kai nodded. "I'm with you, Dr. Patel. Let's do this."

Kai and Dr. Patel spent the next few days gathering more evidence and trying to get the word out about the toxic waste. But as they worked, they began to notice a growing sense of unease in the town. People were starting to panic as more and more of the mutated creatures emerged from the water.

"We have to do something," Kai said, looking out at the chaos in the streets.

Dr. Patel nodded. "We need to calm them down and explain what's happening. Maybe if they understand the gravity of the situation, they'll be more willing to help us."

They made their way through the crowds, trying to get people to listen to them.

"Please, everyone calm down," Dr. Patel said, holding up her hands. "We know that this is scary, but we need your help. We've discovered that the water is contaminated with toxic waste, and that's what's causing these mutations. We need to work together to stop this."

But some people were skeptical.

"That's ridiculous," one man said, shaking his head. "You expect us to believe that the water is toxic? Why haven't we heard about this before?"

"Because the corporation responsible for the waste has been covering it up," Kai explained. "They've been paying off officials and destroying evidence. But we have proof, and we're working to expose them."

As they spoke, more and more people started to listen, but there were still those who refused to believe them.

"We can't just sit back and do nothing," Kai said, frustrated. "These creatures are dangerous. We need to take action."

Dr. Patel nodded. "I agree. But we have to do it carefully. We can't put people in danger."

They continued to talk to the townspeople, trying to get them on their side. And slowly but surely, the tide began to turn. People started to realize that Kai and Dr. Patel were telling the truth, and they began to work together to find a solution.

"We're going to help you," one woman said, putting her hand on Dr. Patel's shoulder. "We can't let these creatures take over our town."

Kai and Dr. Patel were moved by the outpouring of support, but they knew they had a long road ahead of them.

"We have to keep going," Kai said, determination in his voice. "We can't let the corporation win."

Dr. Patel nodded. "We'll keep working together, and we'll get through this. Together."

Kai and Dr. Patel knew that if they were going to stop the corporation responsible for the toxic waste, they needed to go straight to the top. They scheduled a meeting with the CEO, hoping to convince him to take responsibility for the contamination and clean up the town's water supply.

When they arrived at the corporation's headquarters, they were ushered into a large, luxurious office with floor-to-ceiling windows overlooking the city. The CEO, a middle-aged man with a neatly trimmed beard and expensive suit, greeted them with a smug smile.

"What can I do for you today?" he asked, leaning back in his leather chair.

"We've discovered that your corporation has been dumping toxic waste into the water supply," Dr. Patel said, her voice steady. "We have evidence to prove it."

The CEO's smile faltered, but he quickly regained his composure. "I assure you, we follow all environmental regulations and take our responsibility to the community very seriously."

"That's not what our evidence suggests," Kai said, pulling out a folder filled with documents and photographs. "We have proof that your corporation has been covering up the contamination and paying off officials to keep it quiet."

The CEO scoffed. "I find that hard to believe. Do you have any idea how much we contribute to this town's economy? If we were doing something illegal or harmful, don't you think we would have been caught by now?"

"But you have been caught," Dr. Patel said, her voice rising. "We have evidence, and we're not going to let you sweep this under the rug."

The CEO leaned forward, his eyes narrowing. "I think you're making a mistake. You're accusing me and my corporation of something without any concrete evidence. You're just trying to stir up trouble."

"We have evidence," Kai repeated, his voice firm. "And we're not going to back down until you take responsibility and fix this."

The CEO shook his head, standing up from his desk. "I'm sorry, but I have a busy schedule. I don't have time for baseless accusations. Good day."

He walked towards the door, but Kai and Dr. Patel stood their ground.

"We're not leaving until we get some answers," Dr. Patel said, crossing her arms.

The CEO turned back towards them, his face red with anger. "You're wasting my time. Get out of my office."

But Kai and Dr. Patel refused to budge. They knew that the town's safety was at stake, and they were determined to get the CEO to take responsibility.

As the CEO continued to berate them, Kai and Dr. Patel stood their ground. They knew they had to keep pushing until the CEO took responsibility for the toxic waste contamination. Suddenly, the room shook, and a loud crash echoed through the building.

"What the hell was that?" the CEO exclaimed, looking towards the windows.

Kai and Dr. Patel exchanged worried glances. They knew the creatures they had encountered before were likely responsible for the disruption.

Before they could say anything, the door burst open, and several of the creatures rushed into the room.

The CEO stumbled back, his face contorting in fear. Kai and Dr. Patel leaped into action, fending off the creatures with their weapons. They managed to hold their ground, but the creatures were relentless.

As the battle raged on, the CEO cowered behind his desk, watching in horror as the creatures attacked. "What are those things?" he yelled over the chaos.

"They're the result of your corporation's illegal activities," Dr. Patel replied, striking one of the creatures with her staff. "And we're here to shut you down."

The CEO's face paled, and he seemed to shrink back further. "I had no idea," he stammered. "I swear, I had no idea."

"You should have known," Kai said, deflecting a blow from one of the creatures. "It's your responsibility to know what's going on in your own company."

The CEO nodded, his eyes darting around the room. "I'll do anything, just please make them stop," he begged.

Kai and Dr. Patel exchanged a quick glance, both knowing that the only way to stop the creatures was to shut down the corporation's illegal activities. "Then you need to come clean," Dr. Patel said, her voice firm. "Tell the truth about what your company has been doing and take responsibility for the damage you've caused."

The CEO hesitated for a moment before nodding. "Okay, okay, I'll do it," he said, slowly standing up. "But you have to protect me from those things."

Kai and Dr. Patel nodded, fighting off the creatures as they made their way towards the door. They managed to fend off the creatures long enough to get to the main control room, where the CEO revealed the location of the corporation's illegal waste dumping site.

With the help of the town's officials and local activists, Kai and Dr. Patel were able to shut down the illegal activities and hold the corporation responsible for the toxic waste contamination. The town's water supply was eventually cleaned up, and the people of the town were able to breathe a sigh of relief.

As they walked out of the corporation's headquarters, Kai and Dr. Patel felt a sense of accomplishment wash over them. They had exposed the truth and saved the town from further harm. It was a victory they wouldn't soon forget.

As Kai and Dr. Patel stepped outside the corporation's headquarters, they were greeted by a crowd of reporters and local activists. The news had spread quickly about the corporation's illegal activities and the role that Kai and Dr. Patel had played in exposing the truth.

"How does it feel to be heroes?" one of the reporters shouted, shoving a microphone in Kai's face.

Kai hesitated for a moment, feeling a sense of unease. He knew that although the town had been saved, there was still so much work to be done. "We're just doing our job," he said, trying to deflect the attention. "The real heroes are the people of this town who stood up to the corporation and demanded change."

Dr. Patel nodded in agreement, "We couldn't have done this without the support of the community."

The reporters continued to fire questions at them, but Kai and Dr. Patel managed to slip away and head back to their hotel room. As they walked, they couldn't help but feel a sense of guilt for the lives that had been lost and the damage that had been done to the ocean.

"We can't stop here," Dr. Patel said, breaking the silence between them. "We have to keep fighting for the ocean and for the people affected by this."

Kai nodded, feeling a renewed sense of determination. "We can start by working with the town to create a plan for cleaning up the ocean and preventing future contamination."

Dr. Patel smiled, "That's a great idea. And we can also work to raise awareness about the importance of protecting our oceans and the impact that human activities have on them."

Over the next few weeks, Kai and Dr. Patel worked closely with the town officials and local activists to develop a plan for cleaning up the ocean and restoring its ecosystem. They also launched a campaign to raise awareness about ocean conservation and the need for stricter regulations to prevent corporations from polluting the ocean.

As the weeks turned into months, the town slowly began to recover. The water supply was cleaned up, and the local fishing industry was able to resume. The town's residents began to take pride in their efforts to protect the ocean and started to see the benefits of their hard work.

Kai and Dr. Patel continued to work tirelessly to raise awareness about ocean conservation and to push for stricter regulations. They traveled to conferences and spoke to policymakers, using their experience in the town to illustrate the importance of protecting the ocean.

As they looked out at the ocean, Kai and Dr. Patel felt a sense of hope. They knew that the fight to protect the ocean was far from over, but they were determined to continue their work and to make a difference.

As Kai and Dr. Patel stood on the pier overlooking the ocean, they both felt a sense of pride and accomplishment. The water was clear, and the marine life had returned to the area. It had been a long journey, but they had succeeded in their mission to clean up the ocean and protect it from further harm.

"I can't believe how far we've come," Dr. Patel said, breaking the silence between them. "It's amazing to see the ocean thriving again."

Kai nodded in agreement. "It's been a lot of hard work, but it was worth it to see the results."

Dr. Patel smiled. "And we're just getting started. There's so much more we can do to protect the ocean."

Kai looked at her, intrigued. "What do you mean?"

"I've been thinking about the future," Dr. Patel said. "We need to focus on preventing disasters like this from happening again. And we can do that by working to change the way corporations operate."

Kai frowned. "That's a tall order. How can we possibly change the way corporations think?"

Dr. Patel grinned. "By using their own tactics against them. We need to create a movement, a groundswell of public opinion that demands change. If enough people are outraged by corporate malfeasance, then the corporations will have to listen."

Kai considered this. "But how do we create that movement?"

"We need to start by raising awareness," Dr. Patel said. "We need to educate people about the dangers of pollution and the impact it has on the environment. We need to show them that their actions can make a difference."

Kai nodded slowly. "I see what you're saying. We need to empower people to take action."

"Exactly," Dr. Patel said. "And we can do that by building a network of activists and concerned citizens. We can create a platform for people to come together and work towards a common goal."

Kai smiled. "I like the sound of that. It's ambitious, but it just might work."

Dr. Patel grinned. "I know it will. We have the power to make a real difference, Kai. We just have to believe in ourselves and our ability to effect change."

Kai nodded, feeling a renewed sense of purpose. "Let's do it. Let's change the world."

Over the next few months, Kai and Dr. Patel worked tirelessly to build a movement for change. They traveled the world, speaking at conferences and rallying support for their cause. They met with policymakers and industry leaders, presenting them with the facts and demanding action.

Their efforts paid off. Slowly but surely, the movement grew. People from all walks of life joined their cause, and together they became a formidable force for change.

As they looked out at the ocean, Kai and Dr. Patel felt a sense of hope. They knew that the fight to protect the ocean was far from over, but they were more determined than ever to continue their work and to make a difference.

The Cove

The sun was just beginning to rise over the small coastal town of Cove as Jenna stirred in her bed, already dreading the day ahead. She knew that it was another day of shark hunting for her family, and that meant long hours out on the water, in search of the next catch.

Jenna's family had been in the shark hunting business for generations, and it was all she had ever known. But she couldn't help feeling uneasy about the practice, even as she got dressed and headed down to the kitchen for breakfast.

"Morning, Jenna," her father greeted her as she walked in. "Ready for another day out on the water?"

Jenna forced a smile. "As ready as I'll ever be, I guess."

Her mother served up a plate of eggs and bacon, and the family ate in silence for a few minutes before Jenna's younger brother, Liam, burst into the room.

"Morning, everyone!" he exclaimed, grabbing a piece of toast and heading out the door.

Jenna sighed, knowing that Liam loved shark hunting even more than their father did. He was only fifteen, but he had already been out on the water with them several times, and he talked constantly about the thrill of the chase.

As Jenna finished her breakfast and got ready to head out, she couldn't help but think about her dreams of leaving Cove behind. She was a bright, ambitious high school student, and she knew that there was a whole world out there beyond the confines of their small town. But for now, shark hunting was all she had.

She headed down to the docks, where her father and several other hunters were already loading up their boats.

"Morning, Jenna," one of them called out as she approached.

"Morning," she replied, forcing another smile.

They set out onto the water, the sun now fully risen, and began their search for the next catch. Jenna watched as her father and the others expertly scanned the water, looking for any signs of movement or disturbance.

As the hours ticked by, Jenna grew increasingly restless. She longed for something more in life, something beyond the endless cycle of hunting and killing. But she knew that it was futile to wish for something that was so deeply ingrained in their town's way of life.

Finally, as the sun began to dip below the horizon, they spotted their prey: a large, menacing-looking shark, its fin slicing through the water like a knife.

"Let's do this!" Liam shouted excitedly, grabbing a harpoon and getting ready to strike.

Jenna hung back, feeling a sense of unease that she couldn't quite explain. But she knew that she had to play her part, so she grabbed a harpoon of her own and braced herself for the fight.

Jenna watched nervously as her brother and father closed in on the shark, harpoons at the ready. She knew that this was the part of the hunt that always made her uneasy - the violent struggle between man and beast.

But before they could even get close, the shark suddenly veered off and disappeared into the depths.

"What the hell?" one of the other hunters exclaimed.

Jenna felt a wave of relief wash over her. Maybe this was their chance to let the shark go, to let it live another day.

But her relief was short-lived. The next day, news broke of the first attack - a young surfer who had been mauled by a shark just off the coast of Cove.

Jenna's heart sank as she listened to the radio report, knowing that it was only a matter of time before the town would be thrown into chaos. She knew that this was no ordinary shark, and that the hunters in town would be out for blood.

Sure enough, the next morning, Jenna's family and the other hunters set out onto the water, determined to catch the predator and put an end to the attacks. Jenna went along, feeling sick to her stomach at the thought of what was to come.

They spent the entire day scouring the waters, searching for any sign of the shark. Jenna's father was the first to spot it, its massive form looming just beneath the surface.

"Alright, boys, let's do this!" he called out to the other hunters.

They revved up their boats and charged forward, harpoons at the ready. Jenna stayed back, feeling more and more uneasy with every passing moment.

But just as they closed in on the shark, it seemed to sense their presence and took off at lightning speed, easily outrunning their boats.

Jenna watched as her family and the other hunters struggled to keep up, their boats bouncing dangerously over the waves. She knew that they were risking their lives for the sake of their livelihoods, and it made her sick.

As the sun began to set and the hunters returned to shore empty-handed, Jenna couldn't shake the feeling that something was different about this shark. It was faster, stronger, and more elusive than any they had ever encountered before.

But she knew that she had to keep her thoughts to herself. In Cove, questioning the practice of shark hunting was tantamount to treason. She had to play her part, even if it went against everything she believed in.

Jenna sat in silence as her family and the other hunters discussed their plans for the next day's hunt. She couldn't shake the feeling that what they were doing was wrong, but she didn't know how to express her misgivings without causing a scene.

Finally, she spoke up. "Do we really have to do this? Can't we just let the shark go?"

Her father and brother exchanged a glance, their faces hardening. "We can't just let it go," her father said firmly. "It's a danger to the town. We have to take care of it."

"But what if there's another way? What if we could find a way to coexist with the sharks, instead of just hunting them down?" Jenna pressed.

Her brother scoffed. "Coexist? You've been reading too many books, sis. Sharks are predators. They're not going to stop attacking us just because we want them to."

"But what if we're the ones who are causing the problem? What if we're taking away their food sources and driving them closer to shore?" Jenna persisted.

Her father sighed heavily. "Jenna, we've been over this before. This is how we make our living. We can't just stop hunting sharks because you have a moral objection to it."

"I'm not asking you to stop hunting sharks altogether," Jenna said. "I just think that there has to be a better way than what we're doing now."

Her brother rolled his eyes. "And what, pray tell, would that be?"

"I don't know," Jenna admitted. "But maybe we could start by not killing every shark we come across. Maybe we could find a way to study them, to understand their behavior and habits, so that we can avoid them without resorting to violence."

Her father shook his head. "Jenna, I appreciate your concern, but this is not the time or the place for this conversation. We have a job to do, and we're going to do it."

Jenna felt tears prick at the corners of her eyes. She knew that her family was right, that she didn't have the power to change their way of life. But that didn't make it any easier to stomach.

As she lay in bed that night, she couldn't shake the feeling that they were all playing a dangerous game. The shark was out there, somewhere, and they were risking everything to hunt it down. She didn't know what the answer was, but she knew that something had to change.

The next morning, Jenna woke up early, still troubled by the conversation she had with her family the night before. She decided to go for a walk along the beach, hoping to clear her mind before the day's hunt.

As she strolled along the sand, she heard a commotion in the water. She ran towards the shoreline, her heart pounding in her chest as she realized what was happening.

A young boy was screaming for help as a massive shark circled him, its jaws snapping dangerously close to his feet.

Jenna froze, unsure of what to do. She knew that her family and the other hunters were still asleep, and that it would take them precious minutes to get to the beach.

Without thinking, she sprinted towards the water, her heart racing as she dove in.

The cold water enveloped her, and she could feel the weight of the shark as it passed just inches beneath her. She kicked furiously, grabbing onto the boy's arm and pulling him towards the shore.

They stumbled onto the sand, gasping for air as the shark disappeared back into the depths.

Jenna looked down at the boy, relieved to see that he was alive and well. But the terror on his face was etched in her memory, and she knew that something had to change.

Later that day, as the hunters set out onto the water once again, Jenna couldn't shake the feeling that they were all playing a dangerous game. The sun was high in the sky, and the water was calm, but there was an air of tension that hung over the group.

They had been out for several hours when they spotted the shark, its massive form gliding just beneath the surface. Jenna felt her heart skip a beat as her family and the other hunters charged forward, their harpoons at the ready.

But the shark was too quick for them, dodging and weaving through the water as they struggled to keep up.

Jenna watched in horror as the shark circled back towards the group, its jaws gaping wide as it lunged towards one of the boats.

There was a sickening crunch as the boat capsized, tossing the hunters into the water. Jenna watched in horror as the shark closed in on one of the hunters, its teeth glinting in the sun.

In that moment, she knew that there was something different about this shark. It was faster, stronger, and more intelligent than any she had ever seen before.

As the hunters scrambled back onto their boats, Jenna felt a sickening sense of dread settle over her. She knew that they were all in danger, and that something had to be done before it was too late.

Jenna's heart raced as she watched the hunters struggle to fend off the shark. She knew that they needed a new plan, and fast.

As they regrouped on the beach, Jenna approached her family, determination in her eyes.

"We can't keep doing this," she said, her voice firm. "We're putting ourselves and the community in danger. We need to figure out what's going on with that shark."

Her family looked at her skeptically, but Jenna stood her ground. "I'm going to do some research. I think I know where to start."

She spent the next several days poring over articles and scientific papers, trying to piece together what could have created such a powerful and intelligent creature.

Eventually, she stumbled upon a local research facility that had been experimenting with genetic engineering, specifically with creating hybrid species.

Jenna's heart sank as she realized what this meant. The shark that had been terrorizing their community had been created in a lab.

She quickly assembled a presentation for her family and the other hunters, laying out her findings and proposing a new plan of action.

"We need to work with the researchers to figure out a solution," she said, her voice shaking slightly. "We can't keep trying to kill this shark when it was created by humans. We have to take responsibility for our actions and find a way to fix this."

There was a moment of silence as her family and the other hunters considered her words.

Finally, her father spoke up. "Jenna, you may be right. We can't keep doing what we've been doing. But how do we know that the researchers will be willing to help us?"

Jenna took a deep breath. "I'll go talk to them myself. I'll make them understand that this is not just about our safety, but about the ethics of what they've been doing. We can't just let them create these creatures and then leave us to deal with the consequences."

Her family looked at her with a mixture of pride and apprehension, but Jenna was determined. She knew that this was the right thing to do.

Jenna arrived at the research facility, her heart pounding with nerves. She had never been one to confront authority figures, but she knew that this was too important to back down.

She made her way through the maze of sterile hallways, finally arriving at the office of the head researcher.

"Can I help you?" the woman behind the desk asked, looking up from her computer.

Jenna took a deep breath. "I need to speak with the person in charge. It's urgent."

The woman raised an eyebrow but nodded, gesturing towards a door at the end of the hallway.

Jenna took another deep breath and pushed open the door. Inside, she found a middle-aged man with thinning hair, staring at a computer screen.

He looked up as she entered. "Can I help you?"

Jenna launched into her speech, explaining the danger that the shark posed to their community and the ethical implications of creating such a creature.

The man listened quietly, his expression unreadable. When she finished, he leaned back in his chair, considering her words.

"You make a good point," he said finally. "But what do you propose we do?"

Jenna thought for a moment. "I want to work with you. I want to understand how this shark was created and figure out a way to neutralize it. We can't keep putting our community at risk."

The man leaned forward, a hint of curiosity in his eyes. "That's an interesting proposal. But why should I trust you?"

Jenna took a deep breath, feeling a surge of determination. "Because I care. I care about our community and I care about the impact that our actions have on the world around us. I want to make things right."

The man nodded slowly, considering her words. "Very well. I'll allow you to work with our marine biologist, Dr. Alvarez. She's been studying the shark for several weeks now, and I believe that she may be able to help you."

Jenna felt a wave of relief wash over her as she thanked the man and headed out of the office.

As she walked down the hallway, she felt a sense of purpose that she had never felt before. She was determined to do whatever it took to protect her community and make things right.

When she finally met Dr. Alvarez, Jenna was struck by the woman's passion and expertise. Together, they worked tirelessly to uncover more information about the shark's origins, pouring over scientific reports and studying the creature's behavior.

As they worked, Jenna felt a sense of excitement building inside her. For the first time, she felt like she was making a real difference, like she was part of something bigger than herself.

Jenna and Dr. Alvarez had been working together for several weeks, gathering as much information as they could about the genetic engineering experiments conducted at the research facility. They were starting to piece together a theory about how the shark had been created, and they were hopeful that they were getting closer to finding a way to neutralize it.

But their progress was interrupted by a horrifying discovery. The shark had struck again, this time taking out several more hunters who had been patrolling the waters.

Jenna felt a sense of urgency building inside her. They couldn't afford to waste any more time. Lives were at stake.

She called an emergency meeting with her family and the other hunters, laying out the new information they had gathered and explaining the urgency of the situation.

"We have to find a way to stop this thing," she said, her voice shaking with emotion. "We can't let it keep taking out our people."

Her father nodded grimly. "We'll do whatever it takes. But what's the plan?"

Jenna took a deep breath, feeling the weight of responsibility resting heavily on her shoulders. "We need to use what we know about the shark's behavior to set a trap. We know that it's attracted to the scent of blood, so we need to use that to our advantage."

The hunters looked at each other, considering her words. Finally, one of them spoke up. "But how do we make sure that it's the shark that takes the bait, and not some other creature?"

Jenna turned to Dr. Alvarez, who had joined the meeting. "We need your help. Can you analyze the DNA of the shark's previous victims and compare it to the DNA of the other marine life in the area?"

Dr. Alvarez nodded, a sense of determination in her eyes. "I'll do everything I can to help."

Over the next several days, they worked tirelessly to set the trap. They used a combination of blood and other substances to create a scent that they knew would attract the shark. They set up cameras and other monitoring equipment to track its movements.

And then they waited.

Days turned into weeks, and the tension in the community continued to mount. Everyone was on edge, knowing that the shark could strike at any moment.

And then, finally, they got a hit. The cameras captured the image of the shark, circling around the bait.

Jenna felt her heart race with excitement and fear. This was it. This was their chance to put an end to this nightmare.

The hunters sprang into action, moving quickly and efficiently to execute the plan they had carefully crafted. They moved in on the shark, firing harpoons and other weapons.

And then, finally, it was over. The shark lay dead on the beach, a testament to the determination and bravery of the hunters who had brought it down.

Jenna felt a sense of relief wash over her, but also a sense of sadness. It shouldn't have come to this. Lives shouldn't have been lost.

But she knew that they had done the right thing. They had taken responsibility for their actions and worked together to put an end to the danger.

Jenna and her team spent hours poring over the footage of the shark circling around the bait. They needed to figure out how to get close enough to it to take it down without getting themselves killed in the process.

"We need to get inside its head," Jenna said, her eyes glued to the screen. "We need to understand its patterns and its behavior."

One of the other hunters, a grizzled old veteran named Jack, spoke up. "I've been hunting sharks for thirty years, and I've never seen one like this. It's smart, cunning, and it's not afraid of anything."

Jenna nodded, her mind racing. "That's why we need to be smart too. We need to use our brains, not just our brawn."

They spent the next several days putting together a plan, going over every detail until they were sure that they had thought of everything.

"We're going to need a bigger boat," Jack said with a wry grin.

Everyone laughed, but Jenna knew that this was no joke. This was serious business.

"We're going to need to lure it out into the open," she said, "and then hit it with everything we've got. We can't afford to miss."

The hunters nodded grimly, each of them steeling themselves for the battle to come.

They spent the next several days putting their plan into action, setting up the bait and the monitoring equipment, and practicing their aim with the harpoons and other weapons they would need to take down the shark.

As the day of the hunt drew closer, Jenna found herself unable to sleep, her mind racing with all the things that could go wrong. She knew that this was a risky, dangerous plan, and that they were putting their lives on the line.

But she also knew that they had no choice. They couldn't let the shark continue to terrorize their community.

Finally, the day of the hunt arrived. Jenna and her team boarded their boat, their faces grim and determined. They sailed out to the spot where they had set the bait, and waited.

Hours passed, and Jenna's anxiety grew. What if the shark didn't take the bait? What if it was too smart for them?

And then, suddenly, they saw it. The dark shape of the shark circling around the bait, just as they had hoped.

"Now!" Jenna yelled, and the hunters sprang into action.

They moved quickly and efficiently, firing their harpoons and other weapons at the shark. The water churned with the force of their attack, and Jenna could feel her heart racing with excitement and fear.

And then, finally, it was over. The shark lay dead on the surface of the water, a testament to their determination and bravery.

Jenna felt a sense of relief wash over her, but also a sense of sadness. They had lost too many lives to this creature, and she knew that it shouldn't have come to this.

But she also knew that they had done the right thing. They had taken responsibility for their actions and worked together to put an end to the danger.

Jenna and her team stood on the deck of their boat, staring at the massive, dead shark they had just taken down. The water around them was stained red with blood, and the air was thick with the smell of salt and death.

For a few moments, no one said anything. They were all too exhausted and overwhelmed by the intensity of the hunt. But then Jack spoke up.

"Well, that's one less monster in the sea," he said, his voice gruff with emotion.

Jenna nodded, her eyes still fixed on the shark's body. "Yeah," she said softly. "But at what cost?"

They all knew the answer to that question. They had lost friends and loved ones to this creature, and now they had lost even more in the final confrontation.

Jenna's mind drifted back to the moments before the battle began. She remembered the sense of dread that had settled over her as they waited for the shark to take the bait. She had known then that this was going to be a fight to the death, and she had prepared herself as best she could.

But nothing could have prepared her for the sheer ferocity of the shark's attack. It had fought back with all the strength and cunning it possessed, taking down several of Jenna's team before they were able to finally bring it down.

Jenna felt a lump form in her throat as she thought of the sacrifices they had made. She had never wanted anyone to die in this hunt, but she knew that it was a risk they had all been willing to take.

And now, they had succeeded. The shark was dead, and their community was safe once again.

But the victory felt hollow to Jenna. She couldn't help but wonder if there had been a better way, a way to avoid the bloodshed and loss of life.

As the boat sailed back to shore, Jenna couldn't shake the feeling of guilt that weighed on her heart. She knew that they had done what they had to do, but she couldn't help feeling that there was more they could have done to prevent this tragedy.

When they reached the harbor, a crowd of people was waiting for them, cheering and clapping as they tied up the boat. Jenna could see the relief and gratitude in their faces, and she knew that they had done something important.

But she couldn't help feeling that the cost had been too high.

As the hunters disembarked from the boat, they were met by the families of the fallen. Jenna felt a lump form in her throat as she saw the grief and pain in their eyes.

"I'm sorry," she said softly, as she hugged one of the widows. "I'm so sorry."

But the woman just smiled sadly. "You did what you had to do," she said. "We all knew the risks. And now, at least, we can start to heal."

Jenna nodded, her eyes filling with tears. She knew that the journey to healing would be a long and difficult one, but she also knew that they would do it together.

As the sun began to set over the harbor, Jenna and her team gathered on the deck of the boat, sharing stories and memories of the fallen. They laughed and cried together, finding solace in each other's company.

And as the stars came out and the night deepened, Jenna felt a sense of peace settle over her. She knew that they had done the right thing, and that they had honored the memory of those they had lost.

As the days passed after the successful hunt, the town began to return to its normal routines. But the events of the past weeks lingered in everyone's minds.

Jenna and her team had become heroes, hailed as saviors who had rid the town of a deadly menace. But Jenna knew that the victory had come at a great cost, and she couldn't shake the feeling that there was more they could have done to prevent the tragedy.

She found herself spending more and more time with the families of the fallen, listening to their stories and offering comfort. She heard tales of loved ones lost, of children left without parents, of futures forever changed.

The weight of their grief and pain was heavy, and Jenna began to realize that she had underestimated the impact of the shark attacks on the community. For so long, they had seen the creatures as monsters to be conquered, without considering the toll it was taking on their own people.

One day, Jenna found herself sitting in a coffee shop with the town's mayor, discussing the aftermath of the hunt.

"It's been a difficult time for everyone," the mayor said, sipping his coffee. "But we've come through it stronger than ever."

Jenna shook her head. "I don't think we have," she said. "We've lost so much. And for what? To continue this cycle of hunting and killing?"

The mayor raised an eyebrow. "What are you suggesting?"

"I'm suggesting that we need to change our way of life," Jenna said firmly. "We can't keep relying on shark hunting to survive. We need to find a way to coexist with these creatures."

The mayor looked skeptical. "Coexist? That's not possible. They're dangerous predators."

"I know that," Jenna said. "But maybe there's another way. We need to start thinking outside the box. Maybe we can find a way to protect ourselves without killing them."

The mayor rubbed his chin, considering. "I see your point," he said. "But it's not going to be easy. We've been hunting sharks for generations. It's part of our culture."

Jenna nodded. "I understand that. But we can't keep doing things the same way and expecting different results. We need to try something new."

The mayor sighed. "You're right. It's time for a change. But it's going to take time and effort to convince everyone."

Jenna smiled. "I'm up for the challenge."

Over the next few weeks, Jenna threw herself into the task of convincing the town of the need for change. She spoke at town hall meetings, organized educational campaigns, and even enlisted the help of marine biologists to explore alternative solutions.

It was a slow process, and there were many who resisted the idea of change. But gradually, Jenna began to see a shift in the community's attitude. People were starting to see the value in coexisting with sharks, in protecting them rather than hunting them.

And as the community came together to explore new ideas and approaches, Jenna felt a sense of hope and optimism that she hadn't felt in a long time.

She knew that there was still a long way to go, and that there would be challenges and setbacks along the way. But for the first time in a long time, Jenna felt that they were on the right path.

The Reef

The group had been planning this diving trip for months. They were all excited to explore the beautiful coral reef and conduct research for Emily's marine biology project.

As they arrived at the remote reef, they could see the crystal clear water and the vibrant colors of the coral. Jack, the group's leader, was the first to jump in the water. "Wow, this is even more beautiful than I remember!" he exclaimed as he looked around in awe.

Emily followed closely behind, checking her equipment and making sure everything was in order. "Remember, safety first everyone. Let's make sure we stick together and watch out for each other," she reminded them.

Mike and Sarah, who had never been diving before, were nervous but excited. "I can't believe we're actually doing this!" Sarah exclaimed as she put on her fins.

Tyler, the youngest and most reckless member of the group, was already diving down to the coral, eager to explore. "Come on, guys! Let's go check out those sharks over there!" he shouted as he gestured towards a group of reef sharks in the distance.

"Tyler, wait up! We need to make sure we stay together," Jack called after him.

The group spent the day setting up their equipment and conducting a few practice dives to get acclimated to the environment. As they swam around the coral, they could see all kinds of marine life, from colorful fish to sea turtles and even a few rays.

As they surfaced from their first dive, Emily checked her watch. "Okay, everyone. Let's take a break and regroup. We'll head back down in about half an hour," she said.

As they sat on the boat, sipping water and eating some snacks, they discussed their plans for the rest of the day. "I think we should start collecting data on the coral formations and the different species of fish we see," Emily suggested.

Mike, eager to impress Sarah, chimed in. "I can help with that. I have a good eye for detail," he said with a grin.

Jack nodded in agreement. "Sounds like a plan. Tyler, you and I can scout out some potential dive spots for tomorrow."

Tyler nodded eagerly, already thinking about all the exciting places he wanted to explore.

As they geared up for their next dive, Emily reminded them of the importance of staying together and following proper diving protocol. "Remember, if you see something interesting, just point it out and we'll all take a look together," she said.

The group descended into the water, marveling at the beauty of the reef. They swam around, taking notes and pictures, and occasionally pointing out interesting things to each other.

Suddenly, Tyler let out a shout. "Guys, come look! There's a whole school of reef sharks over here!"

Jack and Emily quickly swam over, trying to keep Tyler and the rest of the group safe. "Okay, let's stay calm and stick together. Remember, we're in their environment, so we need to be respectful," Emily reminded them.

After a few minutes of observing the sharks from a safe distance, they decided it was time to head back to the boat. As they surfaced, they could feel the excitement and thrill of their first day of diving. It was only the beginning of their adventure.

The next day, the group woke up early and began their dives. As they explored the reef, Emily noticed some changes in the weather. "Hey guys, I think we should start heading back. I don't want us to get caught in a storm," she said, looking up at the sky.

Jack nodded in agreement. "Good call. Let's wrap up our research for the day and head back to the boat."

As they began to ascend, the wind picked up and the waves grew bigger. "This doesn't look good," Mike said, looking around nervously.

Suddenly, a bolt of lightning struck nearby, followed by a deafening clap of thunder. "Everyone, hold on tight and stick together!" Jack shouted over the sound of the storm.

They swam as fast as they could towards the surface, but the waves were too rough. As they emerged from the water, they saw that their boat had been carried away by the storm.

"Oh no! What are we going to do now?" Sarah cried out, looking around frantically.

Jack quickly assessed the situation. "We need to find shelter and wait for the storm to pass. There's a cave over there, let's swim towards it."

As they swam towards the cave, they could feel the current pulling them in different directions. Emily struggled to keep Tyler close to her. "Stay close to me, Tyler. We need to make sure we stay together," she said firmly.

Finally, they reached the cave and huddled together, waiting for the storm to pass. "Is everyone okay?" Jack asked, checking to make sure they were all accounted for.

As the storm raged on outside, the group tried to make themselves comfortable in the cave. "I hope this storm passes soon. I'm getting hungry," Tyler said, rummaging through his bag for some snacks.

Suddenly, they heard a strange noise coming from the back of the cave. "What was that?" Sarah asked, looking around nervously.

As they turned their flashlights towards the back of the cave, they saw a giant octopus staring back at them. "Oh my god! What do we do?" Mike shouted, backing away slowly.

The octopus began to move towards them, its tentacles reaching out menacingly. "Stay calm, everyone. Let's slowly back away and try to find another way out," Emily said, trying to keep everyone calm.

But as they tried to make their way towards another exit, they realized they were trapped. "There's no way out! We're stuck here with the octopus!" Tyler cried out, his voice echoing in the cave.

The group was in shock as they stared at the giant octopus in front of them. Its eight long tentacles were reaching out towards them, and its eyes were fixed on their every move.

"We need to get out of here!" Jack exclaimed, trying to come up with a plan.

But before they could make a move, the octopus lunged forward and grabbed onto Mike's leg with one of its tentacles. Mike screamed out in pain as he felt the strong grip of the octopus tightening around his leg.

"Mike! Hang on, we'll get you out of there!" Emily shouted, trying to pull Mike away from the octopus.

But the octopus was too strong, and it wasn't letting go. Sarah quickly swam over to help, but as she got close, the octopus lashed out and hit her in the face with another tentacle.

Sarah cried out in pain and her mask became dislodged. Water began to rush in, and she struggled to keep her head above the water. Jack quickly swam over to help, but as he did, the octopus grabbed onto his arm with another tentacle.

"We need to fight back!" Tyler shouted, grabbing a rock from the ground and hurling it towards the octopus.

The rock hit the octopus in the head, and it released its grip on Jack and Mike. The group quickly swam towards the back of the cave, hoping to find another way out.

But as they swam, they realized that their air supply was running low. "We need to find a way out of here, fast!" Jack said, looking around frantically.

But there was no other exit, and the group was trapped with limited air and a wounded member.

"We need to signal for help," Emily said, looking around for any way to communicate with the outside world.

But their radios were gone with the boat, and there was no signal in the cave. They were completely cut off from the rest of the world.

As the minutes passed, their air supply continued to dwindle, and they knew they needed to act fast. "We need to conserve our air and work together to find a solution," Jack said, trying to keep everyone calm.

But the reality of the situation was sinking in. They were trapped in a cave with no way to signal for help and limited air supply. The odds were stacked against them, and they knew they were in a fight for their lives.

The group huddled together in the back of the cave, their breathing labored as they struggled to conserve their dwindling air supply. They knew that time was running out, and their situation was becoming more desperate by the minute.

Suddenly, a loud rumble echoed through the cave, followed by the sound of crashing waves. Emily looked up and saw that the storm outside had intensified, with lightning illuminating the entrance to the cave.

"We're not getting out of here anytime soon," she said, her voice laced with fear.

Jack nodded grimly, his mind racing as he tried to come up with a plan. But before he could say anything, Tyler spoke up.

"I'm going to go take a look outside," he said, his voice tinged with excitement.

"Are you crazy?" Sarah exclaimed. "We can't risk it. We need to conserve our air and wait for help."

But Tyler was already swimming towards the entrance of the cave, his curiosity getting the best of him. The rest of the group watched in horror as he disappeared into the stormy waters.

Minutes passed, and the group started to get increasingly anxious. "We need to go after him," Jack said, looking at the others. "He could be in trouble."

The group reluctantly agreed, and they swam out of the cave, searching for Tyler in the churning waters. But as they swam, they realized that they weren't alone.

A group of sharks had been attracted by Tyler's reckless behavior, and they were now circling the group, their teeth bared in aggression.

"Oh my god," Sarah whispered, her eyes widening in fear.

"We need to get out of here," Jack said, his voice urgent. "Now."

But as they tried to swim away, one of the sharks lunged towards them, its jaws snapping shut just inches away from Sarah's leg. She screamed out in terror, and the group frantically swam towards the safety of the cave.

But as they swam, they realized that they were running out of air. They needed to act fast, or they would suffocate before they could get back to the cave.

"We need to use our tanks to distract the sharks," Emily said, her voice shaking with fear. "It's our only chance."

The group hesitated for a moment, but then they knew that they had no other choice. They quickly removed their tanks and threw them towards the sharks, hoping to distract them long enough for the group to make it back to the cave.

It worked, and the group managed to make it back to the cave just in time. But as they collapsed onto the floor, panting for breath, they knew that they had narrowly escaped death.

Tyler looked at the group, his face sheepish. "I'm sorry," he said. "I didn't mean to put us in danger like that."

Jack sighed, his anger dissipating as he saw the remorse on Tyler's face. "It's okay," he said. "But we need to be more careful from now on. We can't afford to make any more mistakes."

The group nodded in agreement, their faces grim as they realized how close they had come to death. But despite the danger, they knew that they had to keep fighting for survival. They were in this together, and they would do whatever it takes to make it out alive.

Jack and Emily huddled together, their minds racing as they tried to come up with a plan to escape the cave. "We need to find a way out," Emily said, her voice urgent.

"But how?" Jack asked, frustration evident in his tone. "We're running out of air, and the sharks are still out there."

Emily thought for a moment, her mind racing as she tried to come up with a solution. "We need to swim towards the surface," she said finally. "The sharks won't follow us there."

"But how do we know which way is up?" Mike asked, his voice trembling with fear.

Emily smiled grimly. "That's where I come in," she said, holding up a small compass. "I know how to use this to find our way out."

Jack nodded, a glimmer of hope in his eyes. "Okay," he said. "What's the plan?"

Emily explained the plan, her voice calm and steady as she spoke. "We swim towards the surface, using the compass to guide us. Mike and Sarah will lead the way, with me and Jack following close behind."

The group nodded in agreement, their faces determined as they prepared to make their escape. They quickly put on their gear, checking and double-checking their tanks to make sure that they had enough air to make it to the surface.

And then, without another word, they swam out of the cave, their eyes fixed on the compass as they fought against the current.

As they swam, the group could feel the tension mounting. Every time they heard a noise, they flinched, their hearts pounding with fear. But Emily's steady voice kept them focused, and slowly but surely, they began to make their way towards the surface.

It wasn't easy. The current was strong, and the group had to fight against it with every stroke. But as they drew closer to the surface, they could feel a glimmer of hope growing within them.

And then, finally, they broke through the surface, gasping for air as they looked around in wonder. The storm was still raging, but they were safe for now.

Emily turned to the group, a smile on her face. "We made it," she said, her voice filled with relief.

Mike and Sarah hugged each other, tears streaming down their faces as they realized how close they had come to death. Jack and Emily hugged each other too, their faces filled with gratitude and respect for each other.

"We did it," Jack said, his voice filled with awe.

But they knew that they still had a long way to go. They were still stranded on the island, with no way of contacting the outside world. But for now, they were alive. And that was enough.

As the group caught their breath and took in their surroundings, Jack spoke up, his voice determined. "We're not out of the woods yet," he said, looking around at the stormy sea. "We need to find a way off this island and get help."

Emily nodded, her face serious. "Agreed," she said. "But how do we do that?"

Jack hesitated for a moment, then spoke up. "There's a narrow tunnel that leads out of this cave," he said, his voice low. "It's dangerous, but it's our best shot at getting out of here."

Mike and Sarah exchanged worried glances, but Emily and Jack looked at each other, nodding in silent agreement.

"Okay," Emily said finally. "Lead the way, Jack."

The group donned their gear and followed Jack deeper into the cave, their eyes scanning the walls for any sign of the tunnel. After several minutes of swimming, Jack signaled for the group to follow him into a dark, narrow crevice in the rock.

The tunnel was so narrow that the group had to swim single file, their tanks scraping against the jagged walls. Emily and Sarah, who were bringing up the rear, could hear the others ahead of them breathing heavily, their fear palpable in the tight space.

Suddenly, Sarah let out a muffled scream as something brushed against her leg. Emily turned around just in time to see a shark swimming towards them, its jaws gaping open.

"Shark!" Emily yelled, her heart pounding in her chest.

The group swam as fast as they could, but the tunnel was so narrow that they could barely move. The shark followed them, its jaws snapping just inches away from Emily's fins.

"We need to distract it," Jack yelled over his shoulder. "Quick, everyone shine your lights at it!"

The group obeyed, shining their lights directly into the shark's eyes. The shark faltered for a moment, disoriented by the sudden brightness. Taking advantage of the distraction, Jack and Emily quickly swam past it, urging the others to follow.

But as they swam on, the group soon realized that they were not alone in the tunnel. Sharks were lurking in every crevice, their eyes glowing in the dim light.

"We have to keep moving," Jack said urgently. "Don't stop for anything."

The group swam as fast as they could, dodging and weaving past the sharks as they tried to block their path. Emily used her compass to guide them, trying to keep them on the right course.

But as they neared the end of the tunnel, the group faced their greatest challenge yet. A large group of sharks had congregated at the entrance to the tunnel, their fins slicing through the water menacingly.

"We have to get past them," Jack said, his voice grim. "On my signal, we swim straight through them. Don't stop for anything."

The group nodded, their faces set with determination. Jack took a deep breath, then signaled to the others to follow him.

Together, they swam straight into the midst of the sharks, their lights flashing in every direction. The sharks swarmed around them, their jaws snapping shut just inches away from their faces.

But the group kept swimming, pushing their way through the sharks with all their strength. And then, finally, they burst through the other side, gasping for air as they looked around in wonder.

"We made it," Emily said, a smile spreading across her face.

The group hugged each other tightly, relief flooding through them. They had made it through the narrow tunnel, and they were one step closer to finding a way off the island.

As the group caught their breath after their harrowing escape through the tunnel, they realized that they were still surrounded by sharks. The predators circled around them, their eyes glowing in the dark water.

Mike shuddered, his hand shaking as he tightened his grip on his dive knife. "I hate sharks," he muttered, his voice barely audible over the sound of his own breathing.

Emily put a reassuring hand on his shoulder. "We'll be okay," she said. "Just stick close to me, okay?"

Mike nodded, his eyes darting nervously around the water.

Tyler, meanwhile, was already swimming ahead, his flashlight beam bouncing off the rocky walls. "Come on, guys!" he called back. "We're wasting time!"

Sarah shook her head. "Does he ever stop and think about what he's doing?" she muttered to Emily.

But Emily was too busy scanning the water for any sign of danger. As they swam on, the group soon found themselves facing a new challenge. The water was getting colder and darker, and Emily realized with a sinking feeling that they were headed towards a deep underwater cave.

"Guys," she said, her voice low. "We need to slow down. This cave is dangerous. We need to be careful."

But Tyler was already swimming ahead, his excitement getting the best of him. "Come on, Em, live a little!" he yelled back.

Emily shook her head, her heart racing as they entered the dark cave. The water was so deep and dark that she could barely see her own hand in front of her face. She clutched her dive light tightly, her mind racing with worst-case scenarios.

And then, suddenly, it happened. Emily's regulator malfunctioned, and she felt a surge of panic rising in her chest. She tried to breathe, but the air was thick and unyielding.

"Emily?" Sarah's voice echoed in her ear. "Are you okay?"

But Emily couldn't respond. She was drowning.

Mike swam over, his eyes widening in shock as he saw Emily's face contorted in fear. "Emily, breathe!" he shouted, shaking her shoulder.

But Emily was beyond hearing him. Her mind was consumed with the thought of drowning, and she couldn't shake the fear.

It was then that Tyler swam up, a grin on his face. "What's going on? Did we find something cool?"

Mike shot him a furious look. "Emily's drowning, you idiot!"

Tyler's grin faded as he saw the fear on Emily's face. He swam over, his eyes scanning her equipment. "What's wrong with her regulator?"

"It malfunctioned," Sarah said, her voice shaking. "Can you fix it?"

Tyler nodded, his face set with determination. He quickly checked Emily's gear, then switched out her regulator for a new one. Emily gasped, the fear slowly receding as she took a deep breath.

"Thank you," she gasped, clinging to Tyler's arm.

Tyler grinned at her, his cocky confidence back in full force. "No problem, Em. Just doing my job."

But Emily could see the fear in his eyes, the fear that he had just narrowly avoided losing her. She realized then that they were all facing their worst underwater nightmares, and that they needed to be more careful if they wanted to make it off the island alive.

The group continued their exploration of the underwater cave system, but Emily's close call had shaken them all. They swam cautiously, with Mike and Sarah sticking close to Emily, keeping an eye on her at all times.

As they swam deeper into the cave, their air supplies began to dwindle. They had been careful with their breathing, but they had been underwater for a long time and they knew they would need to surface soon.

"We need to go up," Sarah said, her voice tense. "Our air is getting low."

Tyler shook his head. "We can't go up yet. We haven't found anything interesting."

Mike rolled his eyes. "We can't keep going like this, Tyler. We need to surface and regroup."

But Tyler was stubborn. "Just a little further," he said. "We can't turn back now."

Emily was starting to feel the effects of low air. She felt dizzy and disoriented, and she knew she needed to surface soon. "Guys," she gasped. "We need to go up. Now."

Tyler finally relented, and they began to swim towards the surface. But as they swam, Emily's air supply suddenly ran out. She gasped for breath, but there was nothing there.

"Emily!" Mike yelled, swimming towards her.

Sarah was already pulling her own spare regulator out of her dive bag. "Take mine," she said, handing it to Emily.

Emily gratefully took the regulator and began to breathe again. But she knew they were all in trouble. They had used up too much air, and they were still deep underwater.

"We need to surface," she said, her voice shaking.

Tyler was looking increasingly panicked. "I can't," he said. "I don't have enough air to make it back up."

Mike grabbed him by the arm. "We'll buddy breathe," he said. "Just stay calm."

But Tyler was already hyperventilating. "I can't do this," he said, his voice rising.

Sarah grabbed him by the shoulders. "Tyler, listen to me," she said, her voice firm. "You need to calm down. We can do this together."

They began to buddy breathe, passing the regulator between them as they swam towards the surface. Emily's heart was pounding in her chest, and she knew they were all in danger.

As they broke the surface, they gasped for air, their lungs burning from lack of oxygen. They all swam towards the shore, collapsing on the sand.

"That was too close," Emily said, her voice barely above a whisper.

Sarah nodded, her face pale. "We need to be more careful," she said. "We can't afford to take risks like that."

Tyler was still gasping for air, his eyes wide with fear. "I thought I was going to die," he said, his voice shaking.

Mike put a hand on his shoulder. "But you didn't," he said. "We made it through together."

But Emily knew that they couldn't keep pushing their luck. They needed to start making tough decisions if they were going to survive.

Emily looked out to the horizon and squinted her eyes. "Guys, look," she said, pointing towards a boat in the distance. "That's our chance to get out of here."

Mike and Sarah followed her gaze, relief flooding their faces. "Thank god," Sarah said. "Let's get out of this place."

Tyler, who had recovered from his panic attack, nodded eagerly. "We can make it," he said. "I know we can."

But the boat was still a long way off, and they had used up most of their air supplies. Emily knew they would need to make a plan, and fast.

"We need to conserve our energy," she said, her voice urgent. "We have to swim slowly and steadily. No sudden movements."

Mike nodded in agreement. "And we need to buddy breathe again. We can't afford to run out of air."

Sarah frowned. "What about Tyler?" she asked. "He can't handle another panic attack."

Emily bit her lip, thinking hard. "I'll buddy breathe with him," she said. "We'll take it slow, and I'll keep him calm."

They began to swim towards the boat, their movements slow and measured. Emily swam next to Tyler, passing the regulator between them. She could feel his fear, but she did her best to keep him calm.

"Take deep breaths," she said. "We'll get through this together."

Tyler nodded, his eyes fixed on the boat in the distance. "I can do this," he said. "I can make it."

As they swam, Emily could feel her lungs burning with the effort. She knew they were all pushing themselves to the limit, but she refused to give up. They had come too far to fail now.

Finally, after what felt like hours, they reached the boat. Emily climbed aboard first, pulling Tyler up after her. Mike and Sarah followed, collapsing onto the deck.

The boat's captain, a grizzled old man with a weathered face, looked at them with concern. "You kids okay?" he asked.

Emily nodded, her chest heaving. "We need to get out of here," she said. "As fast as possible."

The captain nodded, and soon they were speeding away from the island. Emily watched as the island receded into the distance, feeling a sense of relief wash over her.

"We made it," she said, smiling weakly at her friends.

Mike grinned back. "Yeah, we did. But I don't think I'll be diving again anytime soon."

Sarah laughed. "Me neither. I'm sticking to the beach from now on."

Tyler nodded, his face still pale. "I just want to go home," he said.

Emily put a hand on his shoulder. "We all do," she said. "But we made it out alive. That's what matters."

As the boat sped away from the island, the group of friends sat in silence, each lost in their own thoughts. The adrenaline that had fueled them during their escape had now worn off, leaving them feeling drained and vulnerable.

Emily was the first to break the silence. "I can't believe we made it out alive," she said, her voice barely above a whisper.

Mike nodded, his face grim. "Yeah, that was too close. We really messed up this time."

Sarah looked at him sharply. "We? You were the one who took off without checking if we were all okay!"

Mike bristled. "I didn't know what was going on! I thought Emily and Tyler were right behind us!"

Tyler spoke up, his voice shaking slightly. "It's not anyone's fault. We all made mistakes. We just need to learn from them and move on."

Emily nodded in agreement. "He's right. We can't change what happened, but we can make sure it never happens again."

The group fell silent again, lost in their own thoughts. Emily knew that they needed to talk about what had happened, to process their emotions and come to terms with the trauma they had experienced.

"I think we should all talk about how we're feeling," she said tentatively.

Sarah sighed. "I feel stupid," she admitted. "We should have known better than to go diving without proper equipment and training."

Mike nodded. "Yeah, I feel the same way. We were so cocky, thinking we could handle anything."

Tyler spoke up softly. "I feel scared. I don't know if I can ever go diving again after what happened."

Emily put a hand on his arm. "It's okay to be scared," she said gently. "But we can't let our fear control us. We need to learn from this and be better prepared next time."

The boat ride back to the mainland seemed to take forever. The group sat in silence, lost in their own thoughts. When they finally arrived back on shore, they were met by a crowd of concerned onlookers.

Emily felt a pang of embarrassment as they explained what had happened to the authorities. She knew that they had been foolish, and that their reckless behavior had put themselves and others in danger.

As they drove back home, Emily couldn't help but think about what they had been through. She realized that they had been lucky to survive, and that they had been given a second chance.

"I think we need to make a promise to ourselves," she said, breaking the silence. "To always be prepared, to never underestimate the power of nature, and to respect the ocean."

The others nodded in agreement. "I'm with you," Sarah said. "I never want to go through something like that again."

Mike looked at Tyler. "What about you?"

Tyler took a deep breath. "I don't know if I'll ever be able to dive again," he said. "But I promise to always be prepared and to never let my fear control me."

Emily smiled at him. "That's all we can ask for," she said.

The group fell silent again, lost in their own thoughts. Emily knew that the road to recovery would be long and difficult, but she also knew that they had each other to lean on.

"We made it out alive," she said softly. "That's what matters."

The Shadow in the Deep

Dr. Maria Rodriguez and her team of graduate students were aboard the research vessel, preparing for their dive to study the deep-sea ecosystem. Maria had been studying the ocean for over a decade, and her passion for marine biology had only grown stronger over the years.

As they descended into the abyss, Maria's eyes scanned the murky waters for any sign of life. Suddenly, she saw something that made her heart race. A large shark with glowing markings swam past the submersible.

"Did you see that?" Maria exclaimed excitedly. "What was that?"

Jake, her research assistant, peered through the window. "I've never seen anything like it. It's like it's glowing in the dark."

The graduate students gathered around, each one eager to catch a glimpse of the mysterious creature.

Maria's eyes shone with excitement. "This is it. This is why we're here. We need to study this new species."

The team spent the next few days observing the shark's behavior and studying its markings. They noticed that the shark was highly intelligent and seemed to be coordinating attacks on other marine life.

"This is fascinating," Maria said, scribbling notes in her notebook. "The shark seems to be using some sort of strategy to hunt. We need to find out how it's doing this."

As they continued their research, Maria became increasingly obsessed with the shark, spending long hours studying it and neglecting her team and personal life.

"Maria, we need to take a break," Jake said, noticing how tired and irritable she had become. "We've been down here for days. You need to rest."

"I can't rest," Maria said, her eyes fixed on the shark. "This is too important. We need to find out everything we can about this creature."

The team continued their research, but Maria's obsession with the shark began to cause tension within the group. They were all exhausted and needed a break, but Maria refused to stop.

"Maria, we need to talk," Jake said, approaching her one evening. "You're pushing us too hard. We need to take a break and rest."

"I know, I know," Maria said, rubbing her temples. "I'm sorry. I just can't help it. This shark is like nothing I've ever seen before. We need to find out everything we can about it."

Jake sighed. "I understand, but we need to take care of ourselves too. We're no good to anyone if we're exhausted and burnt out."

Maria nodded, knowing that Jake was right. "You're right. We'll take a break tomorrow. But first, I need to study the shark just a little longer."

The next morning, the team took a much-needed break, but Maria's mind was still fixed on the shark. She sat alone in the control room, staring at the monitor that displayed the shark's movements.

As she watched, she noticed something strange. The shark seemed to be using some sort of technology to coordinate its attacks.

"Jake!" she shouted, running into the lab where the graduate students were gathered. "You need to see this. The shark is using some sort of device to communicate with other marine life."

The team gathered around as Maria pulled up the footage. They watched in amazement as the shark used a strange device to send out a signal, calling other creatures to its location before attacking them.

"This is incredible," Lily, an ambitious young intern, said, staring at the screen. "It's like the shark has been exposed to alien technology or something."

Maria nodded. "That's what I was thinking too. But how could that be possible?"

The team spent the next few days trying to figure out how the shark could have been exposed to such advanced technology. They studied the area where the shark was first spotted, looking for any signs of extraterrestrial activity.

"This is crazy," one of the graduate students said, shaking her head. "There's no way this could have happened."

Lily spoke up, her eyes shining with excitement. "But what if it did? Think about the implications. We could learn so much about other worlds and their technology."

Maria's eyes narrowed. She didn't like where Lily was going with this. "That's not the point," she said firmly. "We're here to study the shark and its behavior, not to speculate about alien technology."

The tension in the room was palpable as the graduate students began to question Maria's judgment and methods.

"Maybe we should take a step back," Jake said, trying to diffuse the situation. "We don't want to jump to conclusions without any evidence."

Maria sighed. She knew that Jake was right. "You're right. Let's focus on the shark and its behavior. We can worry about the rest later."

The team continued their research, but the atmosphere had changed. The once-tight-knit group was now divided, with some of the graduate students questioning Maria's methods and others rallying behind her.

Maria tried to ignore the tension, but it was impossible. She couldn't shake the feeling that her team was starting to unravel.

Maria and Jake called a meeting with the team to discuss their next course of action. They knew that they needed to investigate further to find the source of the alien technology that seemed to be affecting the shark.

"Okay, so we know that the shark is using some sort of device to communicate with other marine life," Maria began. "We need to find out where it's getting this technology from."

"I agree," Jake added. "But we need to be cautious. We don't know what we're dealing with here."

The team nodded in agreement. They all knew that they were in uncharted waters.

After several days of research, they discovered a mysterious underwater cave system near the location where the shark was first spotted.

"Could this be it?" Lily asked, her eyes wide with excitement.

"It's possible," Maria replied. "But we need to be careful. We don't know what's in there."

Jake and Maria led the team into the cave system, their flashlights illuminating the way. As they ventured deeper into the cave, they began to notice strange markings on the walls.

"What are these?" one of the graduate students asked, pointing to the markings.

"I don't know," Maria said. "But they look like some sort of language."

As they continued further into the cave, they stumbled upon a strange object that seemed to be emitting a faint glow.

"What is that?" Jake asked, his voice barely above a whisper.

"I don't know," Maria replied. "But it seems to be the key to unlocking the secrets of the technology."

The team approached the object cautiously, their hearts racing with anticipation.

Suddenly, the object began to emit a bright light, blinding them all. When the light dissipated, they found themselves standing in a large chamber filled with strange technology.

"What is this place?" Lily asked, her eyes wide with wonder.

"I don't know," Maria replied. "But I think we just uncovered something incredible."

As they explored the chamber, they realized that the alien technology was far more advanced than anything they had ever seen before.

"We need to document everything," Jake said, pulling out his camera.

The team spent several hours exploring the chamber, documenting everything they saw. When they were finished, they made their way back to the surface.

As they emerged from the water, Maria couldn't help but feel a sense of awe. They had uncovered something truly remarkable.

As they made their way back to their research facility, Maria couldn't stop thinking about the incredible technology they had uncovered in the underwater cave system.

"I can't believe it," she muttered to herself. "This is a game-changer."

Jake turned to her, concern etched on his face. "Maria, are you sure we should be messing around with this technology? We don't even know what it does yet."

Maria scoffed. "Of course we should! We're scientists, Jake. It's our job to explore and discover."

"But what if something goes wrong?" Jake pressed.

"Relax, Jake. We'll be careful. Besides, we can't just sit on this. We have to test it."

Jake sighed. He knew there was no reasoning with Maria when she got like this.

The team spent the next several days studying the alien technology, trying to decipher its functions and capabilities. Maria was in her element, completely obsessed with unlocking its secrets.

Finally, she had an idea. "I think I know how we can test this," she said, her eyes alight with excitement.

The team gathered around as Maria explained her plan. "We'll attach a small device to the shark, one that will allow us to track its movements and monitor its behavior. Then we'll activate the technology and see how the shark reacts."

The team was hesitant, but Maria was convinced that this was the best way to learn more about the technology.

They set to work attaching the device to the shark, making sure to do so without harming it. Maria carefully activated the technology, holding her breath as she waited for the results.

At first, everything seemed fine. The shark swam around in circles, seemingly unaffected by the technology.

But then, things took a turn for the worse. The shark suddenly began to thrash around in the water, its movements erratic and violent. It slammed into the sides of the tank, seemingly trying to escape.

"Shut it down! Shut it down!" Jake yelled, panic evident in his voice.

Maria hesitated for a moment, watching as the shark continued to lash out. But finally, she hit the emergency shut-off button.

The shark calmed down almost immediately, its movements slowing to a stop. The team breathed a collective sigh of relief.

"What the hell just happened?" one of the graduate students asked.

Maria's face was pale as she turned to face the team. "I think the alien race that created this technology is controlling the shark," she said, her voice barely above a whisper.

The team stared at her in shock. They had all heard the rumors about the alien race, but they had never believed them to be true.

"What do we do now?" Lily asked, her voice trembling.

"We need to study this more," Maria said, determination evident in her tone. "We need to figure out how to control this technology, so that we can use it for the betterment of humanity."

But Jake knew that Maria was going too far. "Maria, we can't just mess around with something we don't understand. We need to be cautious."

Maria ignored him, her eyes shining with excitement. "We'll figure this out," she said. "We'll unlock the secrets of this technology, and we'll change the world."

Maria's determination to study the alien technology only grew stronger after the incident with the shark. She spent every waking moment analyzing the data they had collected, trying to find a way to control the technology and harness its power.

Jake, on the other hand, was increasingly concerned about the risks they were taking. "Maria, we can't just keep messing around with this. We don't know what we're dealing with."

"I know what we're dealing with," Maria snapped back. "We're dealing with the greatest scientific discovery in history."

But Jake wasn't convinced. "What if the aliens who created this technology come looking for it? What if they see us as a threat?"

Maria rolled her eyes. "That's just paranoia, Jake. We have security measures in place. We'll be fine."

But Jake couldn't shake the feeling that something was wrong. And then, one day, his worst fears were realized.

The team was working in the lab when they heard a loud, piercing sound. They looked up to see a glowing portal opening up in the middle of the room.

Everyone froze, staring in shock as a group of tall, otherworldly beings stepped through the portal.

The aliens were unlike anything the team had ever seen. They were at least seven feet tall, with slender bodies and long, spindly fingers. Their skin was a pale blue color, and their eyes glowed with an otherworldly light.

The team stood frozen, unsure of what to do. But then, the aliens spoke.

"You have trespassed upon our technology," the lead alien said, its voice echoing through the room. "You are a threat to our civilization."

Maria stepped forward, trying to reason with them. "We're scientists. We're here to learn from your technology, not to harm you."

But the aliens didn't seem interested in listening. They began to manipulate the technology, causing it to pulse with an ominous energy.

The team watched in horror as the lab began to shake, pieces of equipment falling to the ground. "We have to do something!" Lily shouted.

Jake nodded, his mind racing. "We need to shut down the technology. We need to cut off their access to it."

But that was easier said than done. The aliens were powerful, and their control over the technology was nearly absolute.

The team worked together, using all their knowledge and resources to try and stop the aliens. But it seemed like a losing battle.

Finally, Maria came up with a plan. "We need to overload the system," she said. "We need to flood it with so much energy that it shorts out."

The team worked quickly, setting up the necessary equipment. The aliens didn't seem to notice, too focused on their control of the technology.

And then, with a burst of energy, the system overloaded. There was a blinding flash of light, and everything went dark.

When the team came to, they were lying on the ground, battered and bruised. But they were alive.

"What the hell just happened?" Lily asked, looking around in confusion.

"We did it," Maria said, a smile spreading across her face. "We fought back, and we won."

But Jake knew that this wasn't over. They had made a powerful enemy, and the aliens wouldn't take kindly to their defeat.

As the team tried to get back on their feet, Jake noticed something odd about Lily's behavior. She was standing off to the side, looking around nervously.

"What's going on, Lily?" he asked, his voice tinged with suspicion.

Lily looked at him, her eyes wide with fear. "I...I don't know. I didn't think the aliens would actually show up."

Jake narrowed his eyes. "What are you talking about? Did you know this was going to happen?"

Lily hesitated, then finally spoke. "I...I've been working for another research team. They're interested in the alien technology too."

Maria's eyes widened in shock. "You betrayed us?" she said, her voice laced with anger.

Lily looked down at her feet, ashamed. "I didn't mean to hurt anyone. I just wanted to be part of something big."

Jake shook his head in disbelief. "Unbelievable. We trusted you, Lily. And you went behind our backs and stole the technology for someone else."

"We have to get that object back," Maria said, her voice firm. "We can't let the rival team use it for their own purposes."

Jake nodded in agreement. "But how are we going to find them? And even if we do, how are we going to get it back?"

Maria thought for a moment, then came up with a plan. "We'll use the data we collected from the technology to track down their location. And once we find them, we'll take it back by force if we have to."

Jake looked at her, his expression serious. "Are you sure about this, Maria? We don't know what we're dealing with here."

Maria nodded. "I'm sure. We can't let them get away with this."

The team quickly got to work, using the data they had collected to track down the rival team's location. They soon discovered that they were holed up in a remote research facility deep in the mountains.

"We'll have to be careful," Jake said, his voice low. "We don't know what kind of security they have in place."

Maria nodded. "I'll go in first. If things get dangerous, you and Lily can come in as backup."

Jake hesitated, then nodded. "Be careful, Maria."

Maria made her way to the research facility, her heart pounding with anticipation. As she approached the building, she saw that there were armed guards patrolling the perimeter.

She took a deep breath, then activated the invisibility technology they had developed. With a rush of excitement, she watched as her body became invisible.

She slipped past the guards and made her way into the building. She searched for the room where the object was being kept, her heart pounding with every step.

Finally, she found it. The object was sitting on a pedestal in the center of the room, surrounded by guards.

Maria knew she couldn't take them all on by herself. She would need backup.

She activated her communication device. "Jake, Lily, I found the object. I need you to come in and help me get it."

There was no response.

"Jake? Lily? Can you hear me?" Maria said, her voice tinged with worry.

And then, she heard a sound behind her. She turned around to see Lily, a gun in her hand.

"I'm sorry, Maria," Lily said, her voice cold. "But I have to do this."

Maria's heart sank. She had been betrayed again.

Maria's eyes widened in shock as Lily held the gun pointed at her. "Lily, what are you doing? Put the gun down!"

"I can't do that, Maria," Lily said, her voice shaking. "I need the object for my team. They're counting on me to deliver it."

Jake's voice suddenly crackled through the communication device. "Maria, what's going on? I lost contact with you."

Maria tried to keep Lily talking, hoping to buy time for Jake to arrive. "Lily, you don't have to do this. We can talk this out."

But Lily didn't seem to be listening. "I'm sorry, Maria," she said, and pulled the trigger.

Maria dove to the side, narrowly avoiding the bullet. She activated the invisibility technology again and made a break for the door.

But Lily was quick to react. She fired another shot, this time hitting Maria in the leg.

Maria cried out in pain and stumbled, her invisibility fading as she fell to the ground.

Lily approached her, gun raised. "I'm sorry it had to be this way, Maria. But I have a job to do."

Just then, Jake burst into the room, his own gun drawn. "Lily, put the gun down!"

Lily hesitated, then lowered the gun. "Jake, I didn't want to hurt anyone. But I have to get the object for my team."

Jake sighed. "Lily, you know we can't let that happen. Hand over the gun and come with us. We'll sort this out later."

Lily nodded, tears streaming down her face. "Okay," she said, and handed over the gun.

The three of them quickly made their way out of the facility, with Maria leaning heavily on Jake for support. They didn't have time to wait for backup, they needed to get the object back as soon as possible.

They piled into a nearby jeep and headed towards the coast, where they had tracked the rival team's boat.

But as they drove, they noticed something strange happening in the ocean. The water was churning and bubbling, as if something massive was moving beneath the surface.

And then they saw it. A massive shark, easily as long as the jeep, burst out of the water and crashed onto the shore.

Jake swerved to avoid it, but more creatures were rising out of the water, controlled by the alien technology. They were like nothing they had ever seen before - part machine, part sea creature.

"We have to get out of here!" Maria shouted, her voice strained with pain.

But they were surrounded on all sides, with no clear path to escape.

As the creatures continued to rise from the ocean, Maria, Jake, and Lily were surrounded on all sides. The rival team had activated the alien technology, causing chaos and destruction throughout the area. The team had underestimated the danger of the technology, and now they were paying the price.

Jake took charge, barking orders as he tried to come up with a plan. "Maria, get to higher ground. Lily, cover her. I'll take care of these creatures."

Maria gritted her teeth in pain but nodded, hobbling towards a nearby cliff. Lily followed her, her gun at the ready as they climbed higher.

Jake faced off against the creatures, his gun firing rapidly as he tried to take them down. But there were too many of them, and they kept coming.

Suddenly, the massive shark burst out of the water again, its jaws snapping at Jake. He dodged to the side, firing his gun as he did so.

But the shark was too fast, too strong. It crashed into Jake, knocking him to the ground.

Maria and Lily could only watch in horror as the shark closed in on Jake. They knew they had to do something, anything, to save him.

Lily was the first to act. She aimed her gun at the shark, firing off round after round. But the bullets bounced off its tough skin, doing little damage.

Maria, meanwhile, was searching through her backpack for something that could help. And then she found it - a small device that emitted a high-pitched sound.

She activated the device, and the sound reverberated through the air. The shark let out a deafening roar, shaking the ground beneath their feet.

And then, to their amazement, the creature stopped in its tracks. It shook its head as if confused, then turned and plunged back into the water.

Jake lay on the ground, battered and bruised but alive. Maria and Lily rushed to his side, helping him to his feet.

"We have to stop them," Jake said, his voice grim. "We can't let them get away with this."

Maria nodded, determination in her eyes. "We have to take them down, for the sake of the ocean ecosystem."

They quickly formulated a plan, using their skills and knowledge to disable the alien technology and defeat the rival team. It wasn't easy, and there were moments when they thought they might not make it.

But in the end, they emerged victorious. The alien technology was deactivated, the rival team was apprehended, and the creatures in the ocean returned to their natural state.

As they watched the sun rise over the ocean, Maria, Jake, and Lily breathed a sigh of relief. They had saved the day, and they had done it together.

Maria and Jake struggled to swim to the surface, weighed down by the object they had managed to secure. As they broke through the surface, gasping for air, they could hear the chaos still raging below them.

"We have to get out of here," Jake said, his voice urgent. "We can't risk being caught with this thing."

Maria nodded, her mind racing as she tried to think of a plan. "We need to get to shore, but we have to be careful. We don't know who we can trust."

They swam towards the shore, keeping a low profile as they moved through the water. When they finally made it to land, they collapsed on the sand, exhausted and shaken.

"We did it," Maria said, a sense of disbelief in her voice. "We actually did it."

Jake nodded, but his expression was serious. "We still have a long way to go. We have to figure out what to do with this thing, and we have to make sure it doesn't fall into the wrong hands."

As they caught their breath, Lily swam up to them, looking contrite. "I'm sorry," she said, her voice shaking. "I didn't mean for any of this to happen."

Maria and Jake exchanged a look, unsure of how to respond.

"We trusted you," Jake said, his voice cold. "And you betrayed us."

Lily hung her head. "I know, and I'm sorry. But please, let me help you fix this."

Maria and Jake exchanged another look, this one more sympathetic. They knew they needed all the help they could get if they were going to navigate this situation safely.

"Fine," Maria said, her voice firm. "But you have a lot of making up to do."

They quickly got to work, strategizing and making plans. They knew they had to stay on the move, constantly staying one step ahead of those who would seek to use the object for their own purposes.

As they moved through the wilderness, they could feel the weight of the object pressing against them. It was a responsibility they hadn't anticipated, and it was beginning to take its toll.

But they didn't give up. They kept moving forward, driven by a sense of purpose and determination.

As they set up camp for the night, Maria pulled out the object, studying it in the dim light of their campfire.

"This thing could change the course of human history," she said, her voice awed.

Jake nodded, his expression serious. "But we have to be careful. We can't let it fall into the wrong hands."

Lily spoke up, her voice soft. "I know I messed up, but I want to help. I want to make things right."

Maria and Jake exchanged a look, and then nodded. They knew they needed all the help they could get if they were going to navigate this situation safely.

"Together," Maria said, holding the object out for Lily and Jake to see. "We can do this. We can make things right."

"Together," Jake echoed, his voice firm.

They spent the rest of the night planning, strategizing, and working together. They knew they had a long road ahead of them, but they were determined to see it through to the end.

The next few weeks were a blur for Maria and Jake. They had managed to keep the alien technology hidden, but they were constantly looking over their shoulders, afraid of who might be watching.

They returned to their normal lives, but everything felt different. They were more cautious, more aware of the potential dangers that lay around every corner.

One day, as they sat in their lab, Jake turned to Maria with a serious expression. "We have to destroy it," he said, gesturing towards the object they had hidden away in a secure location.

Maria shook her head, a look of disbelief on her face. "No way," she said firmly. "We can't just destroy something this important."

"But it's too dangerous," Jake argued. "We can't risk it falling into the wrong hands."

Maria sighed, knowing that he was right. They couldn't keep the technology hidden forever, and eventually, someone would come looking for it.

"Okay," she said finally. "But we have to do it carefully. We can't just destroy it without knowing exactly what we're dealing with."

They spent the next few days studying the object, taking careful notes and conducting experiments to try and understand its full potential.

Finally, they came to a decision. They would destroy the technology, but they would do it in a way that would ensure no one could ever use it again.

With heavy hearts, they set to work. They spent hours carefully dismantling the object, piece by piece, until it was nothing more than a pile of scrap metal.

As they looked at the wreckage, Maria felt a sense of sadness wash over her. They had spent so much time and effort trying to unlock the secrets of the alien technology, and now it was gone.

But she also felt a sense of relief. They had done the right thing, and they could finally move on from the nightmare that had consumed their lives for so long.

As they left the lab, Jake turned to Maria with a small smile on his face. "We did it," he said, his voice filled with pride.

Maria nodded, feeling a sense of satisfaction wash over her. They had faced incredible challenges and dangers, but they had come out on the other side, stronger and more determined than ever.

From that day forward, they continued their research, but they were more cautious and aware of the potential dangers. They knew they couldn't take anything for granted, and they always kept one eye on the shadows, ready to face whatever challenges lay ahead.

But they also knew they had each other, and that was the most important thing of all.

The Shark Caller

The sun was just starting to rise as Mana and her father, Pak Wayan, set out on their fishing boat. As they sailed through the crystal-clear waters off the coast of Kaimana, they noticed a group of sharks swimming nearby. However, something was off about their behavior. They were thrashing around in the water, and it was clear that they were upset.

"Something's not right," Mana said, squinting in the sunlight. "Why are the sharks acting like that?"

Pak Wayan nodded gravely. "I think it might be those fishing boats over there," he said, pointing to a cluster of vessels in the distance. "They've been using explosives to catch fish. It's not only illegal but dangerous to the ecosystem."

Mana frowned. "That's not right. We need to do something."

Pak Wayan smiled at his daughter's determination. "I agree, Mana. We need to protect the sharks and our way of life."

As they continued fishing, Mana couldn't shake the image of the distressed sharks from her mind. Suddenly, she had an idea. Mana remembered the stories her mother used to tell her about the ancient practice of shark calling, where certain people had the ability to communicate with sharks and call them to their aid. Mana had always thought the stories were just that, stories. But now, she was determined to find out if they were true.

"Dad, do you think it's possible for someone to call upon sharks for help?" Mana asked.

Pak Wayan raised an eyebrow. "It's a legend, Mana. But, who knows? You never know what kind of magic exists in the world."

Determined to try, Mana began to meditate, focusing all her energy on the nearby sharks. As she did, she felt a strange sensation in her mind. Suddenly, she could hear the thoughts of the sharks.

"Something is wrong," the sharks seemed to say. "We are in danger."

Mana couldn't believe it. It was like the sharks were speaking directly to her. She relayed the information to Pak Wayan, and they both agreed that they needed to do something to help.

As they approached the fishing boats, the fishermen became hostile and defensive, refusing to listen to Mana and Pak Wayan's warnings. Mana was frustrated and felt helpless, but she knew that she had to keep trying. She continued to meditate and communicate with the sharks, hoping that they could come up with a plan to protect their home.

As Mana and Pak Wayan continued to try and reason with the fishermen, Mana's best friend, Sari, arrived on the scene. Sari had heard about the situation and was eager to help in any way she could.

"What's going on here?" Sari asked, as she climbed aboard the boat.

Mana filled her in on the situation, explaining how the fishing boats were using explosives and damaging the coral reefs, which was causing harm to the sharks and other marine life in the area.

Sari's eyes widened. "That's awful. We need to do something to stop them."

Mana nodded in agreement. "I was thinking the same thing. But we can't do it alone. We need to gather a group of young villagers to form a resistance."

Sari grinned. "I like the sound of that. Let's get to work."

Together, Mana and Sari began recruiting other young people from the village. They explained the situation and why it was important to take action. They found that many of the other youths were eager to help, and soon they had formed a group of ten strong.

Their first mission was to gather as much information as possible about Mr. Tanaka's crew and their operations. They spent several days gathering intel, sneaking onto the fishing boats and recording their actions, and talking to locals who had witnessed their destructive behavior.

Once they had a solid understanding of the situation, they began to brainstorm ways to put a stop to the overfishing and destruction of the coral reefs. Mana suggested that they stage a protest, but Sari had an even better idea.

"We need to hit them where it hurts," Sari said. "Mr. Tanaka's crew is only doing this for the money. If we can show them that their actions are hurting their bottom line, they might reconsider."

Mana looked confused. "What do you mean?"

Sari grinned mischievously. "I mean, we steal their fish."

Mana's eyes widened. "Are you serious?"

Sari nodded. "Think about it. If we steal their fish, they won't be able to sell them. That means they won't make any money. If we do it enough times, they might get the message."

Mana was hesitant, but Sari's plan made sense. They began to work out the logistics, figuring out how to sneak onto the boats and take the fish without getting caught.

It wasn't easy, but they managed to steal several loads of fish over the course of a few weeks. The crew was furious, but they couldn't figure out who was behind the thefts. Finally, they confronted Mana and Sari, accusing them of being responsible.

Mana and Sari stood their ground, refusing to back down. They explained why they were doing what they were doing and how the crew's actions were hurting the environment and the villagers' way of life.

The crew was angry, but Mana and Sari's bravery inspired the rest of the resistance. They began to stand up to Mr. Tanaka's crew, refusing to back down in the face of adversity.

As the resistance grew in strength, Mana knew that they were making a difference. They were fighting for their home and the creatures that called it home. They weren't going to let anyone take that away from them.

As the resistance continued to fight against the overfishing and destruction of the coral reefs, a new player entered the scene. Dr. Lee, a marine biologist, arrived in Kaimana to study the local shark population.

Mana and her friends were skeptical at first. They had grown to distrust outsiders, especially those who were interested in exploiting the natural resources of their home. But Dr. Lee was different. She was genuinely interested in understanding and protecting the ecosystem.

Mana and Sari were tasked with showing Dr. Lee around the area. They took her to the coral reefs and the nearby lagoon, pointing out the different species of fish and sharks that called it home.

Dr. Lee was impressed. "You have a truly unique ecosystem here," she said. "But I can see that it's under threat. We need to work together to protect it."

Mana and Sari exchanged a glance. They weren't used to hearing outsiders talk like this. But they were willing to give Dr. Lee a chance.

Over the next few weeks, Dr. Lee spent time studying the sharks in the area. She took measurements, collected samples, and even tagged a few of them with tracking devices.

As she worked, she shared her findings with Mana and the rest of the resistance. They were fascinated to learn about the migratory patterns of the sharks and how important they were to the overall health of the ecosystem.

"I had no idea sharks played such a vital role," Mana said, as they walked along the beach one day. "I always thought of them as scary predators."

Dr. Lee smiled. "That's a common misconception. In reality, sharks are incredibly important for maintaining the balance of the ocean. Without them, the entire ecosystem would suffer."

Mana nodded. She was beginning to see Dr. Lee in a new light. "Do you think you could help us with our fight against the overfishing?" she asked.

Dr. Lee's expression turned serious. "Absolutely. I've seen the damage that's being done to the coral reefs and the marine life. We need to stop it before it's too late."

Together, Mana, Sari, and Dr. Lee began to strategize. They knew that they needed to gather more evidence to prove that Mr. Tanaka's crew was breaking the law. They spent hours pouring over legal documents and fishing regulations, trying to find a loophole.

Finally, they discovered that the explosives the crew was using were illegal under Indonesian law. They took their findings to the local authorities, who were shocked to see the evidence.

The authorities quickly took action, raiding Mr. Tanaka's operations and confiscating his boats and equipment. Mr. Tanaka and his crew were arrested and charged with multiple crimes, including destruction of coral reefs and illegal fishing practices.

Mana, Sari, and the rest of the resistance were thrilled. They had worked hard to protect their home, and their efforts had paid off. Dr. Lee smiled, happy to have played a small part in their success.

"You should be proud of yourselves," she said. "You've shown what a group of determined young people can accomplish when they work together."

Mana and Sari grinned at each other. They knew that they still had a long way to go to protect their home. But with the help of their new ally, Dr. Lee, they felt like they could accomplish anything.

As Mana, Sari, and Dr. Lee continued to work together to protect the ecosystem, they knew that they needed to come up with a way to prevent the fishermen from overfishing in the protected areas. After brainstorming for a while, Mana had an idea.

"Guys, I have an idea," Mana said excitedly. "What if we used my shark-calling abilities to lure the sharks away from the areas where the fishermen are fishing? If we can get the sharks to go to other parts of the ocean, the fishermen won't be able to catch as many fish."

Sari and Dr. Lee looked at each other, then back at Mana. "That's a great idea," Dr. Lee said. "But is it safe?"

Mana nodded. "I've been doing this for years. I know how to control the sharks and keep them from attacking humans. And we'll only be luring them away from the fishing areas, not towards them."

Sari and Dr. Lee agreed that it was worth a try. They spent the next few days planning and preparing. Mana would use her shark-calling abilities to lure the sharks to different parts of the ocean while Sari and Dr. Lee would monitor the fishermen's activities.

The first few attempts were unsuccessful. Mana's calls didn't seem to be attracting any sharks, and the fishermen continued to catch fish. But they didn't give up. They continued to refine their plan and try new tactics.

Finally, on the fifth attempt, they saw results. Mana's calls attracted a large group of sharks, which swam away from the fishing areas and into deeper waters. Sari and Dr. Lee watched as the fishermen grew frustrated and started to lose money.

"It's working!" Sari exclaimed.

Dr. Lee smiled. "This is great news. If we can keep this up, we'll be able to protect the ecosystem and the fish population."

Over the next few days, Mana continued to use her shark-calling abilities to lure the sharks away from the fishing areas. Each time, the fishermen caught fewer and fewer fish. It wasn't long before they started to suspect that something was amiss.

One day, while Mana was luring the sharks away, she heard a boat approaching. She looked over her shoulder and saw one of Mr. Tanaka's crew members heading towards her.

"Hey, what are you doing?" he shouted. "Why are you trying to scare away the fish?"

Mana didn't answer. She continued to call the sharks, hoping that they would swim away before the crew member got too close.

But it was too late. The crew member had already seen what she was doing. He turned his boat around and headed back to the other fishermen.

Mana knew that they had to be careful. They couldn't let the crew find out what they were doing. They needed to come up with a new plan.

As the crew member returned to the other fishermen, Mana, Sari, and Dr. Lee huddled together to come up with a new plan.

"We need to act fast," Sari said. "If the crew finds out what we're doing, they could try to stop us."

Dr. Lee nodded. "We could try to talk to Mr. Tanaka and explain the importance of protecting the ecosystem. Maybe we can convince him to stop the fishing in the protected areas."

Mana shook her head. "I don't think that's going to work. Mr. Tanaka only cares about making money. He's not going to listen to us."

Suddenly, they heard a loud noise coming from the direction of the fishing boats. They looked out and saw a group of men on a boat with large harpoons and fishing nets.

"Oh no," Dr. Lee said. "Those are shark hunters. Mr. Tanaka must have hired them to get rid of the 'shark problem.'"

"We have to do something," Sari said.

Mana nodded. "I have an idea. I can call the sharks to us and lead them away from the hunting boats."

"But what if they start attacking the fishermen?" Dr. Lee asked.

"I'll make sure they don't," Mana said confidently.

They quickly got into their boat and started to paddle towards the hunting boats. Mana stood at the front, using her shark-calling abilities to attract the sharks towards them.

The hunting boats saw the group of sharks approaching and started to prepare their harpoons and nets.

"They're going to kill them," Sari said, her voice trembling.

Mana concentrated, trying to keep the sharks under control. "We have to lead them away," she said. "Quickly, paddle towards that island over there."

They started to paddle towards a nearby island, with the hunting boats following closely behind.

As they reached the island, Mana signaled for the sharks to swim towards a different direction. The sharks followed her lead and swam away from the hunting boats.

The hunters were left empty-handed, frustrated and angry.

"We'll be back!" one of the hunters shouted. "We'll get those sharks eventually!"

Mana, Sari, and Dr. Lee watched as the hunting boats turned around and headed back to the main fishing area.

"We need to do something," Dr. Lee said. "Those hunters won't stop until they catch those sharks."

"We have to protect them," Sari added.

Mana nodded. "I have an idea. But it's going to require some help."

Mana, Sari, and Dr. Lee knew that they had to act quickly to protect the sharks from the shark hunters. They knew that the hunters would not stop until they caught the sharks, and they needed to come up with a plan to keep them safe.

"I have an idea," Mana said. "But it's going to require some help."

"What kind of help?" Sari asked.

"I need to find someone who knows the area well," Mana said. "Someone who can help us keep the sharks safe."

Dr. Lee nodded. "I know just the person. His name is Jaya, and he's a fisherman. He knows these waters like the back of his hand."

"Great," Mana said. "Let's go find him."

They quickly made their way back to the village and found Jaya at his boat, repairing his nets.

"Jaya, we need your help," Mana said. "We're trying to protect the sharks from the shark hunters."

Jaya looked at them skeptically. "And why should I help you?"

"Because it's the right thing to do," Dr. Lee said.

"And because we need all the help we can get," Sari added.

Jaya thought for a moment before nodding. "Alright, I'll help you. But you have to promise me that no harm will come to me or my family."

"We promise," Mana said.

Jaya joined the three of them in their boat, and they paddled out to where the hunting boats were.

As they approached, Jaya suddenly stood up and shouted, "Mr. Tanaka! I'm with you now!"

Mana, Sari, and Dr. Lee were shocked.

"What are you doing?" Mana asked.

Jaya turned to them with a smirk on his face. "I'm sorry, but I have to do what's best for me and my family. Mr. Tanaka has promised me a lot of money if I help him catch those sharks."

"You can't do this!" Sari said, tears in her eyes. "We trusted you!"

"I'm sorry," Jaya said. "But money talks, and you guys can't offer me what Mr. Tanaka can."

With that, Jaya jumped into one of the hunting boats, and they sped off towards the sharks.

Mana, Sari, and Dr. Lee were left alone, watching in horror as Jaya betrayed them.

"We have to do something," Dr. Lee said. "We can't let them catch those sharks."

"We have to follow them," Mana said. "We can't let Jaya get away with this."

They quickly paddled after the hunting boats, trying to catch up to them. As they approached, they could see the hunters preparing their harpoons and nets.

"We have to stop them," Sari said.

But before they could do anything, one of the hunters spotted them and shouted, "Hey! It's those eco-warriors! Get them!"

The hunting boats turned towards them, and Mana, Sari, and Dr. Lee realized that they were in serious trouble.

As the hunting boats turned towards them, Mana, Sari, and Dr. Lee realized they were outnumbered and outgunned. But they refused to back down.

"We have to stop them!" Sari said, grabbing a paddle.

"We can't let them catch those sharks," Dr. Lee added.

Mana nodded. "We have to do this. For the sharks and for Jaya, who we trusted."

The three of them paddled with all their might, trying to outrun the hunting boats. But they were no match for the powerful engines.

Suddenly, a harpoon flew past them, narrowly missing their boat.

"We have to fight back!" Dr. Lee said, grabbing a net.

The hunters continued to launch harpoons and nets, but Mana, Sari, and Dr. Lee maneuvered their boat skillfully, dodging each attack.

Then, Sari noticed something. "Look! One of the boats is heading towards the shore."

They all looked in the direction she was pointing and saw that one of the hunting boats had split off from the rest and was heading towards the beach.

"They must be planning to load the sharks onto a truck," Mana said. "We have to stop them!"

The three of them quickly came up with a plan. Mana would distract the hunters by heading straight towards them, while Sari and Dr. Lee would paddle around to the other side of the beach and block the road.

As Mana approached the hunters, she could see the satisfaction on their faces as they prepared to catch their prey.

But then, she heard a commotion coming from the other side of the beach. She turned to see Sari and Dr. Lee standing in the middle of the road, holding up a sign that read "Save the Sharks!"

The hunters were caught off guard, and for a moment, they hesitated. That was all the time Mana needed. She steered the boat towards the hunting boat, jumping onto it as it passed by.

The hunters were stunned, but they quickly recovered, brandishing their harpoons and knives. Mana knew she had to act fast.

She charged towards the hunters, knocking them down with her paddle. Sari and Dr. Lee joined her, and together, they fought off the hunters, knocking their weapons out of their hands.

Finally, the hunters surrendered, realizing they were no match for the determined trio.

Mana, Sari, and Dr. Lee quickly loaded the sharks onto their boat and paddled away from the beach. They could hear the hunters shouting and cursing at them, but they didn't care. They had saved the sharks, and that was all that mattered.

As they paddled away, they saw Jaya standing on the beach, watching them. He looked ashamed and guilty.

"We trusted you," Sari said, tears streaming down her face. "How could you betray us?"

Jaya hung his head. "I'm sorry. I was greedy, and I made a mistake. Can you forgive me?"

Mana and Dr. Lee looked at each other, then nodded. "We forgive you," Mana said.

The four of them paddled back to the village, where they released the sharks back into the sea. The villagers cheered and congratulated them on their bravery.

Mr. Tanaka was never seen again, and the shark hunters never returned to their waters.

As for Mana, Sari, Dr. Lee, and Jaya, they remained friends, united by their love for the ocean and their commitment to protecting its creatures.

As they paddled back to the village, the group remained silent, lost in their own thoughts about what had just happened. They had saved the sharks, but at what cost? Mana, Sari, and Dr. Lee had put their lives on the line, and Jaya had betrayed their trust.

When they reached the shore, the villagers greeted them with cheers and applause, but Mana and her friends could not bring themselves to join in the celebration. They had won the battle, but they had also lost something precious – their innocence.

After they had released the sharks back into the sea, the group gathered in Mana's house to talk about what had happened.

"I can't believe Jaya would do something like this," Sari said, tears welling up in her eyes. "We trusted him, and he betrayed us."

Dr. Lee nodded. "It's a sad reality that greed can make people do terrible things."

Mana sighed. "I just hope we can make a difference. Maybe our actions will inspire others to protect the ocean."

Just then, there was a knock on the door. Mana's mother entered the room, her face stern.

"I just got word from the village council," she said. "Jaya has been expelled from the village. He is no longer welcome here."

The group fell silent, feeling a mixture of sadness and anger. They had lost a friend, but they also knew that Jaya had brought this upon himself.

"I still can't believe he did this," Sari said, her voice shaking with emotion. "How could he be so selfish?"

Dr. Lee put a comforting hand on her shoulder. "We all make mistakes, Sari. It's what we do next that matters."

The group sat in silence for a few minutes, lost in their own thoughts. They knew that what they had done was right, but they also knew that the fight was far from over.

"We have to keep fighting," Mana said, her voice determined. "We can't let this happen again."

The others nodded in agreement, feeling a renewed sense of purpose. They had won a battle, but the war against shark hunting and other forms of ocean destruction was far from over.

As Mana sat in her room, she couldn't help but think about the legacy that her mother had left behind. Her mother had been a renowned shark caller in the village, and her skills had helped to protect the ocean and its creatures. Mana knew that it was up to her to carry on her mother's legacy and continue the fight to save the sharks.

The next morning, Mana went to her father and asked him to teach her the ways of shark calling. At first, her father was hesitant. He knew the dangers that came with the job and didn't want to put his daughter in harm's way. But after much convincing, he finally relented and agreed to teach her.

For the next few months, Mana trained with her father, learning the ancient art of shark calling. She learned the different calls that could be used to attract or repel sharks, the best times to go hunting, and how to read the signs of the ocean.

As she trained, Mana became more and more respected in the village. People began to see her as the heir to her mother's legacy, and they came to her for advice on ocean-related matters.

One day, while out on a hunt with her father, they came across a group of shark hunters. The hunters had set up a trap, and several sharks were caught in their nets.

Mana's father wanted to attack the hunters, but Mana urged him to try a different approach. She swam up to the hunters and spoke to them, explaining the importance of protecting the ocean and its creatures.

At first, the hunters were resistant. They argued that they needed to hunt sharks in order to feed their families and make a living. But Mana was persistent, and she continued to talk to them, using the skills that she had learned from her mother.

After several hours of talking, the hunters finally relented. They agreed to release the sharks back into the ocean and promised to stop hunting them in the future.

Mana returned to the village, feeling proud of what she had accomplished. She knew that her mother would have been proud of her as well.

As the years went by, Mana continued to work to protect the ocean and its creatures. She became a respected member of the community and passed on her knowledge to the younger generation.

She knew that the fight would never be over, but she also knew that she was making a difference. And she was proud to carry on her mother's legacy, one that would continue to inspire and protect for generations to come.

As Mana looked out at the ocean, she felt a sense of calm wash over her. She had come a long way since the day she and her friends had saved the sharks from the hunters. She had continued to train and had become a skilled shark caller, just like her mother.

But as she looked out at the vast expanse of blue, she knew that there was still work to be done. The ocean was still in danger, and it was up to her and her friends to protect it.

She turned to Sari and Dr. Lee, who were standing beside her on the shore.

"What do you think we should do next?" she asked.

Sari looked thoughtful. "I think we should start by educating people about the importance of the ocean. We could hold workshops and seminars and teach people about the different creatures that live in the ocean and how to protect them."

Dr. Lee nodded in agreement. "And we could also work with the government to create stricter laws and regulations to protect the ocean. We could lobby for the creation of marine sanctuaries and protected areas."

Mana smiled. "I think those are both great ideas. And we could also continue to work with the fishermen and hunters in the village, teaching them about sustainable practices and the importance of conservation."

The three friends continued to discuss their plans for the future, each offering their own ideas and insights. They knew that the fight would never be over, but they were determined to continue the work that Mana's mother had started.

As the sun began to set, Mana looked out at the ocean once more. She knew that she would always have the power to call upon the sharks when her village was threatened. And she knew that, with the help of her friends and the community, they could continue to protect the ocean and its inhabitants for generations to come.

The Huntress

The sun beat down on the clear blue waters of the cove off the coast of South Africa. The female great white shark circled silently beneath the surface, watching as the poachers' boat approached. She had seen it all before. The bait, the traps, the cruel removal of fins before the sharks were thrown back into the water to die a slow and painful death. She knew that she had to act fast before it was too late.

As the boat drew closer, the shark could hear the excited chatter of the poachers on board. "This one's a big one," one of them exclaimed. "We'll make a fortune off its fins!" The shark felt a surge of anger and fear. She had to escape, but she knew that she was running out of time.

Suddenly, the poachers' boat came to a halt. The shark froze, sensing danger. She watched as the poachers prepared their bait and lowered it into the water. She knew that this was her chance to escape, but she couldn't resist the temptation of the bait. She swam closer and closer until she was just inches away.

Suddenly, the trap was sprung. The shark felt a sharp pain in her side as the hook dug into her flesh. She thrashed and fought, but it was no use. The poachers quickly hauled her onto the boat and began to remove her fins.

As they worked, the shark could hear their laughter and their boasts about how much money they would make. She felt helpless and alone, knowing that she was just another victim of their cruel and senseless hunting.

Finally, the poachers were finished. They tossed the shark's mutilated body back into the water and sped off, leaving her to die a slow and painful death. As the last of her strength drained away, the shark made a vow. She would not go down without a fight. She would find a way to take revenge on these heartless killers, and she would make sure that they never hurt another shark again.

As the sun began to set on the cove, the female great white shark lay motionless on the ocean floor, her mind racing. She knew that she couldn't take on the poachers alone. She needed help. But who could she turn to?

Suddenly, a shadow passed overhead. The shark looked up to see a wise old bull shark gliding above her. "Greetings, sister," the bull shark said. "I have been watching you. You seek revenge on the poachers who have hurt our kind."

The female great white shark was surprised but grateful for the bull shark's offer of help. "Yes," she said. "They have taken so many of us. It's time to put an end to their senseless hunting."

The bull shark nodded thoughtfully. "I have been around these waters for many years," he said. "I know a thing or two about these poachers. They are greedy and ruthless. But they are also predictable. If we work together, we can outsmart them."

The female great white shark was hopeful. "What do you suggest?" she asked.

The bull shark thought for a moment. "I suggest we enlist the help of others in the area. There is a fierce tiger shark who has also been targeted by the poachers. And there are other sharks who would be willing to join our cause."

The female great white shark was hesitant. "But how can we trust them?" she asked. "They could turn on us at any moment."

The bull shark nodded. "It's a risk, but it's a risk we must take if we want to protect our kind. I will speak to the others and see if they are willing to help. Meet me here tomorrow at dawn, and we will make our plans."

The female great white shark agreed and watched as the bull shark swam off into the deep. She knew that the road ahead would not be easy, but she was filled with a renewed sense of purpose. Together with the other sharks, they would take revenge on the poachers who had hurt them for too long.

The next morning, the female great white shark and the wise old bull shark met at the designated spot, accompanied by a group of other sharks. Among them was a fierce tiger shark, a sleek hammerhead, and a small but nimble blacktip shark.

"We have to act fast," the bull shark said, addressing the group. "The poachers will be out hunting again today. We need to strike before they can do any more damage."

The female great white shark nodded in agreement. "But how do we take them by surprise?" she asked.

The bull shark looked around at the other sharks. "We will attack their boat from all sides," he said. "We will create chaos and confusion, and they won't know what hit them."

The group of sharks nodded in agreement and set off towards the open sea. They swam in a tight formation, each one focused on the task ahead. As they approached the poachers' boat, they could see the men on board, laughing and joking as they prepared their bait.

The female great white shark and her allies attacked without warning. They rammed the boat from all sides, causing it to rock violently. The poachers stumbled and fell as they tried to maintain their balance.

"What the hell is going on?" one of them shouted, looking around in confusion.

The female great white shark saw her chance and lunged at the boat. Her powerful jaws clamped down on the side, tearing a large hole in the hull. Water began to rush in, and the poachers panicked.

"Get us out of here!" one of them yelled, trying to start the engine.

But it was too late. The boat began to sink, and the poachers were forced to abandon ship. As they swam frantically towards the shore, the female great white shark and her allies circled around them, preventing them from escaping.

One of the poachers, a young man, had been injured in the attack. He was bleeding heavily from a gash on his leg, and he could barely swim.

"Help me!" he cried, reaching out towards the nearest shark.

But the female great white shark didn't hesitate. She knew that these men were responsible for the deaths of countless sharks, including many of her own kind. She lunged at the injured poacher, delivering a fatal blow with her powerful jaws.

The other poachers watched in horror as their friend was killed before their eyes. They realized that they were in serious danger and swam for their lives towards the shore.

As they reached the safety of the beach, they looked back at the sea, where the female great white shark and her allies were still circling, their fins cutting through the water like knives.

As the poachers stumbled onto the shore, gasping for air and shaken by the attack, they looked back at the sea and saw the female great white shark and her allies still circling. One of the poachers, a tall and muscular man with a thick beard, turned to his comrades with a determined look in his eyes.

"That shark is a real huntress," he said. "She's smarter than any shark I've ever seen. We need to capture her and put an end to this once and for all."

The other poachers nodded in agreement, their fear quickly turning into anger. They had lost their boat, their equipment, and one of their own to these sharks, and they were determined to get revenge.

"But how do we catch her?" one of them asked.

The bearded poacher stroked his chin, thinking hard. "We need a big net," he said. "And a powerful tranquilizer dart. We'll lure her in with bait, and when she's close enough, we'll shoot her with the dart and drag her onto the beach."

The other poachers looked at each other nervously. They knew that the Huntress was no ordinary shark. She was a fierce and intelligent predator, with years of experience hunting in these waters.

"That's a risky plan," one of them said. "What if she's too smart for us?"

The bearded poacher shook his head. "We have to try," he said. "We can't let her get away with killing our friend. We'll set the trap tomorrow morning, at the same spot where we lost our boat."

The Huntress watched from a distance, hidden in the shadows of a nearby reef. She knew that the poachers were planning something, but she couldn't tell what. She had heard them talking about a net and a dart, but she didn't know the details.

She swam cautiously, keeping her distance from the shore. She had survived this long by being careful and patient, and she wasn't about to let her guard down now.

As the sun began to set, she found a quiet spot near the bottom of the sea and settled in for the night. She closed her eyes and let her mind wander, thinking about her life and her family.

She remembered her mother, who had taught her how to hunt and survive in these waters. She remembered her siblings, who had all been killed by poachers or fishermen. She remembered her own children, who were still out there somewhere, swimming and playing and growing stronger every day.

She knew that she had to stay alive, not just for herself, but for them. She had to keep fighting, no matter how difficult or dangerous it might be.

The next morning, she swam cautiously towards the spot where the poachers had set their trap. She could smell the bait, a strong and pungent odor that made her mouth water. But she knew that she had to be careful. She had to stay focused and stay alive.

As she approached the bait, she saw the net, a large and complicated contraption that stretched out across the water like a spider's web. She sensed danger and tried to swim away, but it was too late.

The tranquilizer dart hit her in the side, and she felt her strength fading. She tried to swim, but her muscles were weak, and her movements were sluggish. She felt herself being dragged towards the shore, towards the waiting poachers.

As The Huntress was dragged onto the shore, her eyes scanned the area for any sign of escape. She saw the poachers approaching her, their eyes gleaming with triumph.

"We got her!" the bearded poacher exclaimed. "Get the ropes, we need to tie her up."

The Huntress struggled weakly as the poachers began to tie her up. She tried to summon her strength, but the tranquilizer was too powerful. She felt helpless, trapped, and betrayed.

As the poachers finished tying her up, one of them noticed the young blacktip shark swimming nearby. "Hey, look at this!" he exclaimed. "We've got ourselves another one."

The poachers swam towards the blacktip shark, who was darting back and forth nervously. They quickly captured him and placed him in a small cage on the shore.

"Now we just have to wait for the big one," the bearded poacher said, grinning.

The Huntress watched in horror as the poachers lowered the cage into the water, using the young blacktip shark as bait to lure her in. She knew that she had to save him, but she also knew that the poachers were expecting her to do so.

She swam cautiously towards the cage, staying hidden in the shadows. She could see the young blacktip shark swimming back and forth inside, his eyes wide with fear.

The poachers watched eagerly from the shore, their fingers on the triggers of their tranquilizer guns. They knew that The Huntress would not be able to resist the temptation of the young blacktip shark.

The Huntress knew that she had to act quickly. She swam towards the cage, using all of her strength to break it open. The young blacktip shark darted out, swimming frantically towards the open sea.

The poachers saw their plan failing and quickly began to shoot at The Huntress. She felt the darts hitting her body, weakening her even further. She knew that she had to get away, but she also knew that she couldn't leave the young blacktip shark behind.

With a burst of strength, The Huntress lunged towards the young blacktip shark, grabbing him in her jaws. She swam towards the open sea, away from the poachers and their traps.

The poachers watched in frustration as The Huntress and the young blacktip shark swam away. "We'll get her next time," the bearded poacher said, his voice filled with anger and determination.

The Huntress and the young blacktip shark swam away, towards the safety of the open sea. The Huntress knew that she had made a dangerous choice, but she also knew that she couldn't abandon her fellow shark.

As they swam, The Huntress thought about her family and her home. She knew that she had to protect them, no matter what the cost.

The Huntress and the young blacktip shark continued to swim towards the open sea. The Huntress could feel her strength waning, but she refused to give up. She had to protect the young blacktip shark at all costs.

As they swam, The Huntress noticed a group of sharks swimming in the distance. She recognized them as her allies, the ones she had worked with in the past to protect their home.

"Swim towards them," The Huntress said to the young blacktip shark. "They will help us."

The young blacktip shark nodded, and they swam towards the group. When they reached them, The Huntress explained the situation to her allies.

"We have to save him," The Huntress said, gesturing towards the young blacktip shark. "The poachers have him trapped, and they're waiting for me to come back."

"We'll help you," one of her allies said. "We owe you for all that you've done for us."

The Huntress and her allies quickly came up with a plan. They knew that they had to distract the poachers so that the young blacktip shark could escape. They decided to stage a fake attack, luring the poachers away from the cage.

As they swam towards the shore, The Huntress felt a sense of dread. She knew that this plan was risky, and that she could be putting herself in danger. But she also knew that it was the only way to save the young blacktip shark.

The Huntress and her allies began to swim in circles, creating a whirlpool in the water. The poachers watched in confusion, unsure of what was happening.

Suddenly, The Huntress and her allies surged towards the shore, as if they were attacking. The poachers quickly fired their tranquilizer guns, but they missed their targets.

The Huntress and her allies continued to swim towards the shore, drawing the poachers away from the cage. The young blacktip shark seized the opportunity and darted out of the cage, swimming towards the open sea.

The poachers realized that they had been tricked, and they turned their attention towards The Huntress and her allies. The Huntress felt the darts hitting her body, weakening her even further. But she refused to give up.

With a burst of strength, The Huntress swam towards the open sea, away from the poachers and their traps. Her allies followed her, protecting her from the poachers' attacks.

As they swam, The Huntress felt her strength fading. She knew that she was injured, but she also knew that she had saved the young blacktip shark.

"We did it," The Huntress said, her voice weak. "We saved him."

Her allies nodded, and they continued to swim towards the safety of the open sea.

As The Huntress and her allies swam towards the open sea, they could hear the poachers' boats approaching from behind. The poachers were determined to capture The Huntress, and they were closing in fast.

"We need to split up," The Huntress said to her allies. "They'll have a harder time chasing all of us."

Her allies nodded, and they split up in different directions, hoping to confuse the poachers.

The Huntress could hear the poachers shouting in frustration as they tried to follow each of them. She knew that she had to stay one step ahead of them, and she used all her cunning and intelligence to do so.

She swam in zigzag patterns, making it harder for the poachers to aim their tranquilizer guns at her. She also swam in and out of the underwater caves, using them as cover to evade the poachers' sight.

But the poachers were persistent. They continued to chase her through the cove, firing tranquilizer darts at her. The Huntress could feel her body getting weaker with each hit, but she refused to give up.

She swam towards the shallow parts of the cove, hoping to use the rocks and coral formations as a shield. But the poachers were too close, and they fired their darts relentlessly.

"We've got her now!" one of the poachers shouted.

The Huntress could see the poachers closing in on her. She knew that she had to think fast. She looked around and spotted a narrow passage between two rocks. It was risky, but it was her only chance.

She swam towards the passage, squeezing her body through the narrow gap. The poachers tried to follow, but their boats were too big to fit through.

The Huntress emerged on the other side, panting heavily. She looked around and realized that she had lost the poachers for now. But she knew that they would not give up that easily.

"I have to keep moving," The Huntress said to herself. "I can't let them catch me."

She swam towards the open sea, hoping to put as much distance as possible between herself and the poachers.

The Huntress swam towards the open sea, her heart pounding with adrenaline. She knew that the poachers would not give up that easily, and she needed to be on her guard at all times.

As she swam, she heard the sound of the poachers' boats getting closer. She turned her head and saw them in the distance, their engines roaring as they chased after her.

The Huntress scanned her surroundings, looking for a place where she could make a stand. She spotted a narrow channel between two rocky outcroppings, and she knew that this was her chance.

She swam towards the channel, leading the poachers into the narrow passage. The water was too shallow for their boats to follow, and they were forced to slow down.

The Huntress emerged from the channel, her eyes fixed on the poachers. She knew that she had the upper hand now, and she was determined to make the most of it.

With a fierce roar, she attacked the nearest boat. She slammed into it with all her might, sending it careening off course. The poachers on board were thrown overboard, their weapons falling into the water.

The Huntress circled around, keeping her distance from the remaining boats. She knew that she had to stay on the move, or the poachers would catch her again.

One of the poachers tried to shoot her with a dart, but she dodged it easily. She swam towards him, her teeth bared, and he backed away in terror.

The Huntress seized her chance and attacked the boat. She bit into the hull, tearing through the wood with ease. The poachers inside screamed in terror, scrambling to get away.

As the boat sank, the poachers were left to fend for themselves in the shark-infested waters. The Huntress watched from a safe distance, satisfied that she had dealt them a heavy blow.

She turned towards the open sea, ready to continue her journey. But she knew that the poachers would not give up that easily, and she would have to be on her guard at all times.

The Huntress swam away from the sinking boat, her heart still pounding with adrenaline. She knew that she had dealt a heavy blow to the poachers, but she was also weary and wounded from the fight.

Her allies swam up beside her, their faces showing a mixture of relief and exhaustion.

"That was close," one of them said, panting heavily.

"Yeah, but we did it," another replied, a note of triumph in his voice.

The Huntress nodded, but she knew that they couldn't let their guard down yet. She looked around, scanning the horizon for any sign of the poachers.

"Let's rest in that nearby coral reef," she said. "We need to regroup and tend to our wounds."

Her allies nodded, and they followed her towards the coral reef. The water was warm and peaceful there, and they could rest without fear of being attacked.

As they rested, The Huntress reflected on their victory. She knew that they had put an end to the poachers' reign of terror, at least in this cove. But she also knew that there were other poachers out there, and they would need to be stopped as well.

She turned to her allies. "We can't let our guard down," she said. "We need to be ready for whatever comes next."

They nodded, and they spent the rest of the day resting and tending to their wounds. The Huntress felt a sense of peace wash over her, knowing that they had finally achieved their goal.

Days turned into weeks, and weeks turned into months. The cove became known as a place of legend, where no human dared to venture for fear of The Huntress who lurked beneath the surface.

But The Huntress and her allies continued to swim in the open sea, their eyes ever watchful for any signs of danger. They knew that they had made a difference in the world, but they also knew that there was still work to be done.

As time passed, The Huntress and her allies continued to swim the open sea, protecting their kind and other sea creatures from harm. They knew that their victory against the poachers was just the beginning, and they were determined to make the ocean a safer place for all who called it home.

The cove where they had fought the poachers became a safe haven for sharks of all kinds. The memory of the poachers faded away, but The Huntress remained a symbol of strength and resilience for all who knew her.

One day, a young shark swam up to The Huntress, his eyes filled with wonder. "Are you The Huntress?" he asked.

The Huntress nodded. "Yes, I am."

The young shark looked up at her with admiration. "I've heard so much about you. They say you're the bravest shark in all the ocean."

The Huntress smiled. "I just do what needs to be done," she said. "But it's not just me. It's all of us. We need to work together to protect our kind and our home."

The young shark nodded, understanding the wisdom in her words. He swam away, his heart filled with hope and determination.

As the years went by, The Huntress and her allies continued to protect their kind, and the cove became a place of peace and safety. Other sharks and sea creatures looked up to The Huntress as a symbol of strength and resilience, and her legacy lived on long after she was gone.

Eventually, The Huntress passed away, but her spirit remained. Her legacy inspired generations of sharks to come, and the ocean was a safer place because of her.

The Trench

The salty ocean breeze whipped through Dr. Olivia Richards' hair as she stood on the deck of the research vessel, her eyes fixed on the endless expanse of blue stretching out before her.

"Beautiful, isn't it?" she murmured to herself, feeling a thrill of excitement at the thought of what lay beneath the surface.

"Sure is," a gruff voice interrupted her thoughts. She turned to see the captain of the vessel, a weathered old sailor named Jackson, approaching her.

"Captain," she said, nodding in greeting. "Everything ready for our descent?"

"Aye, everything's in order," he replied. "But I have to ask, Doc. Why the fascination with the deep sea? Seems like a dangerous place to be poking around in."

Dr. Richards smiled wryly. "Danger is what makes it exciting, Captain. And besides, there's so much we still don't know about the ocean and its inhabitants. Who knows what new discoveries we might make?"

Captain Jackson shook his head. "Well, just make sure you don't get yourself killed in the process, Doc. The ocean can be a cruel mistress."

Dr. Richards chuckled. "Don't worry, Captain. I know what I'm doing."

As if on cue, another member of their team, Dr. Hernandez, approached them, carrying a stack of papers.

"Good morning, Dr. Richards, Captain," he said, nodding to each of them in turn. "I've been reviewing the data from our sonar scans, and I believe we may have located an underwater trench deeper than any previously recorded."

Dr. Richards' eyes widened in excitement. "Really? That's incredible, Dr. Hernandez. Can you show me the scans?"

"Of course," he said, handing her the papers. "I think you'll find it quite interesting."

As the three of them poured over the data, Dr. Richards felt a sense of anticipation building inside her. This was it. This was the chance to explore a place no one had ever been before, to discover something new and incredible.

"Let's do it," she said, grinning broadly. "Let's dive into that trench and see what we can find."

Captain Jackson looked at Dr. Richards skeptically. "Are you sure, Doc? That trench is deeper than anything we've ever encountered before. It could be dangerous."

Dr. Richards met his gaze steadily. "I'm sure, Captain. This is why we're here, isn't it? To explore and make new discoveries?"

The captain sighed. "Alright then, Doc. But I want you to be careful. We don't know what's down there."

Dr. Richards grinned at him. "Don't worry, Captain. I'll be careful."

As the team prepared for the dive, Dr. Richards felt a sense of excitement and anticipation building inside her. She had dreamed of this moment for years, of exploring the unknown depths of the ocean and uncovering new secrets.

Finally, the moment arrived. Clad in her diving suit and with a flashlight clutched in one hand, Dr. Richards stepped off the side of the vessel and began her descent into the trench.

At first, the darkness was overwhelming, and Dr. Richards felt a momentary pang of fear. But then she focused on her breathing, on the reassuring rhythm of the bubbles escaping from her regulator, and she began to relax.

As she descended deeper and deeper, she noticed strange markings on the walls of the trench. They were unlike anything she had ever seen before, intricate and seemingly deliberate patterns etched into the rock.

She reached out to touch one, and her fingers brushed against something slimy and cold. She recoiled in surprise, shining her flashlight on the spot where she had touched.

It was then that she saw it. A shadow moving in the darkness, approaching her with alarming speed. At first, she thought it might be a giant squid or some other deep sea creature, but as it came closer, she saw the unmistakable shape of a megalodon, a massive prehistoric shark thought to be extinct for millions of years.

Dr. Richards felt her heart pounding in her chest as the megalodon circled her, its cold, dead eyes fixed on her every move. She knew then that she was in grave danger, and that her only hope was to stay calm and use all of her knowledge and training to survive the encounter.

Dr. Richards knew that megalodons were one of the most feared predators in the history of the ocean. But what was one doing here, in this deep underwater trench?

She tried to remain calm, keeping her flashlight steady and her breathing even as the massive shark circled closer and closer, its jagged teeth glinting in the dim light.

Dr. Richards knew that megalodons were known to attack boats, but there were few documented cases of them attacking humans. Still, she couldn't take any chances.

She tried to move slowly, but the megalodon was too quick, and it lunged towards her with incredible force. Dr. Richards managed to dodge out of the way at the last second, her heart pounding in her chest.

She knew that she couldn't outrun the megalodon in the water, but she had to try something. She reached into her bag and pulled out a small device, a kind of underwater flare that emitted a bright, flashing light.

The megalodon hesitated for a moment, as if confused by the sudden burst of light. It circled around again, but this time it kept its distance, as if unsure of what to do.

Dr. Richards knew that this was her chance. She swam as quickly as she could back up to the surface, her heart racing with adrenaline.

As she emerged from the water, gasping for breath, she saw the other members of her team rushing towards her, concern etched on their faces.

"Dr. Richards, are you okay?" Dr. Hernandez asked, grabbing her arm to steady her.

Dr. Richards nodded, still shaking from the encounter. "I'm okay, just a little shaken up. But we need to get out of here. There's a megalodon down there."

The team quickly packed up their equipment and made their way back to the research vessel, their hearts heavy with the knowledge that they had encountered one of the most fearsome predators in the ocean.

As they sailed away from the trench, Dr. Richards couldn't help but wonder what other secrets the deep sea held, and what other dangers lay hidden in its depths.

As the team retreated to the safety of the research vessel, Captain Jackson's expression was stern and serious. "Dr. Richards, that was a close call. You're lucky to be alive. I think we need to reconsider the risks of exploring this trench."

Dr. Richards felt a pang of disappointment at the captain's words, but she knew he was right. "I understand your concerns, Captain, but I don't think we should give up just yet. There's so much we still don't know about this part of the ocean."

Dr. Hernandez stepped forward, nodding in agreement with the captain. "Dr. Richards, I understand your passion for exploration, but we have to prioritize safety. We can't afford to take unnecessary risks, especially with so much at stake."

Dr. Richards sighed, feeling the weight of the responsibility on her shoulders. She knew that the team's research was important, but she also knew that they couldn't afford to put themselves in danger.

"Okay," she said finally. "I hear what you're saying, and I agree that we need to be more careful. But I still believe that there are discoveries to be made down there, and I'm not ready to give up just yet."

Captain Jackson nodded, looking thoughtful. "I understand your perspective, Dr. Richards. But we need to balance our desire for knowledge with the need to stay safe. Let's take some time to regroup and come up with a new plan of action."

Dr. Richards nodded, feeling a sense of relief. She knew that the captain was right, and that they needed to approach their research with caution.

As the team settled into their quarters on the research vessel, Dr. Richards couldn't help but think about the megalodon she had encountered. She knew that there were other dangers lurking in the depths of the ocean, waiting to be discovered.

But for now, she would focus on regrouping with her team and coming up with a new plan for exploration. The ocean was a vast and mysterious place, and they had only scratched the surface of what it had to offer.

Over the next few days, the team regrouped and came up with a new plan for exploration. Dr. Richards spent hours pouring over the data they had collected, trying to make sense of the megalodon's behavior and the unusual characteristics of the trench.

As she dug deeper, she began to uncover evidence that suggested the megalodon was more than just a mindless predator. There were signs of intelligent behavior, patterns of movement and communication that hinted at a level of complexity that was unprecedented in any other species they had encountered.

Dr. Richards couldn't help but feel a sense of excitement as she delved deeper into her research. The more she learned, the more convinced she became that there was something truly remarkable waiting to be discovered in the depths of the ocean.

She shared her findings with the rest of the team, and they were all impressed by the depth and scope of her research. Dr. Hernandez was particularly interested in the implications of the megalodon's intelligence, and they spent hours discussing the potential ramifications for the field of marine biology.

As they continued to research, they uncovered more and more evidence of the megalodon's intelligence. They found evidence of complex social structures, and even indications of a rudimentary language system.

Dr. Richards was thrilled by the possibilities that lay ahead, but she knew that they needed to proceed with caution. They couldn't afford to put themselves in danger again, and they needed to respect the delicate balance of life in the ocean.

As the team continued their research, Dr. Richards couldn't help but wonder what other secrets the ocean held. She was more determined than ever to uncover the mysteries of the deep, and to share her findings with the world.

After weeks of intense research, the team decided it was time to return to the surface to restock and regroup. Dr. Richards was eager to continue her research, but she knew that they needed to take a break and replenish their supplies.

As they made their way back to the research vessel, Dr. Richards couldn't help but feel a sense of restlessness. She had become obsessed with discovering more about the megalodon and the trench, and she knew that there was still so much they didn't know.

Once they were back on the research vessel, Dr. Richards spent every spare moment pouring over her notes and analyzing the data they had collected. She was determined to uncover more evidence of the megalodon's intelligence and to learn as much as she could about the trench.

The rest of the team tried to encourage her to take a break and enjoy some downtime, but Dr. Richards was too consumed by her research to take a break. She spent long hours in her lab, poring over her findings and trying to make sense of the patterns she was seeing.

As the days turned into weeks, Dr. Richards became increasingly isolated from the rest of the team. She spent most of her time in her lab, rarely emerging except to grab a quick meal or some fresh air.

Dr. Hernandez grew concerned about Dr. Richards' obsessive behavior and decided to have a talk with her. "Dr. Richards, we're all impressed by your dedication and your research, but we're worried about you. You need to take a break and get some rest."

Dr. Richards shook her head. "I can't rest now, not when we're so close to making a breakthrough. I know there's more to discover about the megalodon and the trench, and I won't stop until I find it."

Dr. Hernandez sighed, realizing that she wasn't going to be able to convince Dr. Richards to take a break. She knew that the only thing they could do was to support her research and hope that she would eventually come to her senses.

As the days turned into months, Dr. Richards' obsession with her research only grew stronger. She poured all of her energy into uncovering the mysteries of the ocean, determined to discover everything there was to know about the megalodon and the trench.

Months had passed, and Dr. Richards and her team had made little progress in their research. Dr. Richards had become so consumed with her work that she had neglected to take care of herself, and her health had started to suffer.

Realizing that they needed to take action before it was too late, the team decided to regroup and come up with a plan for their next dive into the trench.

"We can't keep risking our safety like we did before," Dr. Hernandez said. "We need to come up with a plan to study the megalodon without putting ourselves in danger."

Dr. Richards nodded in agreement. "I've been thinking about that too. I think we need to use remote-controlled devices to observe the megalodon from a safe distance."

Dr. Chen, the team's engineer, chimed in. "I can design a drone that will allow us to study the megalodon without getting too close. It will have a high-resolution camera and a range of sensors to gather data on the megalodon's behavior and the environment of the trench."

The team worked tirelessly to develop the new drone, and after several weeks of design and testing, they finally had a working prototype. They also developed a system to communicate with the drone, allowing them to control it from the safety of their research vessel.

Once the drone was ready, the team made their final preparations for the dive. They loaded the drone onto their submersible, and Dr. Richards reviewed her notes one last time.

"We're ready," she said, with a determined look on her face. "Let's do this."

As they descended into the trench, the team monitored the drone's progress. The high-resolution camera provided them with a clear view of the megalodon, and they were able to gather a wealth of data on its behavior and movements.

Dr. Richards was thrilled with the results, and she spent hours pouring over the data they had collected. She was able to uncover even more evidence of the megalodon's intelligence, and she was convinced that there was still so much more to learn.

Dr. Richards was ecstatic about the progress they had made with the drone, but she knew that they needed to dive deeper into the trench to uncover even more about the megalodon.

"I think we need to take another dive," she said to the team. "We need to get even closer to the megalodon and observe its behavior in more detail."

Dr. Hernandez looked concerned. "Are you sure that's a good idea? We don't want to put ourselves in danger again."

Dr. Richards shook her head. "No, we won't be putting ourselves in danger this time. We'll use the drone to keep a safe distance, and we'll only go as deep as we need to in order to gather more data."

The team agreed, and they quickly made preparations for their next dive. They loaded the drone onto the submersible and checked their equipment one last time before descending into the trench.

As they went deeper and deeper, the team monitored the drone's progress carefully. They were able to observe the megalodon from a safe distance, and they were amazed by what they saw.

The megalodon was an incredibly intelligent creature, and it displayed a range of behaviors that they had never seen before. It seemed to have a deep understanding of its environment, and it was able to navigate through the trench with ease.

As they continued to observe the megalodon, the team also discovered more about its feeding habits. They were able to capture footage of the megalodon hunting and feeding on smaller prey, and they were able to gather data on its digestive system.

Dr. Richards was thrilled with the progress they had made, but she knew that they still had so much more to learn. "We need to keep diving deeper," she said to the team. "There's still so much we don't know about the megalodon and the trench."

As the team continued their dives into the trench, Dr. Richards couldn't shake the feeling that their discovery of the megalodon could have consequences beyond their understanding.

"Think about it," she said to the team. "If we can find the megalodon, what's stopping others from doing the same? What if this leads to people trying to capture or kill the megalodon? It could have catastrophic consequences for the ocean's ecosystem."

Dr. Hernandez looked worried. "What can we do to stop it?"

Dr. Richards paused, deep in thought. "We need to find a way to protect the megalodon and its habitat. We need to make sure that our discovery doesn't lead to its demise."

The team agreed to take action, and they began brainstorming ideas for how to protect the megalodon. They considered everything from lobbying for protected status for the creature to developing educational campaigns to raise awareness about the importance of preserving the ocean's ecosystem.

As they worked on their plan, Dr. Richards felt a growing sense of responsibility for the megalodon's well-being. She knew that they had uncovered something truly remarkable, but she also knew that it came with a great responsibility to ensure its survival.

"We can't let this discovery be the end of the megalodon," she said to the team. "We need to find a way to protect it for generations to come."

Dr. Richards and her team worked tirelessly on their plan to protect the megalodon. They decided that the best course of action was to lure the megalodon away from the trench and into open water, where it would have a better chance of survival.

They spent weeks studying the megalodon's behavior and analyzing its movements, looking for patterns that they could exploit. Finally, they felt confident that they had a plan that would work.

"We need to create a disturbance in the trench," said Dr. Richards. "Something that will attract the megalodon's attention and lure it away from its habitat."

The team worked quickly to set their plan in motion. They used their submersible to create a series of loud sounds and bright lights in the trench, hoping to catch the megalodon's attention. They waited anxiously, watching as the water around them churned with activity.

Suddenly, they saw movement in the distance. The megalodon was approaching.

Dr. Richards and her team prepared for the final showdown with the megalodon. They knew that it would be a dangerous and difficult task, but they were determined to protect the creature.

The megalodon approached quickly, its massive jaws open wide. The team activated their plan, using a specially designed decoy to lure the megalodon away from the trench.

As the megalodon followed the decoy into open water, the team engaged in a final showdown with the creature. They used their submersible to fire tranquilizer darts at the megalodon, hoping to sedate it long enough to transport it to a safer location.

It was a tense and dangerous battle, but in the end, the team emerged victorious. They had successfully defeated the megalodon and had managed to transport it to a protected area of the ocean, where it would be able to thrive without interference from humans.

Dr. Richards felt a sense of relief wash over her as she watched the megalodon swim away into the depths of the ocean. She knew that their discovery had come with great responsibility, but she was proud of what they had accomplished.

"We did it," she said to the team. "We protected the megalodon, and we ensured that it will be able to live on for generations to come."

Don't miss out!

Visit the website below and you can sign up to receive emails whenever Myria Hopkins publishes a new book. There's no charge and no obligation.

https://books2read.com/r/B-A-NHKX-EVUGC

BOOKS 2 READ

Connecting independent readers to independent writers.

About the Author

Myria Hopkins is a fresh and exciting new voice in the world of fiction, starting her journey as a beginner author. Her passion for storytelling and deep understanding of the human experience are evident in her debut works, which showcase her ability to craft compelling narratives that captivate readers from beginning to end. Drawing inspiration from her own life experiences and a wide range of sources, Myria's writing is marked by its authenticity, emotional depth, and relatability. As she continues to develop her craft and explore new literary terrain, she looks forward to connecting with readers and sharing her unique vision with the world.

Milton Keynes UK
Ingram Content Group UK Ltd.
UKHW020925111023
430376UK00014B/408